West Baden Springs

Thomas R. Kill

authorHOUSE®

AuthorHouse™
1663 Liberty Drive, Suite 200
Bloomington, IN 47403
www.authorhouse.com
Phone: 1-800-839-8640

First published by AuthorHouse 2/11/2008

ISBN: 978-1-4343-3954-6 (sc)

Printed in the United States of America
Bloomington, Indiana
This book is printed on acid-free paper.

⊰ Chapter One ⊱

A FOREST IN Southern Indiana lies dense with fog. The dense fog may give way to any number of men who have trod along through the forest at one time or another: a woodland Indian hunter strapped with bow and arrow, a French fur trader dressed in buckskin, a British redcoat armed with musket, a pioneer toting the ax that enabled him to build a home, or even George Rogers Clark and his men on way to Vincennes. Yet, when the fog breaks for an instant, the forest brings forth none of these who have fought with her hardship, but rather she reveals an awesome site—a magnificent site. A great circular structure surrounded by eight Byzantine towers and topped with a mighty dome stands in majesty in all its beauty and strength. Refined enough to be a palace, stalwart as a castle, this strange, imposing building that disappears and then reappears intermittently through the dense fog is perhaps an illusion of the mind starved for fantasy. Surely few sites could be more incongruous with their surroundings. Why should a building somewhat reminiscent of the famed Blue Mosque of Istanbul be placed in the wilderness of Indiana?

An impenetrable thorn hedge, high as the trees, encircles the property on which the structure rests, serving perhaps as a barrier to the encroaching woodland. Interrupting the thick hedge at one point is found a great arched gate that very likely served a main entryway for the property. Words are written in curvature high above on the arch. "West Baden Springs" the words read. Woven with overgrown vines, the gate's wrought-iron bars have apparently been fastened for years with a rusted padlock, a device perhaps permanently rusted shut. Across some tall grass not far from the arched gate, a wooden railway depot sags in neglect. The crumbling building bears a sign in faded letters, spelling out again "West Baden Springs." Running alongside the depot but obscured by thick weeds lay rusted rails that have not felt a locomotive's weight in years. Nature has obscured any evidence of a road that at one time may have led to the property. Hence, all traffic to the place, whether by rail or by road, ceased long ago.

Crossing the arched gate into this property is entering into a mysterious, still land far removed from the rest of the world. Out of tall grass, rusted boulevard lamps similar to those found along the fashionable Champs-Elysee in Paris begin at the arched gate and continue on in parallel along an obscure brick road until both the road and ornate lamps gradually disappear into the fog. As for the grounds, no longer do large oaks dominate the land, like in the forest, but rather a confusing network of overgrown cedar, boxwood, and yew twist about in a lake of tall grass out of which a dissonant chorus of insects resounds. Marble statues drowning in overgrowth are barely visible; ivy strangles the human figures. In all directions of West Baden Springs, the fog periodically gives way to strange, perplexing visions. In one direction a collection of buildings resembling Greek temples stands high over what was once perhaps a sunken garden. In another direction an Oriental shrine appears as one may have appeared during the Han dynasty. Off at a distance, the faint silhouette of a miniature Gothic cathedral rises through the fog as one might rise over a European City.

But the site that dwarfs all of these mentioned is of course the great Byzantine structure with dome and towers. However imposing as the building may have appeared at a distance, the thick fog had politely concealed many scars of decay that give the edifice a tired, effete look when seen from close up—quite the look of a large, ancient ruin. The walls, towers, and crenellated edge all appear weather-beaten. Birds flying in and out of broken windows have made a giant nest of the place. At the foot of the building, a large veranda, hoisted up by crooked columns, is thick with peeled paint. Mangled wicker chairs rot in large piles on the veranda floor.

Inside, beyond the main door, a blanket of dust covers a large, musty-smelling room furnished with large, Edwardian pieces. Landscape paintings of a somber mood cover the walls. Several large pottery planters play host to giant dead ferns. A massive piano on one side of the room is stacked with yellowed sheet music. An enormous ebony clock with its large pendulum at a standstill serves as a constant reminder that time and the rest of the world have long forgotten West Baden Springs.

But the circular area at the center of the building under the great dome is nothing less than magnificent no matter what forlorn conditions have arisen through the years. Light beaming through glass in the dome reveals the area's breathtaking proportions. Twenty-four gigantic Roman columns around the circumference support a dome two hundred feet in diameter. An elaborate mosaic covers the floor below in timeless beauty. Between the columns are intricately painted Florentine designs. The dome itself is a masterwork. Although rust, dust, and mold still prevail, it strikes one as peculiar that, when viewing this magnificent area under the dome resembling a Pompeian court, all recollection of decay is easily forgotten and only the thought of grandeur remains. She readily gives clue to former glory but struggles to uphold her dignity amid depredations. One can only imagine the events that brought this magnificent place to such decay. Far off, secluded in the dense woodland of Indiana, forgotten and neglected, West Baden Springs yearns to tell her story.

⊰ Chapter Two ⊱

NOT EVEN SO long ago as the year 1890, West Baden Springs was no more than leaf-strewn wilderness, yet with a very special feature. As its name would imply, hot mineral springs bubble up from its grounds. A native son by the name of John Everett longed to forge from these springs a magnificent spa as elegant as any in Europe.

At first Everett's resort was no more than a clearing and a few poorly built wooden cabins. But the young man's big break came when the Monon Railroad agreed to run a line through the valley, connecting with Chicago, Indianapolis, and Louisville. Almost instantly people came from these cities to enjoy the therapeutic water of the valley. Again and again, over a period of ten years, Everett expanded his hotel so that by the turn of the century Everett's hotel had grown into an enormous clapboard Windsor Castle complete with round towers, crenellated walls and turrets, multiple piazzas, and nearly five hundred rooms. He added more amusements as well: more bathhouses, an opera house, and even the nation's only covered one-third mile, double-decker bicycles, and pony track. No longer was Everett's West Baden Springs a rustic country retreat, but rather it was now a thriving, sophisticated resort, known throughout all the Midwest. His dream of an elegant spa had come true.

But tragedy struck one ill-fated summer morning. A fire started in the hotel's kitchen, and in a matter of minutes the entire wooden structure was ablaze, lighting the countryside like a giant torch. Stunned by the sound of the clanging alarm, all guests quickly fled the burning hotel and in nightclothes watched Mr. Everett's prosperous hotel collapse in a torrid heap. No lives were lost, but nearly everything was charred to ashes. The destruction was so complete that Everett dismissed any notion of reconstruction. Instead the young man turned his back on the misfortune and departed for Europe.

Of the fine families who received John Everett on his voyage, none was more eminent as the great Randreninoff family of St. Petersburg. For centuries the Randreninoff dynasty had held a prominent place in Russian aristocracy. Peasants regarded them as royalty. Many considered their estate large and grand enough to be a palace. The Randreninoff women were regarded as the epitome of style and fashion. The family had great influence with the Czar. All of Europe knew of the Randreninoffs, and for one reason in particular. Through the centuries the Randreninoffs had accumulated one of the world's greatest collections of jewels. Kept within a great vault on the magnificent estate, the jewels were the talk of St. Petersburg, and at times, all of Russia. Through stories and legends of the famous jewels, the people of St. Petersburg suspected that the dazzling gems worn by the Randreninoff women were but a pittance of the actual collection—a collection envied by all, including the Czar himself. All likewise knew of the Randreninoff prophecy; if the famous jewels were ever to be removed from Russian soil, it would mean the end of the Randreninoff dynasty.

Although initially lured to the hospitality of the Randreninoffs in hopes of witnessing the majesty of these famous jewels, John Everett discovered a single jewel who sparkled more brilliantly than any he could have imagined in the famous collection. Katia Randreninoff was considered one of the most beautiful, charming, and accomplished women in all of St. Petersburg. When she wore any of the family jewels, her beauty would put the dazzling gems to shame. At twenty-two Katia won the hearts of all who laid eyes on her, including Everett. The two would take long walks together on the estate, during which time Everett would tell Katia of his homeland in the new world.

From listening to Everett, Katia gradually realized how empty was her life in the Russian aristocracy. The aristocracy built the grandest homes, hosted the grandest balls, and dressed themselves in the finest clothes yet felt nothing in their hearts, only the necessity to preserve their grand way of life that was in reality as false as their imagined virtues. Cold, insensitive, these people had reaped the material spoils from others to create a selfish, secluded world of ostentation. Katia escaped this world when she was with Everett. He stood apart from them all. His kindness and honor were true and sincere. Here was a man who could take her away from this life she had grown to hate. Here was a man she loved like no other.

Katia implored Everett to talk about West Baden Springs, for nothing he did brought her more joy. It was as though he was describing a fairyland: the clapboard castle of a hotel, the enchanting woodlands, the springs, the bicycle track, all designed to make people happy. How wonderful, she thought, to receive guests no matter who they may be and to work alongside the hotel staff in an attempt to make these visitors happy. How wonderful to be out from under the restraint of Randreninoff standards—to laugh and sing with guests, to run in the open sunshine without assuming the Randreninoff air of superiority. Everett told her of the great fire and of his concern for his former hotel employees who were now without jobs. Touched by Everett's sensitivity for these people, Katia vowed they would not be unemployed for long. With slight misgivings on the part of the Randreninoffs, Katia and John were married on the great estate and returned to America to build a new West Baden Springs Hotel, a hotel that would be magnificent and enjoyed by all!

On the voyage back, the Everetts could do little else but dream about their new hotel. They imagined a great circular structure that would support the world's largest dome. The building would have Byzantine towers to give it a fairytale look. Acres of formal gardens would surround the hotel.

Only, when the Everetts arrived in Southern Indiana, they received an unwelcome surprise. West Baden's longtime rival in the valley, French Lick Springs, had taken full advantage of Everett's misfortune by having done extensive remodeling and advertising. Due to vast improvements, it was now one of the leading attractions in the Midwest. But the Everetts remained undaunted by their rival. They knew their great domed structure would attract people from all over the country.

But leading architects refused to quote on the contract because a two-hundred-foot dome unsupported in the center had never been built. For a time the search was fruitless. The Everetts' approach to leading architects always resulted in "It can't be done." The weight of such an immense dome would cause the walls to fall in—or fall out. The architects pointed out the great temperature changes in Southern Indiana's climate; thermal expansion and contraction would cause severe damage, not to mention the snow load that the dome would have to bear in the winter. "Impossible!" architects would say.

It appeared that the Everetts' dream hotel would not become a reality until a young, unknown Indiana architect, Spencer Albright, volunteered to do the job. He and the Everetts must have been birds of the same flamboyant feather, for Albright seized the Everett's grandiose ideas of extravagant Byzantine harmony with enthusiasm. John Everett persuaded Albright of the importance of having the hotel completed by the next summer in order to compete with French Lick. Jaunty and self-confident, Albright signed a contract that summer of 1901 to construct the hotel within a year.

One can only guess at the hours Spencer Albright must have spent drawing up the staggering logistics for such an undertaking. The principle feature of the hotel would be the great inner court, roofed over by the great dome. Two hundred feet in diameter, it would be the largest unsupported dome in the world. Standing 150 feet above the floor with no support other than the massive columns next to the walls, it would seem more of a home for giants than people. The dome, entirely without support from the center of the floor, was to be held up by twenty-four steel ribs stretching from a hub in the center to the walls. The hub itself was to be ten feet high and sixteen feet in diameter and was to weigh eight and one half tons. The steel girders would rest on the top of massive columns six stories high and five feet thick. The problem of expansion and contraction of the metal was solved by a brilliant yet simple device. Each girder would rest on the columns at its outer edge upon rollers, somewhat like elongated ball bearings.

Seven hundred and eight rooms would have all the modern conveniences. A circular corridor on each of the six floors would give entrance to the rooms. Half of these were to overlook the gardens, and the other half would look out onto the great atrium. Six Italian artisans were commissioned to floor the atrium with marble parquet, the Florentine design to be fashioned from twelve million one-inch squares of marble. The atrium would be faced with a high wainscoting of Hauteville marble.

The feat of the building's construction caused architects and builders to wonder. A force of five hundred carpenters, brick masons, steel workers, stone masons, and laborers were assembled. Tons and tons of bricks, cement, and steel poured into the valley. The Monon Railroad ran a spur to the hotel site to facilitate handling the tremendous amount of material. In a few short weeks, the foundations were finished and the walls began to rise.

While this work was going on, Albright was gathering men and materials for the construction of the dome, which was to be the most difficult and important part of the job. High wooden scaffolding was built to support the girders until they were all in place. Then, as the air rang with cheers, the first steel girder was locked in placed. After such a successful beginning, the job was harried through to completion.

On the great day when the false work tower was to be removed, a great crowd gathered. Many of them expected to see the dome collapse. Police ordered everyone a safe distance away from the building. But the architect, sure that he had built wisely, climbed to the very peak of the dome and from there gave the order to release the props. The dome held! The exulting Albright waved to the cheering crowd, and almost every man there tossed his hat into the air. The determination of the Everetts and their belief in a young architect's ability outdid all existing free-span domed buildings of the era. This wonder of a 708-room resort hotel was completed in 365 days! It was in fact referred to as "the eighth wonder of the world"!

Only a year after the start of construction, the Everetts moved into their apartment within their new hotel and shortly thereafter hosted a magnificent ball for the grand opening occasion. Guests arrived and were overwhelmed by the hotel's splendor and size. Many claimed the grand lobby was the most beautiful room they had ever seen. The great domed atrium, resembling a Pompeian court, was simply too magnificent for words. Lofty palms and hothouse plants were scattered about singly and in clusters up the mosaic floor. At one side of the atrium was a mammoth brick fireplace where fourteen-foot logs might burn in cooler weather. As for the ball, Indiana had never witnessed a more extravagant event. While guests danced to the gentle music, an enormous chandelier was suspended from the hub of the dome and mechanically lowered with its dazzling lights.

Even more dazzling than the extravagant ball, however, was the charming hostess whom most met for the first time there at the ball. In time, months after the ball, the people of Indiana came to adore and admire Katia like no other woman in the state. In their eyes Katia Randreninoff Everett must have seemed like a young misplaced queen from some strange, foreign place who fancied the Byzantine beauty of West Baden Springs as her royal palace. When people came to know of Katia's aristocratic background, they awed in fascination. Legends and stories of the Randreninoff dynasty spread throughout Indiana like wildfire. "Imagine!" people would say, "to have a real Randreninoff so close at hand—and the famous jewels! She must wear some of them. But no! Never! Remember the Randreninoff prophecy." Ladies emulated Katia. "See my new dress," they would say. "It's just like something the stunning Mrs. Everett of West Baden Springs would wear." Visitors to West Baden would gather together in hopes of catching a glimpse of Katia when she came by. Katia was kind to all people, from the lowliest worker to the most prominent guest. She charmed them all, laughed with them, and above all, made them welcome at West Baden Springs. Groups would gather in great numbers to hear Katia play the piano, to marvel at her oil painting, but most of all, to just listen to her strange, beautiful accent and gaze into her lovely face.

John Everett could see that his wife had proved herself the most alluring attraction at West Baden. But nonetheless, he provided an astonishing array of amusements that made the hotel in effect a microcosmic fun city. The list of activities available was spectacular. The opera house offered either musical or theatrical productions each evening. Traveling companies presented current popular dramas. Indoors, there were writing rooms, lounges, a music room, and a playhouse for children. Along a grand promenade, there was a row of bathhouses that were all white and resembled Greek temples. For those who like to just sit and rock, there were platoons of rocking chairs on a long veranda. There was golf, horseback riding on wooded bridle paths, and rides on a trolley to French Lick Springs. There was a grand ballroom, a magnificent dining room, and all the supportive elements were there too: a dairy, a greenhouse and conservatory, an ice-cream manufacturing plant, an ice plant, a filtering plant—even a newspaper.

Although people had long been attracted to the valley for the therapeutic properties of its water, fantastic rumors had spread guaranteeing the water cure for more than fifty ailments, including sprains, cancer, sterility, rheumatism, asthma, and alcoholism. Although many ailments were treated, only the water's mild laxative property had been firmly established. But for this, many sufferers found relief and sang West Baden's praises far and near. Those who wanted to get the full benefit from the water were advised to drink copiously. The standard prescription was two or three glassfuls before breakfast, three or four glassfuls in the forenoon, and a like quantity in the afternoon, with an interval of fifteen to twenty minutes between each glassful. Guest were urged also to take a brisk walk—not too tiring—after drinks, which was to aid in the action of the water. A miniature cathedral stood on a hill where the ailing might ask the Almighty to assist the water.

West Baden Springs was more than a hotel. It was a whole world that wished only to be beautiful and superlative. Only pleasing, graceful elements prevailed here. Exquisite pieces from all over the world filled opulently decorated rooms, representing many periods: Queen Anne, Louis XVI, Empire, Victorian, and above all, Edwardian. Great chefs prepared gourmet food served on the finest china from England and France, to be placed on lavishly decorated tables covered with delicately laced tablecloths. All wine came from the finest vineyards. Orchestras and individual virtuosos played the greatest music of the greatest composers. The library was stacked with the finest authors from every period of civilization. The gardens were as grand as any that might accompany a royal palace in Europe.

Of course Katia's European charms helped to bring about such superlatives to West Baden Springs. Her talents astounded everyone: piano, poetry, paintings—all very accomplished.

When after four years at West Baden the Everetts announced the news of Katia's pregnancy, most people were jubilant. But one lady approached Katia, saying, "Why Katia Everett! I understand you're expecting. You poor thing! It will take you away from all your duties at West Baden. Your talents and accomplishments surpass every lady in the state. Why anyone can have a baby!" To this Katia calmly replied, "Yes, but how gracious of God to make it possible for this most wonderful thing to happen to anyone."

The Everett child was a beautiful baby girl whom they named Lillian. Thinking of Katia's Russian background, John Everett at first suggested a Russian name. But Katia insisted on this popular American name she had come to know from her new American friends. Strange how so much happiness could blossom out of the ashes of a fire. And now there was this new blessing in the form of a child. From the moment she was born, Lillian was the center of attention at West Baden. Guests would spoil her. "My, what a darling little girl," they would say. "How I envy you, Mrs. Everett, for having such a precious child." In John Everett's eyes, the child could do no wrong. He would give her outlandish gifts: ponies, stacks of dresses, mountains of toys.

When Lillian was seven, she and her mother left West Baden for an extended visit to the Randreninoffs in St. Petersburg. After having not seen their beloved Katia in some fourteen years, the Randreninoffs were ecstatic. The Randreninoffs welcomed little Lillian with cheer, but it soon became apparent that her freelance nature was not in accordance with the strict aristocratic manner of the Randreninoffs. For the first time, Lillian was no longer the center of attention. She now had cousins with whom to compete. Adults were appalled at her spoiled nature. Once Lillian's grandmother gave her a brisk slap for bad behavior. It had been the first time Lillian had known fear. She grew more fretful of the Randreninoffs each day, and her mother was her only refuge. Lillian and her mother became very close, and Katia was able to teach her daughter good manners, polite behavior, self-control, and all other elements that make up a well-brought-up young lady. The time in St. Petersburg had turned a little imp into a little lady.

Katia and Lillian's stay with the Randreninoffs that summer of 1914, however, was suddenly cut short. At Serajavo an obscure Serbian student with a single shot touched off the powder keg of military alliances in Europe that had formed since the beginning of the century. It was war, and precariousness blanketed Russia and all of Europe. In the midst of this international turmoil, the Czar's government was continually threatened by ever-strengthening revolutionary groups. With pious heart for the safety of their American relatives, the Randreninoffs urged the mother and daughter to quickly leave precarious Russia. By God's grace the two made their way back to America, though overwhelmed with concern for the Russian family.

Back at West Baden Springs, newspapers tormented Katia with bad new from her childhood home. The bad news never seemed to end. Germany was beating Russia terribly, and the revolutionary parties were gaining more power each day. Katia feared the worst for her family. All of West Baden could see anguish in her face. For three years, blow by blow, the bad news came. Then in March 1917, it happened: the people revolted. Revolution started in St. Petersburg and spread through all of Russia. In October 1917 the Bolsheviks gained control of the government. In March 1918 that government surrendered to Germany. In July 1918 Czar Nicholas II and his family were imprisoned and killed. The mighty Randreninoff family had been overthrown and many of them had been executed. Although Katia had escaped the fate of her family in Russia, she suffered with them vicariously.

Revolutionaries stormed the stately Randreninoff estate to seize the famous family jewels. But when they opened the great vault, they found nothing! Not a single gem of the Randreninoff jewels could be found. They had all completely vanished! For weeks groups searched for the jewels, but their whereabouts remained a mystery!

On April 6, 1917 the United States declared war on Germany, and a year later the West Baden Springs Hotel experienced an astonishing hiatus in its career. Because the war created a need for additional hospital facilities, the hotel became U.S. Army Hospital No. 35. There to greet the soldiers were the Everetts, who were, strange as it may seem, delighted to host the young men and excited upon their arrival. The Everetts became widely involved with the hospital. By devising activities for the convalescing men, they did their best to deep their military guests in good cheer. For Katia, the commotion of the hospital kept her mind off the sorrows of her Russian family. Lillian played junior nurse to the soldiers. While doing nothing more than taking temperature and doing small errands, Lillian thought herself the most envied eleven-year-old in the state for playing an active part in the war effort. In the evenings Katia would play at a concert grand piano in the atrium. The soldiers, opening the French doors that faced the atrium, would sing along. John Everett would stand at the very center of the atrium and conduct the large group of singing men who could be hear for miles. The West Baden wounded did not include the war's worst causalities, and for many of the soldiers, their stay at West Baden was a happy interlude in their lives. The United States Army thanked the Everetts for their hospitality and service to their country.

The war was over, and after extensive renovations, West Baden Springs was ready to pass into a new decade. Early in the summer of 1920, the Everetts hosted a grand reopening celebration. Hundreds of guests, including the governor of Indiana and other personages, joined in a full day of festivity. All were eager to forget the years of war; therefore, the reopening of West Baden Springs was to them a symbolic return to happy days. There was an opulent afternoon banquet on the front lawn. For the evening, a grand ball in the atrium had been planned.

Guests noticed only one thing different when they entered the great atrium for the ball. Except for her absence in Russia, never could the guests remember a ball at West Baden when Katia was not there to greet them at the door. John Everett and his lovely wife would stand hand in hand at the doorway with little Lillian at their side. But this time only Mr. Everett and Lillian were there. "Where is our darling Katia?" guests would immediately ask. Everett would reply to them, "She must be doing a few last-minute arrangements. She'll be right down."

But two hours had gone by and still there was no Katia. The ball was extravagant. Women wore their finest gowns and jewelry. The orchestra made an attempt to please the crowd, but the guests would not be mollified until they saw Katia, for she was much of the majesty of West Baden Springs. While dancing on the marble mosaic, guests imagined that at any minute they would turn and see Katia, whom they all knew would be the most stunning figure among them. But Katia never appeared. Guests would throng to John Everett, saying, "Where on earth is your lovely wife? We must see her." The Governor ordered Everett, "Run and fetch your wife at once! I've heard so much about her. I simply must see if she's for real."

Everett was worried. Katia would never miss greeting guests for any social occasion, let alone a grand reopening. Making his way through the crowd, John arrived at this family apartment on the third floor. He opened the bedroom door to behold with great horror his beautiful wife across the bed in a red silk evening gown. The diamonds that he had given her on their wedding sparkled at her neck. Her eyes closed, Katia's pale cheeks formed a smile of contentment. Dumbfounded, Everett held his wife in his arms, carried her to the balcony facing the atrium, opened the French doors, and stared bewildered down at the dancing people. The music was strong, the chatter loud, but Everett heard nothing. Gradually the orchestra stopped playing and people stopped dancing until not a sound was heard. A somber tone had come under the great dome. The crowd stared up at the balcony where Everett stood holding his wife.

The following day Katia lay in her casket at the center of the atrium under the great dome. A group of people even greater than that of the previous day assembled to bid their friend farewell. Somber yet composed, they would enter the atrium, finding it for the first time invaded with sorrow. At first glance of Katia in the casket, there was not one who did not shed a tear for this woman who had somehow made their lives a little better. Surely the world would be less kind without her.

Intermingled with sorrow and grief for their friend was intrigue and mystery. For the superstitious the fragments were not difficult to piece together. Indeed the Randreninoff prophecy stated that if the great family jewels were to be removed from Russian soil, it would mean the end of the Randreninoff dynasty. Many declared that the jewels had been removed from Russia and that they were hidden somewhere at West Baden Springs. Very likely the

Randreninoff family, finding themselves in a precarious state, ignored the prophecy and instructed Katia to take the jewels with her to America and return them to Russia when conditions improved for the Randreninoffs. But conditions certainly never improved for the Randreninoffs. The fact that the jewels could not be found in all of Russia further strengthened the belief that West Baden Springs was their hiding place. As for Katia, she was likely a victim of the prophecy, as were the rest of the Randreninoffs, for none are known to be living.

⊰ Chapter Three ⊱

KATIA'S MYSTERIOUS DEATH was indeed a tragedy for all those who knew and loved her. But the blessing in that life renews itself helps mitigate such tragedies. Lillian Everett was just that blessing. For the old familiar guest, Lillian was the Katia they remembered at West Baden Springs, still young and beautiful as ever. Everyone was amazed with just how much Lillian resembled her mother. Katia's rare beauty, style, charm, and precocious talents were Lillian's as well. The women seen throughout the decade in places like Chicago wore short, tight dresses and rolled their silk stockings down to their knees. They cut their hair in a boyish style called a bob and wore flashy lipstick and other cosmetics. But all of these would have proved only a mar to Lillian. Her long, dark hair, always groomed neatly, was accompanied with dark, well-defined eyelashes and eyebrows. Her skin was soft and white, her elegant clothes all tailor-made at West Baden. When guests heard the rustle of Lillian's long silk dresses about the halls of West Baden, they would turn with the expectation of seeing Katia again. Sometimes by mistake they would even call Lillian by her mother's name.

Guests adored Lillian just as they had adored Katia and even more so because, for them, Lillian was a link with the old days. Lillian was their queen with the royal duty of maintaining and preserving at West Baden the last traces of the elegant days before the war that Katia had represented so well. Throughout this decade known as the Jazz Age, West Baden remained an isolated memorial to Katia and the world she represented—that graceful, beautiful, neatly ordered life when gallantry took its last bow, when dancing the waltz, wearing elegant clothes, and using polished manners were all important. The old established families from Chicago, Indianapolis, and Louisville would take nostalgic pilgrimages to West Baden, finding it forever locked in the past, locked in the beautiful age they all loved. Groups would gather on the veranda for hours and relive their fond memories of this age. West Baden Springs was their refuge from the noise and confusion of the present Jazz Age, characterized by lax manner and morals, gambling and gangsters, bootleg liquor, and people dancing the energetic Charleston to blaring jazz music. None of these elements had ever entered West Baden Springs, and there was no reason to believe they ever would. Together Lillian and her father preserved a tiny realm of refinement far off in the rolling hills of Southern Indiana.

It was not difficult to see a special relationship between Lillian and her father. They were an inseparable pair, as familiar a sight at West Baden as John and Katia Everett had been decades before. At every sporting event, every grand social affair, every musical event, hand in hand, the two would go about and greet people.

As happy as Lillian and her father appeared, however, Lillian always knew that her father had never fully recovered from her mother's death. John Everett never talked of his late wife, and guests knew never to discuss the matter. Lillian knew that for years her father had suffered in silence, and the effects had taken toll on his health. By the time Lillian had entered college, her father showed every sign of decline: white hair, quivering voice, and slow, labored movements. As much as she avoided thinking about it, Lillian could see that before long she would be alone at West Baden Springs.

One morning in early spring of 1929, during her senior year at college, Lillian received the news of her father's death. Although the news was not a total surprise, Lillian was nevertheless heartbroken as she wept over her father's casket in the center of the atrium where her mother had been nine years before.

Lillian was taken with the same depression that had possessed her after her mother's death. Her father had always been with her as a stable source of encouragement and inspiration. Suddenly this security was pulled out from under her, just as in the case of her mother. When Lillian returned to West Baden after college, everyone there was interested in her loss. The hotel staff whispered sympathetically about her. Men playing cards, alluding to her, shook their heads and smoked in silence for a while. Gardeners told of seeing Lillian as she strayed along the grounds of West Baden with watery eyes.

Lillian found herself forever drawn to the lobby. This was where her father would always sit throughout the day, greeting guests in an armchair. Only when Lillian had entered the lobby and saw the empty armchair would she remember that her father was no longer with her. But in a way Lillian's father was still with her, and her mother as well. Her mother and father and the world they represented were everywhere at West Baden Springs. Everyone still talked of the Everetts; people would never let them die.

Guests at West Baden could see Lillian was unhappy. In an effort to lift her spirits, they invited her to their homes, introduced her to their city's notable citizens, and hosted grand events in her honor. On these visits Lillian was treated as a celebrity. Every person of high society wanted to meet her, for all knew of Katia, the legend of the Randreninoff jewels, and the wide fame of West Baden Springs.

On a visit to Chicago, Lillian herself was captivated with someone she had met. Lillian met the famous Braxton Kingsley. Although not part of the familiar old guard who visited West Baden Springs, he was a wealthy businessman and was considered the most dashing man in Chicago. Women's hearts would flutter for him. Lillian had heard girls at college rave about this dashing man, but she never considered him or any other of the common things her college peers would discuss. But, meeting him for the first time there in Chicago, Lillian could see that Braxton Kingsley was anything but common. She had to admit that with his tall, dark, masculine bearing, he was the most striking man she had ever seen. With his dynamic charisma, he seemed to fascinate everyone. Lillian was at once infatuated with him. Night after night Braxton Kingsley would call at Lillian's Chicago address, rendering his full charm. Lillian became more infatuated with him each time he would call.

After Lillian returned to West Baden, Kingsley would make regular visits there as well. By that summer of 1929, Lillian could see that her relationship with Braxton had turned into more than just a casual friendship. In her world of idealism, Lillian had long known West Baden Springs as the setting, but now Braxton Kingsley had become the principle player. He played the part of the knight in shining armor who had captured her imagination and made her forget much of the sorrow brought on by her father's death. All through the summer, talk of the courtship buzzed from Chicago to Louisville. The two were frequently seen walking the grounds of West Baden hand in hand. Although the announcement of their engagement had been no surprise, many were a little startled, however, that the wedding would take place so soon—as early September.

Lillian's female college peers were electrified at the news of her engagement. None could believe that this goody—whom they regarded as an outcast of their Jazz Age, who always seemed off on her superlative cloud—had captured the very prized they all coveted. They came at once to West Baden, making an effort to rekindle any slight bit of friendship with Lillian. When convinced of the reality of the engagement, they saw Lillian in quite a different light. If the proper and prim Lillian Everett had managed to snag Braxton Kingsley, a man known to prefer more provocative women, perhaps there was something about Lillian they had overlooked. Lillian was flattered that her college peers came rendering their friendship to her at West Baden. It seemed as though she had finally won them over as friends, which was something she could never do at college. Although Lillian did everything to keep her friends pleased, most grew bored with West Baden very quickly. By late August only three female friends and their boyfriends remained regulars at West Baden Springs.

Lillian sat with these three friends at the oriental shrine in the formal garden one week before her wedding. It would be difficult to imagine a more colorful scene than the four girls dressed in bright clothing and surrounded by the vibrant flowers of the garden. The flowers had been blooming all summer long, so by that warm late summer afternoon, they had reached their peak. The surrounding forest was a lush green and overflowing with life. It was late afternoon, and while still bright, the sun had begun to diminish in strength. It was not difficult to distinguish Lillian from her three friends. Minnie, Violet, and Pearl were their names. In their short, tight skirts and flashy cosmetics, they were the epitome of the present-day fashion. As they chattered and moved about energetically, Lillian, never drifting from a demure manner, sat in the middle of her three vivacious friends.

"I don't know why I asked you three here," said Lillian. "I thought you could help me with last-minute arrangements for the wedding, but you three chatterboxes have proven yourselves more a nuisance than anything else. I'd be better off talking to a gardener."

"But Lillian," replied Pearl. "How can you remain so calm when in just a week you'll be standing in this very spot taking the vows of marriage with Braxton Kingsley! I'd be so excited I couldn't stop screaming!"

"How did you ever manage to snag him, Lillian?" asked Minnie. "Why, every single woman in Chicago must have been after him."

"And every married woman too!" added Violet.

"Lillian, are you sure it's such a good idea having a garden wedding?" Pearl suggested. "What if it rains?"

"The sky would not dare rain on my wedding. Everything's going to be nothing but sunshine. It's going to happened again—the Camelot era at West Baden Springs that everyone thought was gone forever." Lillian spoke with a dreamlike voice as she rested her head on one of the columns of the shrine and looked over at the domed hot with its Byzantine towers. "As a little girl I can remember standing next to my parents while they received guests at grand balls and elegant affairs. You should have seen the gleam in people's eyes when they would meet my mother. Why shouldn't we be as happy and admired as they were? Braxton fits in at West Baden perfectly, as if it had all been imagined. Tonight I'm hosting a party for Braxton. I want some old friends of my parents to meet him. I sometimes think of them as my adopted family, and I want their approval of Braxton, even though I don't know how anyone could disapprove of him."

"What!" snapped Minnie. "You're having a party tonight for Braxton and you didn't invite us?"

"I didn't think you'd be interested in socializing with any of the people there."

"Of course we're not interested in socializing with those old goats," replied Minnie. "But as long as Braxton will be there, that's reason enough to come."

"Yes, anything to see Braxton," Violet added.

"Good heavens, girls!" exclaimed Pearl. "What on earth are we going to wear?"

"So this is your plot, Lillian Everett," said Minnie. "You planned to spring this party on us at the last minute, when you'd know we would have left all our best evening attire at home. You want us to look like fools in front of Braxton. Is that your game? But don't worry, girls. We'll still be the only women there in style. Braxton will have to notice that, considering all the chic places one finds him at in Chicago. Lillian, you'd think after being around us all summer you'd take after our good, modern style. Just look at you! You look like something out of another century."

"Always remember, Lillian," said Pearl. "One must be a little scandalous these days to be in style, and that it's much more fashionable to be a divorcee than an old maid."

"It's quite the fashion to break the law," said Violet. "Especially when it comes to drinking. Everyone does it, you know."

Minnie continued. "These are reckless times and there's no limit to the fun people can have now that they've defied the stupid, boring ways of the past. I feel there's nothing I can't do."

"Well, if you're coming to the dinner party tonight," said Lillian, "I'm afraid there is something I will have to ask you not to do. Please don't flirt with Braxton in front of the other guests. It would be very embarrassing for me."

"But, Lillian," replied Violet. "Braxton is always the only handsome man around this place. Who else would we flirt with?"

"You don't have to flirt at all," retorted Lillian.

"Don't worry, girls," said Pearl. "We can always flirt with that waiter again."

"Of course!" said Violet. "He's so cute and innocent looking—like a little puppy dog."

"I'm afraid we can't flirt with him either," replied Minnie. "I overheard Rimsky fire him this morning."

"Fire him?" Pearl replied in astonishment. "That's terrible. What for?"

"How should I know," said Minnie. "I don't keep up on the affairs of servants."

"Lillian, do you know whom we are talking about?" Pearl questioned.

"I think so. You mean the one who always looks lost?"

"Yes, that's the one," Pearl continued. "You're the owner of West Baden Springs, Lillian. Go straight to Rimsky this instant and tell him to rehire that poor waiter."

"I can't very well tell Rimsky to rehire a waiter just because you three want to flirt with him."

"Then make up something," said Pearl. "Oh come on, Lillian. We're so fond of this one."

"What would your boyfriends say about all of this?"

Lillian stopped talking. Something passing through the front gate caught the attention of the four girls and just about every one else. The male counterparts of the three girls had arrived in a sports car, the engine roaring, the horn blaring, and the three young men screaming for joy. Never could Lillian remember these three—Harold, Chuck, and Roy—arriving at West Baden in any other fashion. The boys stopped along the grand driveway, jumped out, and ran to the shrine to join the four girls.

"We won the game of golf!" exclaimed Roy. "It was an incredible victory! We three fearless Spartan athletes totally devastated our opponents! Your heroes have returned for a victory celebration."

The girls looked bored and uninterested.

"What's with this?" Chuck questioned. "We three virile athletes spend an entire day of drudgery under the scorching sun to achieve victory and we come back to this?"

"Sorry, boys," said Minnie. "But golf is a bore!"

"How could anybody not be interested in golf?" said Chuck. "It's the most exciting thing in the world!"

"We know a story, though, that will amuse you for sure," said Harold. "But for acting so glum about our golf victory, we're not going to tell you."

"Oh come on!" shouted Violet. "That's not fair. Tell us!"

"You know you three jokers are just dying to brag about whatever practical joke you pulled," Lillian added.

"Well, all right," said Harold. "Since you're forcing us to tell. Rimsky and some of the staff were in the dining room this morning. Then came the perfect opportunity."

Roy continued with the story. "We went in while they were working, saying that we were looking for a glove one of you girls left behind. That little blond waiter we always pick on walked right passed us with a huge silver punch bowl full of leftover punch. We tripped him!"

"And where do you think the punch landed?" Chuck questioned. "On Rimsky! I've never seen anybody so mad in all my life. And the best part is that little schmuck waiter got fired, all because of us!"

"So you three are to blame for this!" scolded Pearl.

"What's wrong, girls?" said Roy. "Don't you think it's funny?"

"No, we most certainly do not," retorted Pearl. "And Lillian is going straight to Rimsky this instant, to explain everything and make Rimsky rehire that poor waiter, aren't you, Lillian."

"I suppose I should. But can't you three find better things to do than play such nasty tricks?"

"What else is there to do around this place?" whined Chuck.

"Let's have more parties," said Violet. "There must be some local hillbillies who can make some bootleg liquor for us," said Minnie.

"We'll turn the place into a speakeasy," said Roy with excitement. "And do some outlandish things—scavenger hunts, flagpole-climbing, stunts from airplanes."

"I know something all of you can do tomorrow night," said Lillian in a bold, confident manner. "Come to another one of my piano recitals. This time I'm playing Chopin's Mazurka in B Flat Minor, Opus 24, Number 4. It will be marvelous."

"Oh, Lillian, we're so tired of your stupid piano recitals," snapped Minnie. "They are such a bore. Don't you ever do anything fun? I can't imagine why Braxton would want to marry you."

"It can't be for money," Chuck pointed out. "Kingsley's got plenty."

"It must be the jewels!" exclaimed Roy. "Yes, that must be why Kingsley is marrying you, Lillian—to get the famous Randreninoff jewels."

"Don't tell me you believe in that silly legend that the Randreninoff jewels are hidden here," said Lillian. "Father and I never found any hidden jewels at West Baden Springs and nobody ever will. They're not here and that's all there is to it."

"Of course they're here. Where else would they be?" asked Roy.

Lillian tried to reason with Roy. "We're always finding holes on the grounds where people have dug illegally. Don't you think someone would have found them by now?"

"Your mother was a clever woman," Roy continued. "She hid the jewels where nobody would ever think of looking. But don't worry. They'll be found someday, and what a great day that will be."

"A great day for somebody," said Harold. "But not a great day for Lillian or West Baden Springs."

"What do you mean by that?" Pearl asked.

"I can just picture the day the jewels are found. The news of their discovery will spread like wildfire and people will come to West Baden, running across its grounds like cattle to get a handful of gems. These gardens will become nothing but wasteland. This gracious hotel will be reduced to a ruin, just like Sutter's property during the California Gold Rush."

"I'll bet Rimsky has long made off with them," said Violet. "He's so sinister and evil-looking. He scares me to death. Lillian, you must be out of your mind for keeping him on as manager. He probably robs you blind."

"And the worst thing is that he never lets us have any fun around here," complained Violet.

"Wouldn't it be great to have him gone from West Baden Springs," said Roy. "Imagine the fun we would have."

"He doesn't own the place, you know," Minnie pointed out. "Though you'd never think so by the way he acts and by the way people treat him. Lillian, you can't tell us that you like Rimsky. In fact, I can remember several times when you've acted downright petrified of him."

"No, I don't like him at all. I think there's something evil about him. I think everyone does. But he's always done such a good job as manager that father would never let him go."

"That's ridiculous!" declared Roy. "Kingsley probably knows a dozen people in Chicago who can run this place better than Rimsky. Lillian Everett, go over to the hotel right now and tell that old buzzard that he's through!"

"No! I couldn't do that!"

"Do you want him here as manager?"

"No, I don't but—"

"But nothing. Get rid of him. You act like he's the devil or something. You're actually too afraid of him to fire him, aren't you?"

"Maybe …"

"Maybe what, Lillian?"

"Braxton told me he'll need a business manager at West Baden. I could suggest that position to Rimsky. Managing West Baden Springs would be nothing compared to managing Braxton's vast financial empire. Rimsky would be sure to take the position. And then I could get a new manager for the hotel."

"And then we could have better parties because old Rimsky wouldn't be in charge of the hotel to ruin all our fun," said Violet with enthusiasm.

"Then it's settled," said Pearl. "Go to the hotel right now Lillian and tell Rimsky."

"Right now? Couldn't I make it some other time?"

"No, do it right now or else you won't do it," Pearl continued. "You have a way of avoiding unpleasant things, Lillian."

"But I need some time to think about this."

"Lillian Everett," scolded Minnie. "We're not going to say another word until you get up, go over to the hotel, and tell Rimsky."

Lillian's six friends remained silent and looked away from her. Lillian then stood up reluctantly and walked slowly toward the hotel.1

⊰ Chapter Four ⊱

LILLIAN ENTERED THE hotel lobby. She did not want to confront Rimsky. Meandering through the lobby, she small-talked to anyone she could find, surveyed some menus that were posted near the dining room, sifted through some papers behind the front desk—anything to stay clear of Rimsky.

When an hour had passed, Lillian found herself in a secluded corner, lost in one her favorite romance novels. She looked up, however, startled, almost frightened, to find Minnie standing over her. "Did you talk to Rimsky yet, Lillian?" Minnie asked peremptorily.

Lillian saw the other five across the lobby staring at her with blank faces. "Well, ah, I was just about to and …" Lillian knew she had procrastinated. "And I found some things behind the desk that just simply could not wait." Minnie gave a stern look and then turned sharply to a bellboy. "Leave word with Mr. Rimsky that Miss Lillian would like to see him in her office immediately." The bellboy turned at once to Lillian, who reluctantly nodded an approval.

Lillian looked at them both with a fearful face, looked at the other five with the same face, and then proceeded to her office in a feeble fashion.

Lillian's office was an elegant little pink, feminine, Louis XVI style room just off the lobby. As it had been her mother's office at one time, Lillian had long made an effort to preserve the room so that nothing about it had changed since her mother's death. The desk and the rest of the furnishings were light, dainty pieces with elaborate adornment and intricate carving. All around the room in small, ornately carved, gold frames were photographs and paintings of the Randreninoff family. A large portrait painting of Katia rested proudly over a diminutive fireplace. Even with just one window, the little office was the most bright and cheerful in the hotel; the afternoon sunlight would beam vibrantly through white Priscilla curtains.

When building the hotel, Katia had situated her office so as to allow a view of the front entryway in order to see arriving guests. The view farther to the left continued all the way down the grand boulevard to the main gate and train depot. The view farther to the right gave sight to the magnificent formal gardens. The view from the window was Lillian's favorite. She would sometimes stand there for great periods of time in a dreamlike gaze as she watched people stroll through the gardens or arrive at the front gate. The office was Lillian's private little space where she could daydream, where her mind could wander and her thoughts could be free. Lillian was glad she was confronting Rimsky in this office, where the Randreninoffs, from their picture frames, could encourage her with their stern, aristocratic faces. This was one place at West Baden where Rimsky had no control. Just being in the bright, cheerful room increased Lillian's confidence immensely.

Lillian sat at her desk fidgeting, rehearsing things to tell Rimsky. Nothing sounded right. She grew more apprehensive by the minute. Perhaps it was not too late to change her mind. Perhaps when Rimsky came she could simply say she wanted to see how things were coming along with the dinner party preparations. Then what would she tell her friends who would certainly be eager for results? No, she would have to go through with it. She would have to make a proposal to Rimsky. With Rimsky as Braxton's business manager,

Lillian could find someone else to run the hotel, someone whom she could control.

Roy had been right when he said Lillian was afraid to dismiss Rimsky. She dreaded to think of what the old man might do if dismissed. Lillian had feared Rimsky ever since his arrival at West Baden Springs ten years ago when she was but a girl of twelve. She remembered well that infamous day when he came to West Baden bearing the name Igor Sergeavich Rimsky. No one at West Baden save Katia would have recognized this refugee from the Russian Revolution as a once powerful and wealthy land baron. Apparently Rimsky had been a friend of the Randreninoffs, but just why Katia ever hired Rimsky and eventually made him in charge of the hotel administration would always remain a mystery to Lillian. Perhaps as a result of the revolution in her native land and the great engagement of war in her adopted land, Katia thought Rimsky best suited for preserving an old-world manner at West Baden. But Katia had failed to see then that whatever favorable trace of old-world spice that came with Rimsky on that day of his arrival, there also came something evil that outweighed the former tenfold. Lillian could not prove this, but she knew it somehow.

She had wanted to dismiss Rimsky since the day she inherited West Baden, but other than her personal dislike for him, she could not find a reasonable excuse for doing so. Technically there was nothing wrong with Rimsky's administration; in fact, everything ran like clockwork. Lillian's father had long been pleased with Rimsky's efficiency and had never once considered dismissing him. Still, Lillian knew she would never feel entirely at ease at West Baden until Rimsky had been replaced.

Through the years Lillian had always avoided Rimsky. His characteristic slow, lumpy footsteps echoing throughout any hall at West Baden were Lillian's signal to turn and walk in the opposite direction. She listened for his footsteps extra carefully before turning corners and would always make a detour if it allowed her to avoid Rimsky. Traces and clues of Rimsky seemed ubiquitous throughout the hotel: flower arrangements, table displays, furniture arrangements, menu selection—all so characteristically Rimsky, all done just his way. And he had staunch control over the staff, almost as if he had them under a spell of obsequiousness. When Lillian's father was alive, there was never a need to deal with Rimsky. She would surround herself with dozens of admirers and forget his presence. But now, as owner of West Baden Springs, Lillian could no longer avoid Rimsky.

Antagonism arose between the two the instant Lillian returned home from college that spring of 1929. Lillian thought she had returned so educated and sophisticated and that she could run West Baden just as her mother did years ago. But Rimsky frustrated her ambitions by doing everything he could to prove to the staff and to the guests that Lillian was an inept, foolish child, completely incapable of making decisions at West Baden. Lillian tried to prove Rimsky wrong, but usually her efforts would end in disaster.

For Independence Day Lillian had taken it upon herself to order new tablecloths for the dining room. Not until Lillian opened the doors to the dining room to allow her guests entry did she and the guests discover the tablecloths were not long enough to cover the tables. Lillian could remember many other fiascoes, even as far back as Christmas and Easter. She had changed Rimsky's Christmas drink from old English wassail to eggnog. Just when Lillian had proposed a toast of Christmas cheer did she and the guests notice that the eggnog had curded. At Easter, shortly after her father's death, Lillian had organized an Easter egg hunt for the children of the county. Only, the staff had hidden the eggs so well that very few children ever found eggs, and Lillian's grand event turned into nothing but crying children and disappointed parents. Eventually Lillian learned never to interfere with Rimsky's management, but she was nevertheless annoyed that she had so little control over the hotel. Even when Lillian would do something so simple as change a flower arrangement, she would always find that her change had been completely reverted within an hour, and no matter how many times she would make the change, a reversion would always occur shortly thereafter.

Lillian wished she had more control over the hotel. But no matter what Lillian might do, the staff and guests would still adore her. In their eyes Lillian Everett was queen of West Baden Springs and nothing could ever change their opinion of her. Nothing could ever make them see a flaw in her, no matter what fiasco might occur. This was the one thing at West Baden over which Rimsky had no control: he could not keep people from adoring Lillian. Everyone adored and admired her. She knew this by the way she would captivate an audience during a piano recital. She knew this at every grand event when guests would throng to her. She knew this by the way the staff regarded her with almost a degree of sanctity. Rimsky was well aware of Lillian's wide acclaim even though he did everything to remind Lillian and others of her shortcomings. But perhaps Rimsky's inability to defile the staff and guests' opinion of Lillian was as frustrating for Rimsky as Lillian's inability to control the hotel administration was for her.

It was Rimsky. As he walked through the door, the bright, cheerful room was suddenly covered with a blanket of darkness and gloom. A cloud had covered the sun so that the sunshine no longer beamed through the white Priscilla curtains. Meeting Rimsky in Katia's office had given Lillian a false sense of security, for any trace of encouragement present in the room was suddenly obscured by this dark man. Eyes black as coal, face still as stone, Rimsky stood in silence for a moment. He was a short, thin man with black-and-gray gnarled hair. In a Russian accent, he spoke with an irritating whine. "You wish to see me, Miss Lillian?"

Lillian knew that if she did not stop gazing into Rimsky's entrancing eyes she would never say what she had intended. She turned away quickly and looked out the window. "Yes, I have something very important to discuss with you," she said nervously, trying to force the words out. She did everything to avoid looking into his eyes. Words and phrases twisted around in her mind, but nothing seemed coherent. "I, I'm sure that my mother and father would have appreciated everything you've done for West Baden Spring in the ten years that you've been here. You've done everything in your power to maintain West Baden to a state to where both of them, the builders of West Baden, would be proud even today. I want to say that, that I too appreciate everything you've done for West Baden in these ten years, and, and I appreciate your loyalty as well." Everything Lillian had meant to say glibly had come out clumsily. Rimsky looked at Lillian as though she was wasting his time.

Nevertheless, Lillian continued. "Since you've proven yourself so admirably at West Baden through the years, Mr. Rimsky, I now have a much more important position for you to fill. My future husband will be living here after we're married. He plans to establish West Baden as his permanent and official residence. And of course, as anyone would expect, Mr. Kingsley will be requiring a business manager here to handle his vast enterprises, most of all in the stock market. You know we have a broker's branch office of Logan and Bryan right here at West Baden. I feel that there's no one better suited for the job than you, Rimsky, and with your approval I will take every measure to secure the position for you."

There was silence. Lillian wished Rimsky would say something rather than make her endure the tension of silence. She continued to look out the window.

"Your proposal overwhelms me, Miss Lillian," said Rimsky. "I accept with great enthusiasm."

"I am very glad to here this." It seemed too easy. Where was the usual opposition she received from Rimsky? Where was the questioning, criticizing, and scrutiny? Even with knowing very little about Braxton's business, Rimsky accepted the position without hesitation. Lillian's apprehension apparently had not been necessary. For once one of her schemes had worked. "Mr. Kingsley is due back within the hour. I will talk to him immediately about the proposal, and then I'm sure he will be eager to make arrangements with you shortly thereafter. Don't worry about the hotel administration. I'm sure we can find a suitable replacement."

"Replacement?" Rimsky questioned.

"Yes, you will require a replacement as head administrator of West Baden Springs."

"And why should this be necessary?"

"Mr. Rimsky, you did accept my proposal to be Mr. Kingsley's business manager, did you not?"

"Yes, with great enthusiasm."

"Surely you won't be able to continue your present job if you take on this new position."

"Why should this not be possible? I was one of the most powerful land barons in Russia with vast properties and influence. Certainly both positions would not be a great difficulty."

He had done it again. He had confounded Lillian's plan. Somehow at the back of her mind Lillian knew all along this would happen. Why could he not comply with her just once! He always had to make matters difficult. "Mr. Rimsky, I really can't see you handling both jobs. I would hate to think of you wearing yourself out. You were much younger back in Russia."

"One grows wiser and more capable with years."

"Still I would hate to see you overexert yourself with both jobs. If something happened I would never forgive myself."

"Nonsense! I will insist upon remaining head administrator at West Baden Springs."

How foolish of Lillian to think that Rimsky would just up and leave after controlling the hotel for all these years. Her plan had backfired. Lillian did not think she could stand another argument with Rimsky. If only her father were here to handle him. If there was only someone else at West Baden who could deal with Rimsky!

Why not let Braxton handle Rimsky? Yes! Why had she not thought of this before? With Braxton at West Baden, Lillian might not ever have to deal with Rimsky again. Why, Braxton might get rid of Rimsky altogether! How wonderful that would be. She would drop the matter for now and tell Braxton everything when he arrived. Lillian knew that Braxton could deal with Rimsky. "There is really nothing more we can say now, Mr. Rimsky, until I consult with my future husband over the matter."

"As you wish, miss. If there is nothing more, I have many matters of which to attend."

"No, that will be all, Mr. Rimsky."

Just as Rimsky turned for the door, Lillian remembered the matter of the waiter that the girls had brought up. "Oh, Mr. Rimsky, there is just one more small matter I forgot to mention."

"And what would that be, miss?"

"Lillian replied nonchalantly, "There is a young waiter who you discharged today."

"Yes, that is correct."

"There is no need to discharge him now. You see the accident this morning in the dining room was a practical joke. Three of my mischievous friends were responsible for tripping the waiter. So in all fairness, Mr. Rimsky, I feel you should rehire the waiter."

Rimsky's black eyes went into fury. Lillian thought she had escaped Rimsky's temperament, but it showed now. It was the same reaction every time Lillian tried to interfere with Rimsky.

"That will be impossible. Arrangements have already been made. I never relinquish after taking action on anything."

"That hardly seems fair. The whole incident was not his fault."

"It's no matter. I was planning to discharge the waiter anyway. The young man is completely useless. There is no place for him at West Baden Springs. It would be poor judgment to keep on such a useless lad."

"Poor judgment or not, I would still like you to keep him on. There are certain people at West Baden who are quite fond of him."

"Fond of a common waiter?"

"I know that must sound ridiculous to you who are used to such a rigid class structure, but please, Mr. Rimsky, all I ask is that you give him another chance, and if he proves unsuitable then let him go."

"He already proves completely unsuitable."

Lillian had reached her limit with Rimsky. It was bad enough that she had failed at the primary mission of this meeting with Rimsky, but she would not relinquish such a small matter as this. She hardly knew the waiter, but still, it was the principle that mattered. She would not let Rimsky tell her what to do at her own hotel. From deep within her, a spark became ignited, and she spoke words unfamiliar to her demeanor.

"Mr. Rimsky, when I give an order, I expect it to be carried out. Mr. Kingsley will be arriving shortly, and I may have to ask him to intervene if my orders are not carried out. I'm sure you will not be able to get around him as easily as you do me."

Rimsky's eyes were pierced with astonishment at hearing Lillian's bold words. He replied in a calm voice, "As you wish, miss." He then turned and walked out the door somberly, leaving tension between himself and Lillian at a new high.

⊰ Chapter Five ⊱

RIMSKY LEFT LILLIAN'S office and proceeded across the atrium toward the dining room to continue with preparations for Lillian's dinner party. The atrium was crowded with guests gathered in delicate wooden tables and chairs, enjoying afternoon tea amid lofty palms and hothouse plants.

The moment Rimsky passed through the dining room door, the room fell to a hush, though the staff continued yet with ever greater vigor to set the tables ever so punctiliously. As the staff scurried about, Rimsky suddenly shouted "Back!" at which time the entire staff halted at a perfect line back away from the tables. Rimsky then pulled out a measuring device from his pocket. He went around at random to tables, measuring the distance from the dinner plate to the edge of the table, from the bread-and-butter plate to the butter knife, to the wine glass, and then to the water glass, the salad fork, dessert fork, dessert spoon, soup spoon, and so on. Rimsky then stood back and viewed each table at a distance. He picked a few dead petals from some flowered centerpieces, turned to the staff with his usual scowl, and then proceeded calmly out of the room.

The kitchen's reaction to Rimsky was the same. As the cooks continued with their food preparations, Rimsky went about them with menu in hand, observing and sampling in extreme detail: caviare oeuf panier, Lynn haven bays, cream of chicken profitroles, consommé d'Orleans, boiled Columbia River salmon regence, potatoes Sarah Bernhardt, braised gigot fausse vinaison St. Hubert, vol-au-vent of sweetbreads Toulouse, beignet soufflee Marie Louise Sabayon, roast suckling pig stuffed with glazed apples, cauliflower au gratin, roast young turkey stuffed with oysters and cranberry sauce, spiced lobster, English plum pudding, crepe suzette—to name a few items on the chef's menu.

Just as Rimsky began to consult the head cook, a loud thump went off in the pantry. The kitchen, before bustling with commotion, was suddenly subdued. All faces were expressionless as they stared into Rimsky's angry eyes. In the pantry Rimsky found the young waiter, Hans, whom he had discharged that morning but whom Lillian had forced Rimsky to rehire only minutes ago. Rimsky stood silent. The slender young man was only slightly larger than Rimsky. Hair blond, eyes blue, Hans's boyish face looked younger than its twenty-two years.

"I hope I'm not interrupting anything," said Rimsky in a harsh voice.

With these words Hans jumped and faced Rimsky, completely startled. "Oh, Mr. Rimsky! I was just …" Hans paused as if thinking up something to say.

"From all the noise you've been making back here, I could scarcely call your actions clandestine. And so I must assume you are, ah, perhaps, helping to clean the pantry?"

"No, not exactly, Mr. Rimsky," replied Hans uncomfortably. "I'm just taking little break."

"A break? It would appear that your entire existence at West Baden Springs is one break followed by another then another. How many times must I tell you that I do not tolerate breaks! They are a flagrant display of inefficiency. You servants at this hotel sometimes have it better than the guests. American servants are the most useless creatures on earth. The moment they taste the slightest morsel of this idiotic American democracy, it infects them like a chronic disease and off they go in a world of dreams, thinking they will soon aspire to be millionaires, deeming their duties as servants as only a temporary inconvenience. In Russia I ruled over the miserable masses whose very lives were governed by fear. I ruled over these pathetic creatures who were too ignorant to claw their way out of the abyss of misery, whose piercing, bloodshot eyes revealed their longing for some better life that was all too unattainable."

These long-winded orations were so very typical of Rimsky. Hans would hear one every time he had done something wrong, and that was quite often. Rimsky usually ended up saying the same thing every time. Although Hans would always make an attempt to act as though he had paid attention, his response always told Rimsky otherwise.

"I'm always open to a little constructive criticism, Mr. Rimsky," replied Hans. "But considering this is my last day at West Baden Springs, I find your words of limited value with regards to my future aspirations."

"Words of impudence flow through your mouth with such perfect ease." Rimsky's temper began to escalate. "Do you think I would be standing here wasting my time if this was your last day? It should be no surprise to you that I have just received orders from Miss Lillian that you are to remain on my staff."

Hans could not believe what he had just heard. Could it really be possible that Miss Lillian had interposed for him?

"Miss Lillian told you this herself, Mr. Rimsky?"

"Yes."

"I did not think she even knew my name," said Hans softly.

Hans had had a crush on Lillian ever since his arrival at West Baden one year ago. Perhaps Lillian had at last noticed him. She must have been fond of him in some way. Why else would she want to keep Hans at West Baden? It most certainly could not have been for his performance as a waiter.

"You think you're pretty clever, don't you?" continued Rimsky. "You think that by going over my authority and appealing to Miss Lillian that you've outsmarted me, ah?"

"I made no such appeal," retorted Hans boldly. "If Miss Lillian wishes to keep me on at West Baden Springs, she has every right to do so. After all, is she not the owner of this fine hotel?"

"You will shut your stupid mouth concerning matters of which of you know nothing. As for Miss Lillian, I've seen the way you behave around her. You're in love with her, aren't you? You think by her little act of amnesty that she's finally responded to your secret affection. You're a fool for reaching out for the impossible. Miss Lillian would laugh at the very notion of a common servant daring to have the slightest affection for a lady of her status. Obviously, the fact that Miss Lillian is to be married within a week still has not penetrated your head. Or do you intend within a week's time to compete with Mr. Braxton Kingsley for her affection? Mr. Kingsley gives her diamonds and sables, and what have you to offer?"

"It's no matter," continued Rimsky. "I've wasted enough time with you. Only, let me warn you that you will not be able to survive my administration in your present daydreaming condition. You will discover all to soon who is in complete control at West Baden Springs. You will know the full impact of my power and influence that grows steadily each day."

Rimsky left the pantry as quietly as he had entered, leaving Hans alone with nothing but Lillian on his mind. Hans had been in an excited state ever since Rimsky had told him of Lillian's orders to rehire him. Why would she do such a thing if she did not have at least a small affection for Hans? Hans straightened his uniform, combed his hair, and proceeded out the pantry toward the veranda to continue his duties as a waiter. Lillian was Hans's incentive to hurry back to work. Perhaps he might see her on the veranda. If not there, then most certainly in the lobby, and maybe, yes maybe, she might show some interest, whether by something she might do, say, or even by the way she might look at Hans.

As Hans went about the guests on the veranda with lemonade and iced tea, he looked about in hopes of seeing Lillian. The thought of her still preoccupied his mind, as it did much of the time. Even though Hans would see Lillian for only minutes at a time, it was these minutes that were most precious to him. At dinner he would see her the most. Continually he would implore the headwaiter to let him wait on Lillian's table. There Hans would find Lillian each night, scintillating among guests, charming everyone around her. Only recently had she been spending her evening meal with her six friends from college. Lillian was so unlike these children of the Jazz Age. Her moves were not abrupt and energetic, but slow and graceful. Her voice was not loud and brazen, but soft and musical.

Anywhere Hans would see Lillian, whether among guests in the dining room, whether playing the piano in the lobby, or even when he would watch her from the veranda walking by herself about the grounds of West Baden, one thought always remained suppressed at the back of his mind: he could never have her. Any affection for her was pure folly. She was the owner of West Baden Springs at the extreme top of the hierarchy, and he was the lowest, most modest servant. He had built a dream world around her that could never know reality. Yet although only an illusion, this dream world nevertheless made his life meaningful. There was something to look forward to every day, something wonderful that could happen: a moment with Lillian.

As Hans passed a window that looked into the lobby, he saw Lillian at the lobby's grand piano, hovering over some sheet music, skimming through the pages randomly. Of course! Lillian was preparing for an evening concert to accompany her dinner party. This was Hans's golden opportunity to be with Lillian.

After setting down his tray of refreshments on the veranda, Hans entered the lobby and timidly made his way to the vicinity of the grand piano. As

Hans lingered about stupidly, Lillian, still seated, suddenly turned away from the score and addressed him.

"I'm so glad to see you!" she said energetically.

Hans turned toward Lillian nervously.

"Well, ah, I'm glad to see you too, Miss Lillian," Hans said as if flustered.

"Never mind me. Just go ahead and do what you have to."

Hans looked confused.

Lillian continued. "You are here to set up chairs for the concert, are you not? And surely there are others on the way?"

The concert—this was why Lillian was glad to see Hans—so he could help set up for the concert. What a fool Hans had been for thinking otherwise and what a terrible impression he was making as he stood there maladroitly trying to speak.

"Ah, yes, Miss Lillian, the others will be along shortly. I might as well begin."

"Go right ahead," said Lillian without looking up from the score. "You won't disturb me."

Hans would have to make the most of his time alone with Lillian before the other waiters arrived. He went about setting up chairs and stands, clumsily clanging and banging, paying little attention to what he was doing. Lillian ignored him as she sat leafing through the musical score, her thoughts fully immersed in the work. This was Hans's big chance to speak with Lillian, but what on earth could he say? He just had to blurt out something.

"By the way, Miss Lillian," said Hans with a crack in his voice. "Just to refresh your memory, I'm Hans. I've been here at West Baden for about a year now. I usually wait on your table at dinner."

Lillian did not look up as she continued leafing through the score.

"Did you say something?"

"Yes my name is Hans, remember?"

"Hans? Hans as in Hans Richter?" Lillian spoke in a voice as to imply she was paying Hans little attention as she continued to leaf through the musical score.

Who on earth is Hans Richter? thought Hans.

"I beg your pardon, Miss Lillian, Hans Richter?"

Lillian went on in a preoccupied fashion.

"Yes, the famous Hungarian conductor. As a matter of fact he conducted the premiere of Elgar's first symphony in A flat, calling the slow movement the most beautiful since Beethoven. Elgar even dedicated the work to Maestro Richter."

"How interesting, Miss Lillian. It's Hans also as in Hans Christian Andersen who wrote stories for children."

"Very sweet, but I usually stick to things more sophisticated like Shakespeare, Dante, and Tolstoy."

"Of course," said Hans feebly.

There was another quiet spell. Again Hans tried to say something.

"I enjoy your concerts, Miss Lillian." No reaction. "You are certainly the finest pianist I have ever heard." Lillian still paid no attention to Hans. But suddenly Lillian stopped leafing through the score, turned, and looked Hans straight in the eye, giving him her full attention. "Now I remember. I was just talking to Mr. Rimsky about you not less than an hour ago. He had quite a few words to say about you."

"I hope not all bad." Hans gave a boyish grin.

"Well, nothing that would make me change my mind about rehiring you."

"Miss Lillian, I can't tell you how much I appreciate your effort in reacquiring my job. It was very kind of you."

"More than anything else," said Lillian flippantly, "it would appear that you have certain admirers at West Baden Springs." Lillian turned and looked at the score, again giving Hans only half her attention.

But Lillian suddenly stood up from the piano bench and took three quick steps away from Hans, leaving him talking into the air. Something at the doorway had captured her complete attention. It was Braxton Kingsley. At first sight of him standing, tall and bold in a dark suit, his white teeth gleaming, his mustache giving him a distinguished look, Lillian walked quickly toward him. Guests from all over the lobby witnessed Lillian fling her arms around her future husband in great excitement. It would have been impossible to remove the smile from Lillian's face as she took Braxton's arm and strolled through the lobby with him. Eventually the two made their way back to the piano, where Hans was setting up chairs and stands. Hans listened as they talked.

"Let's go over this way to the piano, Braxton, darling," said Lillian. "I want to show you what I'm playing for tonight's sunset concert. Here it is—Chopin's piano concerto No. 1 in E minor." Lillian handed Braxton the score. "It's one of my favorites, although I'm sure you've heard it a thousand times."

As Braxton scanned the orchestral score in a puzzled way, his eyes rolled through the pages in apparent enigma. Hans knew at once Braxton knew nothing about reading music. "Yes, Lillian, I listen to this one all the time," said Braxton. "It looks very familiar."

"Don't be silly, Braxton!" exclaimed Lillian. "You're looking at the score upside down." She turned the score around for Braxton.

"Yes, it looks even more familiar now." Braxton continued to ponder the score. "There are so many notes!"

"Oh, Braxton, I'm sure an important businessman like you has better things to do than capitulate to all my fanciful endeavors here at this sprawling resort hotel. But after we're married, darling, I'm sure I will lose interest in piano and everything else and think of nothing but you."

"Yes, my dear," said Braxton, taking hold of Lillian's hands. "We will stand together as joint rulers of our kingdom of West Baden Springs, united and strong in our love."

As Hans listened he thought the two sounded like something out of sickening romance.

"Oh, Braxton," continued Lillian. "Our wedding is going to be the biggest and grandest in Indiana history, an event long remembered. Why, even the governor is coming."

Braxton had a strange, tense look on his face just when Lillian started talking about the wedding.

"Why do we need a stupid wedding, my darling?" said Braxton. "I hate to think of you wearing yourself out on a bunch of ceremonial nonsense. The noise and confusion of a wedding would only mar the perfect splendor of our love. Let's elope this instant to Paris. I can't stand the thought of not being married to you another instant." Braxton began kissing Lillian's hand.

"Braxton, you're sweet, but we must control our passion. Now the wedding is my department. You leave everything to me. All I ask is that you show up one week from today for the most wonderful day of our lives."

"As for dinner tonight, I thought I'd surprise you with a little dinner party of old friends for you to meet."

"A dinner party of old friends!" said Braxton as if alarmed.

"Yes, friends of my parents. I call them the old guard. I think of them as guardians in a way. Practically all were here at one time or another over the summer, but somehow you just happened to miss them. All quite naturally expressed to me their discontent that the wedding hour is soon approaching and still most have not met you. So I decided to get them all together at one time tonight."

Braxton looked very disturbed.

"This is all so unexpected. You might have given me a little warning, my dear."

"What would it matter, Braxton? You're bound to meet them eventually. You'll love them. Quite a number are established business people from Chicago. So you have a lot in common right there. Most are staying right up until the wedding, so you'll have plenty of time to get to know each other."

Braxton looked nervous.

"Well, well, I won't be able to stay around here during the week."

"I understand, dear. You have important business to conduct in Chicago. That's why tonight's dinner is so important. So you can meet all of these people for sure."

"I really don't know if I'm up to this tonight," said Braxton.

"Braxton, I think it's cute how you're nervous about meeting these people—so old world. But I assure you, my dear, there is nothing to worry about. They're going to love you."

Lillian gave Braxton a big hug.

With Lillian's hug, Braxton suddenly groaned loudly, bent over, put both hands together at an area just below his over left rib, and leaned onto a nearby sofa.

"Braxton, my darling, what on earth is wrong!" cried Lillian.

"It's an old war wound. It flares up every now and then. It must have when you hugged me."

"Braxton, I'm so sorry. Do you think you'll be all right?"

"I don't know. It really hurts."

"Don't think this is going to get you out of the dinner party. I don't care if you're there in a wheelchair. Oh look! Here are some people that I'd like you to meet, Braxton."

"Lillian, my dear, don't you think a nice walk alone of the grounds would be better?"

"Braxton, what a charming idea." Lillian went on in a dreamlike tone. "West Baden is so beautiful at twilight—the summer sunset's reflection in the pristine springs, the tired, weary, twilight sky in its shades of orange and red, dying ever so slowly into darkness, the late summer mist in its gloaming covering the fragrant flowers with slumber."

Braxton looked as though he did not quite know how to respond to Lillian's description.

"Well, we'd better get out there before we miss all the action."

Lillian took Braxton's arm and the two walked off. But just as the two walked toward the main door, Braxton tugged Lillian off in another direction toward a side door, thus circumventing the main door and several people.

⊰ Chapter Six ⊱

LILLIAN STOOD WITH Braxton in the center of the lobby. Both were elegantly dressed in formal evening attire, as were the great number of guests who had assembled for the sunset concert. Women in beautiful evening gowns and men in dashing tuxedos would approach Lillian and Braxton to cordially render their fondest regards. Often a gentleman would inadvertently stumble on the question that always made Braxton tense.

"Just what is your line of business anyway, Mr. Kingsley?"

To this Braxton would hesitate and then answer timidly, "I, ah, play the stock market."

But Lillian would often interpose. "Don't you men talk about anything but business? This is supposed to be a party. Let's talk about the old days at West Baden and other happy things."

The orchestra's warming up signaled the guests to be seated. Lillian sat herself at the piano, and shortly thereafter Chopin's Piano Concerto in E Minor was under way. From the first note of music, guests were captivated by Lillian's delicate touch on the ivories, her graceful runs up and down the keyboard, the intricate parts that she made sound flowing and pleasing, her complete agreement with the orchestra, which, although small, proved its full efficacy. Harmonic richness filled the room, yet Braxton was indifferent to it as he slouched back in a large, well-stuffed leather chair, his eyelids fighting to stay open. The concert ended with a great tumult of applause, and soon afterward a bouquet of roses was presented to Lillian.

Upon entry into the dining room for the fabulous dinner portion of the evening, Lillian was met with a strange imbroglio at discovering that Braxton had taken it upon himself to change seating arrangements. No longer were Lillian and Braxton to sit at the very center of the dinning room to allow maximal exposure to the guests. Braxton had changed things so that the two would sit far off in the most remote corner of the room.

"I thought it might be nice for us to be alone for a while," he used as an excuse.

This did not stop Lillian from seeing people, however. Throughout most of the dinner, she flitted from table to table, leaving Braxton alone at their table, far off, where he was obviously contented to be.

After the sixth course of a meal that demonstrated West Baden's culinary mastery, an elderly gentleman stood up with Lillian in the center of the room and requested that he be given everyone's attention.

"Our dear Miss Lillian Everett of West Baden Springs," the gentleman said eloquently. "What words could possibly express our deep and everlasting fondness to you? You've long held a special place in all our hearts as we've seen you, through the years at West Baden, grow into a perfect rose of a lady. Like the great domed structure that stands here in rustic surroundings, you stand alike to its strength and beauty, a defiant bulwark of goodness unassailable to all things base. Your parents forged from a leaf-strewn desert the magnificence of West Baden Springs—the eighth wonder of the world with its mighty dome. You continue their legacy most admirably, dear Lillian. All of us now offer our sincere congratulations on the occasion of your marriage. Please accept our most ardent blessing. Ladies and gentlemen, I propose a toast to Miss Lillian Everett of West Baden Springs."

Everyone in the room raised their glasses high, smiled, and repeated "to Lillian Everett of West Baden Springs."

The elderly gentleman continued. "And now what we've been waiting for all evening—a word from the groom. So much about you remains a mystery. Stand up, dear boy, and tell us all about yourself—your family, background, schooling. Tell us about your business. Our curiosity is at a zenith. Stand up and speak, dear boy."

Braxton's face went white. Looking out at the large room of guests with wide-open eyes, he realized there in his secluded corner he had suddenly become the focus of everyone's attention. He said nothing, nor did he move.

Lillian briskly walked over to Braxton. "Go on, Braxton," she said. "Don't be shy."

After several seconds of hesitation, Braxton stood up slowly and rather clumsily. He looked about the room of blank faces for a while, then uttered feebly, "Good evening, ladies and gentlemen." Braxton paused. "As you may have guessed, my name is Braxton Kingsley ... and ... and ... I'm from Chicago." Braxton paused again.

The tense silence was suddenly broken with an irritating laughing noise that came from beyond the main door. The door flung open to reveal a very ostentatiously dressed woman. In the sweltering summer heat, the woman wore a mink coat. Her long, black hair was in disarray. Cakes of powdery cosmetic covered a forty-three-year-old face. At her ears was a large pair of diamond earbobs. Nearly every one of her fingers bore a ring with an immense jewel, a different precious stone for each finger. The rings on one hand made a clicking sound as the woman furiously waved a Japanese hand fan. It was not difficult to perceive that the woman was trying to show wealth, or at least an imitation of wealth.

"Hello, hello, everybody!" the woman said in a brazen voice. "Here I am at last. Everyone's favorite girl, Zelda Fairfax! My, what a quaint, little party."

Everyone in the room looked and listened in astonishment to the eccentric Zelda Fairfax, who had invaded the room with a blatantly abrupt manner. Zelda walked briskly to the table of Lillian's six college friends.

"Here you are, my six angels!"

"Zelda, thank goodness you're here," said Minnie. "We've been dying of boredom in the middle of all these old people."

"What den of old geezers has Lillian compiled this time?" replied Zelda. "Reminds me of the time I was in Pompeii. So many ancient ruins about the place."

"Now that you're here, Zelda," said Pearl, "maybe you can put some life into this crowd."

"I'd do better at a wax museum!" answered Zelda. "I dare say," she continued, "Lillian hasn't learned a thing from us all summer. This party is proof of it. You'd think that by now she would have adapted to our style, fashion, and modern ways."

"Let's face it, Zelda," said Roy. "Lillian is a lost cause. She'll never be one of us. You can't say we haven't tried."

"It would seem to appear that I still need to educate Lillian on a few matters," said Zelda.

Upon spotting Lillian, Zelda left the group of six and briskly walked toward the hostess. About halfway there, Zelda shouted, "Lillian, my darling child!" and began running to her. In a great display of emotion, Zelda threw her arms around Lillian, causing everyone to stare in astonishment.

"Why, Zelda," said Lillian. "How nice of you to drop in."

Braxton then greeted Zelda. "Why Zelda! What a surprise. We hardly knew you were here."

Lillian continued. "Zelda, you're just in time to hear a few words from Braxton."

"Yes," said Braxton uneasily. "These wonderful people whom you just passed through want to know all about me—my background, what I do for a living, everything."

"I think that's a fabulous idea," replied Zelda. "What could be more appropriate? But first, Mr. Kingsley, I think it only proper that you take my coat."

Braxton removed the mink to reveal a most appalling pink flapper's dress, excessively adorned with fringe. Zelda's neck was anchored with several sets of beads.

"And while you're at it," continued Zelda, "buy me some cigarettes ... and ... get me a glass of iced tea ... with lemon ... and ... and buy me a postcard in the lobby. Run along now, Mr. Kingsley."

The instant Braxton walked away with Zelda's mink coat, Zelda jerked Lillian aside and, holding her arm like a vice, talked to her in a soft but brisk and peremptory voice.

"Lillian, I thought I should warn you about these people whom you've assembled here without my acknowledgement."

"They're just some old friends of my parents who were interested in getting to know Braxton," replied Lillian. "You remember them from the old days, don't you, Zelda?"

"Yes, Lillian. I remember most from the old days at West Baden, and that is precisely why I must warn you that they and Braxton might not see eye to eye on certain matters. Braxton is more worldly and outgoing ... and provocative. You could say that he runs at a faster speed than all these old friends of your parents, causing perhaps a distortion in, in ... synchronization between the two. Therefore, I would not pay much attention to the comments about Braxton. Some might try to meddle or give you faulty advice. You're so young and innocent. I wouldn't want anybody steering you down a road that leads to a broken heart."

"Zelda, I appreciate your concern, but I'm certain there is noting to worry about. I can tell they like Braxton already. And even if they don't, nothing could ever change my love for Braxton."

"I'm glad to hear that, Lillian. That's just the way it should be. Let your heart guide your decisions. Perhaps I'm being overly cautious for you in light of the promise I gave to your dearly departed mother. I remember when your mother died in my arms nearly nine years ago. I go into fits of tempestuous emotion every time I think about it. She gave to me her last words. 'Take care of my little Lillian,' she said. 'Treat her as if she were your own. You, Zelda Fairfax, are the only person whose integrity I can trust. You, Zelda, are my dearest and closest friend.' I made a promise to look after you, Lillian, to make sure you make the right decisions and do the right things. I shall be true to that promise until my dying days."

"So you've said a number of times, Zelda. But if you made such a promise, why have you been absent from me and West Baden for so many years?"

"I thought you'd get around to asking that question, Lillian." Zelda paused for a moment. "The truth is out there!" Zelda motioned toward all the people seated at their tables. "These crazily possessive people would not let me near you for all these years. But when you began a courtship with my dear friend, Braxton Kingsley, when there was talk of marriage, I could hold back no longer. I was compelled to rush to your side to protect and guide you, my dear."

Braxton returned from the errands.

"But we're forgetting all of our guests!" exclaimed Lillian.

"Yes, how terrible of us," replied Zelda. "Lillian, why don't you go along and greet them. I want to say a few words to your husband-to-be. I want to make sure he intends on giving you every happiness."

"Well, all right," replied Lillian as she departed.

Hans had been waiting on the table all evening. But when he saw that Braxton and Zelda were talking alone at the secluded table, he was determined to wait a while longer to hear what the two were saying. Something did not seem quite right about Braxton and Zelda. If necessary Hans could hide a little behind a large planter—anything to hear what Braxton and Zelda were talking about.

"Zelda," said Braxton. "Don't you think you're going overboard with this 'dearest Lillian' routine? Her mother's dearest and closest friend! This respectable crowd still avoids you like a whore."

"You have no cause to criticize my methods of operation," retorted Zelda. "Everything is going as planned, isn't it? As for just now, I saved your neck! What could you have told these stuffy prigs about yourself?

"And what about this bogus romance with the proper and prim Lillian Everett?"

"Now don't say that, Braxton. You only have another week to go, and after that you'll have joint ownership of West Baden Springs, after which time we can start to talk of ways to relieve our proper and prim princess of her duties. When that ring slips on her finger, we are home free! And just think of the reward!"

"The perfect place for my ... commodity," said Braxton.

"And a whole new crowd will replace these old stuffs. While you're in Chicago this week, Braxton, I'll stay at West Baden to keep Lillian away from these annoying pests. I hope none of them have found out anything yet."

"It's no matter. Lillian would not believe them if they told her. She wouldn't believe me if I told her nor anybody else. She lives a life of dreams that she won't let be destroyed."

Just then Hans looked around from behind the planter. Rimsky had spotted him. Hans pretended that he had dropped something and tried to look efficient as he moved away from the planter to continue his duties as waiter. This seemed to mollify Rimsky, but just then Hans cared little about

Rimsky. All he could think about was the conversation between Braxton and Zelda. It seemed as though they were plotting something against Lillian. Hans must warn Lillian. But what could he say?

Just then Lillian returned to Braxton and Zelda's table.

"Why, Braxton!" said Lillian. "You haven't talked to anyone all evening. Come with me now and I'll introduce you to some people."

"That would be quite impossible, my dear," replied Braxton. "I just received a telegram that I am needed in Chicago right away."

"But the next train does not leave until morning."

"But it leaves very early in the morning, my dear. So I must go to my room to sleep right away."

"I understand, darling, but you'll want me to come with you of course. All of the wedding arrangements have already been made, and I'm really not needed here at West Baden. I want to see what you really do up there in Chicago."

"Nothing but boring, stupid work," replied Braxton. "You would hate every minute. Business in Chicago is no place for a lady of your breeding and distinction, my dear."

"Yes, Lillian," Zelda added. "You're place is here at West Baden, to play the piano for all the grateful multitude of guests who could not do without you."

"But surely, Braxton," said Lillian, "you're not going alone! Why, all summer long you have mysteriously popped in and out of West Baden by yourself. Don't you ever have assistants or business associates to accompany you?"

Braxton gave a bewildered expression, turned around, and jerked Hans quickly to his side.

"Meet my new assistant," replied Braxton, holding Hans tightly by the arm. "His name is—"

"Hans," replied Hans.

"But Braxton…" said Lillian.

"No time to chatter, my dear. I must find Rimsky to assure that I acquire this fine young man as my assistant. We men must run along and do business."

"But, Braxton," Lillian persisted as Braxton walked away briskly with Hans, still holding him tightly by the arm.

The two then approached Rimsky.

"Ah, Rimsky," replied Braxton. "Just the person I want to see."

Rimsky looked bewildered.

"I'm afraid I'll have to withdraw your application for the position as my business manager. I have already found, if not a business manager, a very suitable assistant. And he's right here."

Rimsky said nothing but looked at Hans up and down as if in disbelief.

"Yes, this fine, young man will do quite nicely," Braxton continued. "I hope your staff can spare him, Mr. Rimsky. Get him to bed right away. We are taking the early-morning train to Chicago."

Braxton walked off abruptly, leaving Rimsky's eyes glaring with jealousy and malice.

"Well, well," Rimsky said to Hans. "I must say you certainly get around. Last time it was Miss Lillian and now it's the fabulously wealthy Mr. Braxton Kingsley. However did you manage it? Don't flatter yourself by thinking he's serious. In a few days or so he'll see how incompetent you are. Huh! You won't last two days!"

Rimsky too walked off abruptly, leaving Hans's mind in confusion. But one thing predominated amid the confusion: the conversation between Braxton and Zelda. Although the conversation was vague in meaning, one thing was for sure. Braxton did not love Lillian and was marrying her to get control of West Baden Springs. But why? What possible reason would Braxton want West Baden compared to all his millions? Just what was this "commodity" of which he spoke? How could Hans find out? In Chicago. Yes, in Chicago this week, Hans could investigate Braxton in hopes of finding some sound evidence against him. Although the idea of Hans being Braxton's assistant sounded preposterous, perhaps this was all part of Braxton's scheme against Lillian. The best thing to do just then was to play along with Braxton in hopes of passing information on to Lillian. Hans could present Lillian with evidence and smash her iron infatuation for Braxton. Hans knew Lillian would never believe him from just the conversation he had overheard. Hans would need sound evidence, and it must be obtained before the wedding.

⊰ Chapter Seven ⊱

As THE TRAIN pulled into Chicago, Hans stared out of the window in fascination. In all his life, never had he seen even a small city, let alone the nation's second largest metropolis. He wondered how the earth could support so much concrete and why the tall buildings did not just sink into the ground. The blocks and blocks of streets crammed with automobiles seemed endless. Multitudes of people swarmed through the streets like a colony of ants.

When the train halted at Union Station, Hans and Braxton left the train and passed through the main lobby. More than once Braxton had to pull Hans by the arm to keep him from disappearing into the great number of people. Once outside Union Station, Hans nearly fell on his back when attempting to see the tops of the tall buildings. Many of the well-dressed people on the fashionable streets of Chicago would stare at Hans in his churlish attire.

The first stop for Braxton and Hans was a sophisticated men's store.

"Why, Mr. Kingsley!" said a clerk while approaching Braxton. "How good to see you again. And what have we here?" The clerk surveyed Hans from head to toe with a dismal expression.

The rest of the clerks and well-dressed customers stared at Hans with the same expression. Braxton jerked the bag from Hans's hand, opened it, and conspicuously tossed the wretched articles of clothing out onto a table for everyone to see Hans's torn underwear and forlorn clothing with patches, ragged ends, and parts that Hans had cursorily sewn together himself. Braxton picked up each article one at a time, and then tossed each piece into a nearby garbage can, one by one, until nearly all of Hans's belongings were discarded. Braxton took a suitcase from a shelf, opened it, and filled it with items he had gathered desultorily from about the store. Braxton then ordered that Hans be taken to the dressing area to be fitted for a business suit.

Then it was on to the Chicago Stock Exchange. From the time the two entered the spectator's gallery, viewing the noise and confusion among the brokers down below, Hans could see that a spell had come over Braxton. Although Hans failed to see what could be so fascinating about a bunch of numbers, Braxton was nearly delirious at watching the stock prices.

"Up three quarters from yesterday!" exclaimed Braxton. "Marvelous! Up, up. The stock market always goes up. I tell you, my boy, there are fortunes to be made playing the stock market. One would have to be crazy these days for not investing every dime into it. There is simply no way of losing when the stock prices keep climbing!"

Hans knew little about the stock market. He had frequently seen people at West Baden's Logan and Bryon brokers branch office gather around the stock ticker, but the purpose of this machine had long remained a mystery to him. What better way to learn about the stock market than to listen to those around him? Drifting away from Braxton just a bit, Hans overheard a group of gentlemen.

"Good Lord!" one gentleman said. "Just look at those outrageous prices! Westinghouse 289 and seven-eighths, U.S. Steel 261 and three-quarters, General Electric 396 and a quarter, AT&T 300 points! This ridiculous bull market has gone on for too long now! Prices simply must fall!"

"That's what you've been saying now for two years and prices keep going up!"

"If in 1927 stock prices had seemed high as the clouds, now prices have simply left the earth's atmosphere."

"Anybody who would have predicted in 1927 that the bull market was on the verge of a wild advance which would make that year's dangerously high prices seem trifling would have appeared quite mad."

"Or else inspired with a genius for mass psychology."

"What on earth do you mean by that?"

"Back then, gentlemen, we failed to take into account the ridiculous commercial romanticism of the American people, inflamed by year after plentiful year of Coolidge prosperity which has long since persuaded people to gamble their life savings away on the stock market. Why the market's become a national mania. People are speculating—and without the slightest knowledge of the nature of the company upon whose fortunes they're relying, like the people who buy Seaboard Air Line under the impression that it's an aviation stock!"

"Damn speculators, of course! They're the ones making the market go crazy! Their numbers have been growing over the years so that by now they all but control the market. Damn idiots! Don't they know business is bad and that credit is inflated? Can't they see that the stock price level is dangerously high? Suppose all these madmen who insist on buying stocks at advancing prices tried to sell all at the same moment!"

"You must understand, my dear sir, that the American public has an altogether normal desire to get rich quick, and is ready to believe anything about the golden future of American business. As long as stocks climb, speculators will buy, no matter what the forecasters say, no matter how obscure the business prospect. They simply cannot resist a rising stock market, and money has gradually found its way more plentiful into speculative use despite the many barriers raised by the Federal Reserve Board."

"The confounded reserve authorities have been beaten time and time again. Each time they impose a new restriction to discourage speculation, prices fall drastically at first, but then to our great amazement, not only do prices recover, but they then soar to even higher levels! The lesson is plain. The public simply will not be shaken out of the market by anything short of a major disaster. In economics as in physics, the higher they go, the harder they fall!"

Hans was not quite sure what these gentlemen were saying, but it sounded none too good. This was not at all the way Braxton talked about the stock market. Perhaps this was important inside information Braxton did not know about.

Hans suddenly stepped away from the group of men to realize that as he looked around through the great number of people there in the spectator's gallery, he could no longer find Braxton. What had become of him? Perhaps the best thing to do was to wait right where Hans had last seen Braxton.

But after Hans waited for over two hours, there was still no sign of Braxton. In Braxton's eyes Hans must have seemed insignificant compared to the excitement of the stock market. Perhaps Braxton had forgotten all about him.

Just when Hans was on the verge of panic, a tall man in a dark suit approached him.

"You are Hans?" he said.

"Yes, I am."

"You are to come with me."

Hans followed the man out of the building and onto the street, where a large black limousine was waiting. The man opened the door for Hans and then walked around to the driver's seat. As the limousine drove through the busy streets of Chicago, Hans would often look out the window to find people staring at the limousine. Perhaps they thought Hans was someone important. The limousine drove on through the city center but eventually passed into more suburban surroundings and finally turned into the driveway of a country club.

After letting Hans out of the vehicle, the driver led him through an elaborately decorated main lobby and into a very masculine-looking room with dark walnut paneling, brass chandeliers, and leather sofas and chairs. Braxton was seated at the center of a group of well-dressed men. All listened attentively as he spoke.

"But gentlemen, let me remind you that all the old markers by which the price of a promising common stock can be measured have long since been passed; if a stock once valued at one hundred went to three hundred, what on earth can prevent it from sailing on to four hundred? Why not ride with it for fifty or a hundred points with Easy Street at the end of the journey? Let me also remind you that with every crash of the past few years there has always been a recovery, and that every recovery has always brought prices to a new high point. Two steps up, one step down, two steps up again: this is how the market goes. If you sell you have only to wait for a few months for the next crash and buy again at bargain prices. In fact, there is really no reason to sell at all. You're bound to win in the end if your stock is sound. The best thing to do is buy and hold on."

Braxton paused for a moment to acknowledge Hans with a quick nod, although he did not bother to introduce Hans to the rest. No one bothered to speak to Hans. The gentlemen probably thought he was Braxton's errand boy. Hans sat mute in a corner, becoming more mind-boggled with the discussion as it went on. Although he understood little of the business talk, Hans could tell that what Braxton was saying sounded a great deal more positive than what the men at the stock exchange had said.

Braxton continued.

"Time and again economists and forecasters have cried wolf, wolf, and the wolf has made only the most fleeting of visits, leaving only a slight scratch each time. Time and again the Reserve Board has whined for fear of inflated stock prices, but inflation, as we know, gentlemen, has failed to bring hard times. Business in danger? Why, nonsense! Factories are running at full blast and the statistical indices register maximal industrial health. Is there a threat of overproduction, gentlemen? Nonsense again! Are not business concerns committed to hand-to-mouth buying? Are not commodity prices holding to reasonable levels? Where are the overloaded shelves of goods, the heavy inventories that those irritating business analysts universally accept as a storm, a signal? And just look at the character of the stocks that are now leading the advance in prices! Such solid and conservatively managed companies as U.S. Steel, General Electric, and American Telephone—which are precisely those which the most cautious investor selects with an eye to the future. Their advance is simply a sign that they are beginning to have a scarcity value, that's all."

Just when Hans was nearly unconscious with boredom, his stomach growling from not having eaten lunch, the men began to leave the room. Braxton motioned to him to come with the rest. The group of men, including Hans, embarked on a game of golf. Hans had seen people play the game at West Baden, though he had never golfed himself. He had no apprehensions, however. Hitting a ball with a stick looked easy enough. But the whole afternoon proved a fiasco for Hans. The men were amazed as they witnessed Hans repeatedly hit the grass instead of the ball. Whenever Hans would hit the ball, it would land in the worst possible place: a sand trap, a pond; once he even killed a bird in a tree.

When the rest of the men were not offering instruction to Hans, they continued with business talk.

"Prosperity due to decline? Why, man, we've scarcely started?"

"Be a bull on America."

"Never sell the United States short."

"I tell you, some of these stock prices will look ridiculously low in another year or two."

"Just watch that stock. It's going to five hundred."

"The possibilities of that company are unlimited!"

"Never give up your positioning a good stock."

Braxton took Hans to dinner at the home of a Mr. Clyde C. Duncan, a man who, apparently like Braxton, had amassed a fortune by playing the stock market. The home was a large and showy Victorian mansion in the Hyde Park area of Chicago. Ten other people joined Braxton and Hans in a tastelessly over-decorated dining room. Like the gentlemen at the country club, the people seated at the table talked of nothing but money and the stock market. Hans was surprised to discover that the five women at the table not only listened attentively to the business discussion but joined in as well, speaking out as astutely and avidly about the stock market as any man. Even more to Hans's astonishment was how the household servants seemed preoccupied with the discussion as they loitered about just outside the dining room and lingered on extra long when serving the guests. Perhaps they too had interests in the stock market.

As Hans sat at the table, as the only person who had said nothing all evening, the rest bubbled with enthusiasm as they told fantastic stories of sudden fortunes: a young banker had put every dollar of his small capital into Niles-Bement-Pond and now was fixed for life. A widow had been able to buy a large country house with her winnings in Kennecott. One man pointed out how many millions a man would have made if he bought a hundred shares of General Motors in 1919 and held on. Another man told of a broker's valet who had made nearly a quarter of a million in the market, of a trained nurse who cleaned up thirty thousand flowing the tips given her by grateful patients, and finally of a Wyoming cattleman, thirty miles from the nearest railroad, who bought or sold a thousand shares a day, getting his market returns by radio and telephoning his order to the nearest large town to be transmitted to New York by telegram. One woman told of an ex-actress who had fitted up her Michigan Avenue apartment as an office and had surrounded herself with charts, graphs, and financial reports, playing the market by telephone.

"I like money," said one man. "And I like the lifestyle that money brings—fancy homes, fancy cars, and the like. Why there's nobody on earth who doesn't want the good life that money brings. Why should I care where it comes from as long as I have it? At least I'm not hypocritical like those revolting intellectuals who have money in the stock market. They do nothing but lament the depressing effects of standardization and mass production upon American life yet are all to eager to reap the fruits thereof."

The host, Mr. Duncan, a short, fat, and bold man in his fifties, was seated at the end of the table. Although he had played the role of mediator throughout the evening, now he spoke out in full force.

"The way to wealth is to get into the profit end of wealth production in this country. If one saved but fifteen dollars a month and invested it in a good common stock, allowing the dividends and rights to accumulate, at the end of twenty years one would have at least eighty thousand dollars and an income from investments of a least four hundred dollars a month. It's all so easy!" he insisted. "The gateway to fortune stands wide open!"

Hans had been silent all night. The others probably thought him a bore. He wanted to say something. Trying to remember what the men at the stock exchange had said, Hans timidly spoke up among the vociferously chattering people.

"Wouldn't it be pretty bad for stock prices if everyone should decide to sell all at the same time?"

Mr. Duncan addressed Hans didactically.

"My dear boy, obviously you know nothing about the stock market. Something like that could never happen. Whenever the price of a stock goes down, people will be willing to buy all the more at the new lower price. There is a great propensity to buy the lower the price goes. And besides, investment trusts provide a cushion for the market by making new purchases at low prices. And there are powerful bankers who can support prices at any moment."

"Yes, but isn't all this speculation a bad thing?" Hans questioned.

"Speculation?" responded Mr. Duncan. "What of it? Weren't Columbus, Washington, Franklin, and Edison all speculators! One must always be willing to take a chance. Is America not the land of opportunity? The blood of pioneers still runs in American veins, and if there is no longer something lost behind the ranges, still the habit of seeing visions persists as the American spins a host of wonderful dreams—a romantic day when he can sell his Westinghouse stock at a fabulous price and live in a great house and have a fleet of shining cars and loll at ease on the sands of Palm Beach. And when he looks toward the future of his country, he can envision an America set free from poverty and toil. He sees a magical order built on the new science and new prosperity—roads swarming with millions upon millions of automobiles, airplanes darkening the skies, lines of high-tension wire carrying from hilltop to hilltop the power to give life to a thousand labor-saving machines, skyscrapers thrusting above one-time villages, vast cities rising in great geometrical masses of stone and concrete and roaring with perfectly mechanized traffic—and smartly dressed men and women spending, spending, spending with the money they had won by being foresighted enough to foresee way back in 1929 what was going to happen."

For the rest of the time in Chicago, Braxton generally neglected Hans, leaving him alone at the hotel to do several menial jobs, among which were shining Braxton's shoes and taking Braxton's suits to be pressed. Hans's immediate impression was that, after his apparent faux pas in Mr. Duncan's dining room, Braxton no longer wished to expose the unthinking young man to people, let alone hail him as an assistant. But a far more plausible explanation for Braxton's lengthy absences was likely to be found at the destination of a large black limousine. Braxton would regularly leave the hotel in such a vehicle, along with several tall men in dark suits.

This was the perfect opportunity for Hans to investigate the darker side of Braxton that had long remained a mystery to all at West Baden Springs. Hans tried to follow the limousine several times in a taxi, but the limousine always managed to disappear into traffic. He searched Braxton's room thoroughly but found nothing but some pictures of scantily dressed women. The one time Braxton left the hotel on foot, Hans tried to follow him but ended up getting lost several times over. A policeman finally found it necessary to walk Hans the few blocks back to the hotel. Hans knew very little about anything dishonest. He did not know how to begin investigating Braxton, and hence every effort proved futile. Braxton was just too cunning. It looked as though Hans would have to return to West Baden without the badly needed evidence against Braxton.

On the way back to West Baden, Hans could not help but ponder Braxton's behavior as the two sat on the train. Braxton did not act like a man on his way to be married but rather like a man on his way to conduct an unpleasant business transaction. Thinking back on the week in Chicago, Hans thought it strange that not once could he remember Braxton discussing Lillian or the wedding. The few times that the matter was brought up, Braxton instantly changed the subject, as if he wished to discuss anything else. While Lillian almost certainly had been busy the entire week perfecting the most lavish wedding in Indiana history, Braxton had been hiding out in Chicago, doing his best to forget about the while event. This was all the more proof to Hans that Braxton did not love Lillian and wanted to marry her only to get control of West Baden Springs. Hans must warn Lillian.

On the morning of the wedding, even before anyone else had awakened, Hans took a walk through the forest, trying to think up a way of reaching Lillian before the wedding. There would be so many girls around her, fitting her into her wedding dress and all. The only way to see her alone would be to pass her a note somehow.

Then suddenly, as Hans stood there in the forest, his mind in a maze of confusion, he saw the silhouette of a woman off at a distance amid the dense morning fog. At first he thought it imagination. But as he walked toward her, the dense fog weakened, and she became more real. To his great amazement, Hans could see that it was Lillian walking through the forest in a dreamlike state. What a lucky break! He ran to her quickly.

"Miss Everett! Miss Everett!" he cried.

Lillian turned abruptly as if being awakened from a dream.

"I won't be Miss Everett for long," she said. "But who are you and what do you want? Why such a rumpus?"

"I must speak to you."

"How inappropriate for a bride to be alone in the forest with a stranger. I took this walk to be by myself, to think about personal things before the wedding. You'll have to make it some other time."

Hans was a bit disheartened that Lillian still did not know him even after their few encounters, but this thought was dismissed in light of his more urgent task.

"Miss Lillian, don't you recognized me? I'm Hans, Mr. Kingsley's new assistant."

"So you are," said Lillian. "And might I add that by taking that job away from Rimsky you annoyed me very much. Now I'm stuck with that impossible old man as general manager of West Baden Springs."

"There is something I must tell you about Mr. Kingsley," said Hans impatiently.

"There's nothing you can tell me about Mr. Kingsley that I wouldn't already know."

"It's very important, Miss Lillian. I'm afraid, I'm afraid it's something you won't want to hear."

"Then don't tell me."

"But I must for your protection. It's about a conversation I overheard between Mr. Kingsley and Miss Fairfax. By the way they were talking it sounded as though they're planning some awful scheme against you. I think they want West Baden Springs for some reason."

Lillian laughed. "That's ridiculous. You must have misunderstood them. They were probably making some plans for the wedding, that's all."

"No," urged Hans. "By the way they were talking, I know they wish harm to you in some way."

"Braxton and Zelda? They're as harmless as kittens. When did you overhear this preposterous conversation anyway?"

"During dinner the night before Mr. Kingsley and I left for Chicago. I waited on your table. You left to greet guests, leaving Mr. Kingsley and Miss Fairfax alone. I did not tell you at the time because I thought I could find some kind of evidence in Chicago."

"And what did you find in Chicago?"

"Mr. Kingsley was just too slick for me. Every time I left the hotel in an attempt to follow him, I would always get lost."

"So you have no evidence to support this outrageous story of yours?"

"Miss Lillian, you must believe me. Something is very wrong. I just know it. What do you really know about Mr. Kingsley's business anyway?"

Lillian thought for a moment.

"Well … he's a businessman… and he has a lot of money in the stock market." Lillian paused again. "I don't know anything about business. Why should it matter what kind of business Braxton does. I would love him regardless. Nothing could possibly be wrong. Anyway it's too late to do anything now. I'd look like a fool if I tried to call off the wedding. I've made such a fuss about it. Hundreds of people will be here in a matter of hours expecting a grand and beautiful ceremony. I'd be the laughing stock of Indiana if I were to call off the wedding."

"Miss Lillian, I urge you to reconsider. All I can tell you is that Mr. Kingsley does not love you and he wants to marry you to get control of West Baden Springs."

"Braxton does so love me. Why wouldn't he? Why wouldn't anyone?"

"Then why did he avoid talking about you the entire week I was with him in Chicago? With all the many people we saw, not once did Mr. Kingsley mention you or the wedding."

Lillian paused for a moment to scrutinize Hans's tense expression, as if trying to make rhyme or reason out of his strange disclosure.

"I think I understand now," she said, assuming a more relaxed manner. "I've heard the same things for weeks from all my old beau. 'My dear Lillian,' they all say. 'He just doesn't love you like I love you.' I should have known. I've heard from several sources that you've had a crush on me ever since you arrived at West Baden, Hans. I think that's cute, but very impractical. How could I possibly see anything in you or any other man as long as there's Braxton? You'll just have to be content with young ladies of your own social standing. But have no compunctions about your behavior. I really can't blame you for falling in love with me. And I'm flattered that you would create such a story to keep me from marrying Braxton. Don't think you're the only one that's tried. They all tell me how they can't live without me, and that I'll never be happy with Braxton. They say that Braxton doesn't love me. Huh! I will allow you, my dear young man, the same last privilege I've granted all the rest. You may kiss me on the cheek, but just once."

Hans knew that any further appeal to Lillian would be wasted. There was nothing that would turn that idealistic head from its final verdict. He would just have to accept the fact that he could do nothing but stand by and watch her embark on an episode that might bring great damage. He kissed her gently on the cheek. Although Lillian showed no emotion, Hans was shaking, for he was kissing goodbye a beautiful dream.

All morning West Baden buzzed with enthusiasm while preparing for Lillian's garden wedding. The hotel staff worked diligently to bring about every detail of perfection, covering the lawn with rows of banquet tables dressed in while linen and topped with elaborate rose centerpieces. All tables were punctiliously set and opulently decorated. For days prior, gardeners had trimmed and groomed the hedges and lawn and had tended to the many flower beds and planters. Florists had spent days making intricate flower arrangements and a great arbor of clinging vines to be used for the aisle. The orchestra's warming up among the large stacks of bleachers was an indication to all that the great hour was soon approaching. The sun blazed down with radiant power as an ostensible omen of approval. It appeared as though Lillian's fairy tale wedding would become reality.

Of everyone at West Baden that busy morning, there was only one who stood idle. While standing about watching Rimsky's staff working at full capacity, Hans felt a brief moment of relief to be out from among their ranks. More than once Rimsky passed Hans, rendering a contemptuous jeer—a jeer mixed with jealousy, for even Rimsky would have had to admit that, standing there in his dark suit, Hans was handsome and dignified-looking. Hans may have appeared as thus standing staunchly, face devoid of all emotion, but his mind was active with discontentment and fear for Lillian. The emotion not seen on his face was twisting his mind apart. Many thoughts thronged to his mind at once. The frustration was unbearable. Though Hans loved Lillian, he had accepted the fact that she did not love him. What he could not accept, however, was the trap he was letting Lillian and West Baden fall into. Hans would accept the pain of watching the bogus wedding as punishment for not being able to reach Lillian.

As Hans surveyed the guests who were being seated during the orchestral prelude, he could see from their expressions that the grandeur and the ostentation of the wedding had put them under a spell. The governor's arrival made no arousal, for the grandeur of the sight dwarfed the importance of even the most worthy personage. No document could have been more coveted that summer as an invitation to Lillian's wedding. Nobody but Hans, though, could see the wrongness of it all. No one bothered to analyze. They were all satisfied with the superficial. An almost surreal image was portrayed by their placid, serious faces filled with poignancy against the bright, vibrant flowers of the garden, enhanced by the sun's powerful rays. All of these images, especially the bright sunlight, left Hans powerless. He tried to rationalize that it would be all right. Maybe things were not as he thought. But when he looked at Braxton at the end of the procession line, Hans knew otherwise.

With the piercing shrills of Purcell's Trumpet Voluntary, the processional began. Lillian appeared in a wedding dress said to have been her mother's. Clearly the finest tailor in all of St. Petersburg had spared nothing in making it tastefully opulent. It would be difficult to imagine a face full of more joy than Lillian's face at that moment. Walking through the arbor, she smiled exuberantly, her beautiful dress rustling along the way. If only the sun had not been so powerful, if only the trumpets were not so shrilling, the guests not so sentimental—if only Lillian in her dress was not so beautiful and innocent-looking in white—Hans could have stood much better the pain of seeing her walk through the arbor, down the aisle, on her way to something that might change her life for the worse.

The ceremony would have been unbearable for Hans had Zelda not put on a fake act of tears. She made quite a scene, whimpering and sniffling with an occasional gasp so that everyone as far back as the last row could hear her. She, like Hans, felt that the ceremony was just too perfect. Her deliberate drama could be reckoned as a reminder to Braxton throughout the ceremony of the transgression he was committing.

The time had come for the ring. Braxton pulled the ring from his pocket with a smirk on his face and took hold of Lillian's hand. Not a sound was heard at this moment. But as soon as the ring slid onto Lillian's finger, a great tumult of thunder crackled overhead and the sky became dark with rain clouds that began to release a delicate sprinkle but promised to produce torrents of rain in only minutes. If no one else saw the wrongness of the wedding besides Hans, at least the sky did.

At the first tumult of thunder in an otherwise passive sky, Lillian's face went white with distress and perplexity as she stared at Braxton and nudged away from him just a bit. She had long been confident that the sky would bless the wedding with good weather, but instead the loud tumultuous thunder was acting to shake her fairy tale apart. Braxton gave a brief look of guilt but then resumed his usual jaunty self. He smiled at his distressed bride.

"It does rain, you know," said Braxton.

Braxton's grin could always win Lillian's trust. Her apprehension eventually subsided. As the light sprinkle increased in intensity, the minister hurried to finish; he even left out parts. The trumpets signaled the wedding march, and Lillian and Braxton recessed down the aisle and then proceeded to the lobby of the hotel, where they received their guests.

Rimsky had been prepared for rain. By the time the Kingsleys had received their guests in the lobby, the reception had been efficiently moved to the atrium under the great dome.

The wedding reception began. While sheets of rain could be heard pounding away atop the great dome, guests indulged themselves on gourmet delights while seated at the elegant banquet tables. The great banquet was several hours in length, and then the tables were efficiently removed to make room for a grand ball on the mosaic floor.

With the first note of a Viennese waltz, Lillian and Braxton took the floor. Everyone else stood around the circumference of the atrium and watched them. Lillian's face had resumed its earlier dreamlike glow. The guests were full of joy, and not one of them took their eyes off Lillian in her beautiful dress that swayed in graceful rhythm to the music.

"She's so like her mother," the guests would say. "How charming. What a lovely sight. It's just like the old days again."

Slowly the old familiar friends and guests of West Baden Springs joined in. Some had probably not danced the waltz in ten years, but it seemed to come naturally to them.

⊰ Chapter Eight ⊱

NOT UNTIL LILLIAN stepped foot onto the train the next morning for the voyage to Paris did Braxton inform her that Hans was to accompany them.

"But, Braxton," she said, "I thought we were going to be alone!"

"We will be alone for some of the time," replied Braxton. "But quite naturally I must bring along my assistant. Whenever I go on a voyage for any great length, I always bring along someone to keep correspondence with my business enterprises."

This seemed logical enough to Lillian, but just the same, the scenario was awkward, and it annoyed her. Even thought Lillian and Braxton had their own compartment on the train and a private cabin on the ship, Braxton always insisted on having Hans with them, even when seated in the ship's elegant dining room.

"The poor boy doesn't know a soul on board," replied Braxton. "What would he do? As his employer I feel a responsibility to look after him."

"But doesn't he have some correspondence work to do?"

"Not until Paris. Then he'll be plenty busy. Just ignore him. Pretend like he's not here."

But in effect, whenever the three were together, it was Lillian who was ignored. Braxton showed little interest in her but rather devoted most of his attention to Hans, talking to him about sports, lecturing him on the stock market, and playing cards with him. Occasionally Braxton would ask Lillian to join in the card games, but only at the request of Hans. Apparently the thought that Lillian might want to be alone with her husband on their honeymoon had never crossed Braxton's mind. Hans would regularly insist that he leave the company of the two newlyweds, but Braxton would order Hans to stay.

On the morning before Lillian's wedding, Hans had told her that Braxton did not love her. Lillian knew this was not true. She knew that Braxton adored her, just like everyone else she had ever known. Lillian wanted to prove to Hans that Braxton was deeply in love with her, but this was indeed a frustrating task. Braxton was not the least bit romantic, as he had been all summer long. He seemed totally uninterested in Lillian. Lillian was annoyed with Braxton, but she could not start a quarrel. This would only reaffirm Hans's false belief.

If only Hans was not here things would be all right, she thought. *He's ruining everything. He's making me so nervous. This just isn't the way it should be!*

But then Lillian had an idea.

"Braxton, darling," she said. "I didn't want to tell you this before because I thought you might be jealous. You see, I really don't think it's such a very good idea to have this Hans character around us so much because you see, ah, it's been common knowledge to everyone at West Baden that this Hans, whom you have chosen as your business assistant, has had a crush on me for quite some time."

Braxton's face was expressionless.

"In fact he's made advances at me several times."

Still Braxton did not appear perturbed.

"Well, isn't that just awful!" exclaimed Lillian.

Lillian's confession resulted in the removal of one of the two men from the cabin during the day, not Hans but Braxton. Braxton would spend entire days in the ship's casino and plan things so that Lillian and Hans would be alone together.

Lillian blamed everything on the confines of the ship. But she knew the romance would all begin in Paris. She would bide her time until then and read her romance novels when she was alone with Hans. She tried not to look at Hans, because she knew what he was thinking.

"Braxton doesn't love you. Can't you see that by the way he's acting?"

To defend herself against this, Lillian would frequently create lies.

"After you went to bed early last night, Hans, Mr. Kingsley and I had the most romantic time on the deck in each other's arms, looking up at the stars. It was breathtaking, just like a dream. All of Braxton's hugging and kissing gets a little annoying at times. He's so big and strong that I can hardly breathe when he hugs me. But I try to show I don't mind. It just shows me all the more how much Braxton adores me. Of course he would never show this around you. You see, Mr. Kingsley, being a gentleman, would never dream of displaying affection in public. It's just not fitting."

Braxton was yet to show his gentlemanly conduct in Paris alongside his expatriate friends. He called them the greatest intellectuals of the day. They were one of the few things Braxton had discussed with Lillian on the voyage across the Atlantic. Lillian had always dreamt of being in Europe alongside great writers, artists, and musicians, sharing intellectual talk with the best of them. Her years of study in all these areas would certainly show before them. Lillian was thrilled at the prospect of meeting these acclaimed people. She pictured herself in the middle of a great crowd, glibly discussing the greatest minds from ages past: Goethe, Dante, Shakespeare, Voltaire, Newton, Darwin, Galileo, Mozart, Beethoven, Bach. Lillian would show them all that she was as well read as any intellectual in Paris.

Lillian had prepared for hours for the first party with these friends of Braxton. She wore her mother's beautiful white silk evening gown, the one Katia had worn to the grand opening ball of West Baden Springs. This was the most beautiful and elegant dress Lillian had ever known. She was sure to make a sensation, opulently adorned in her mother's finest jewels. Lillian was determined to be the rage of the party, to be the most popular and attractive of all, just like at West Baden. She would win their hearts with her beauty and charm just as her mother had done in the same dress and jewels nearly twenty-eight years ago at West Baden Springs. Lillian was set for the time of her life. The Paris she knew from books and legend would be hers that night.

But when Braxton and Lillian arrived at the party, Lillian stood at the door in disillusionment, tightly clutching onto Braxton's arm. This was not the Paris of her dreams—of glowing chandeliers lighting opulently decorated Louis XVI rooms, of beautiful people in elegant clothing dancing and swaying to gently music. The room was small and dark with billows of smoke that danced in rhythm to a blaring jazz band. Nearly everyone in the room was seated holding a cigarette in one hand and a drink in the other. All were shabbily dressed, untidy in nature, and very motley looking. No one smiled or gave much expression.

"Braxton are you sure we're at the right place?" asked Lillian.

"Of course we're at the right place," answered Braxton . "Where else would we be?"

As Braxton led her through the smoky darkness, Lillian noticed that the eyes fixed on her were not at all welcoming but rather somber in nature and at times even contemptuous.

"Braxton, the reason I asked whether we're at the right place is that no one here looks as if they know you."

"It's quite the fashion in Paris to look as though you don't know anybody," explained Braxton.

"If it isn't Braxton Kingsley, the Don Juan of Chicago," one woman said as she turned around in her chair, taking a puff from her cigarette. "Who is this with you? You better tell her this isn't a costume party. Who are you supposed to be anyway sweetie, Cleopatra or the queen of Sheba?"

Lillian did not understand what the woman was saying but responded, "I am Mrs. Braxton Kingsley."

"If you're Braxton's wife, honey, I'm the empress of China. Everybody knows that Braxton Kingsley is not a marrying man."

Braxton paused for a moment, chuckled, and then replied, "It happens to the best of us."

The woman laughed. "I don't believe it! Braxton Kingsley is married now!"

The woman stood up abruptly and shouted to everyone in the room. "Hey, people! Hey, people! Get a load of this!" The noisy room was silenced. "Let me introduce to all of you Mrs. Braxton Kingsley!"

Just after the woman pointed to Lillian, acknowledging her to all, someone near the stage band focused a spot light on Lillian. A gentle laughter prevailed. Lillian was stunned. Squinting her eyes from the spotlight, she could perceive nothing but glaring white light and laughter, both addressed at her. Although the spotlight had been placed on Lillian for only a minute or so, her eyes thereafter were unable to adjust to the dark room. With arm somewhat extended, she walked forward, trying to feel for Braxton, but ran into a table of people instead. Apparently Braxton had left with the woman, leaving Lillian there in the center of the room, temporarily blinded. Lillian stood still for about five minutes until her eyes readjusted.

Once the narrow space between the tightly packed tables had become more visible to her, Lillian started out in search of Braxton, maneuvering her way as gracefully as possible through erratic noise and congestion. Trying her best not to bump into people, she managed very well to maintain the reserved, elegant movements so characteristic of Lillian Everett of West Baden Springs.

People stared at her as though a spotlight still followed her throughout the room. Lillian could not blame them for staring; she must have seemed striking in her beautiful evening gown, her jewels shimmering a bright array of color. None of the other women in the room could compare to her. All were rather unladylike in short, straight, long-waist dresses, their hair cut in the boyish bob style, their movements jerky and abrupt. Lillian could see that she had captured the attention of nearly everyone in the room. Now it was time to capture their hearts. Why look for Braxton just yet? Instead let Braxton return to find his charming wife merrily scintillating among a large number of his friends.

But when Lillian's vision had fully adjusted, the darkness gave way to faces not glowing with warm smiles as she had thought but instead faces jeering with laughter. Though it was hard for her to admit, Lillian slowly and painfully saw that the attention she was receiving was not awe for her charm, beauty, and manner but rather derision for something she could not imagine. Never had she known people to laugh at her. What could it be? Perhaps she had spilled something on her dress! Perhaps there was a smudge on her face.

Lillian looked into a mirror. She could see nothing unusual about her appearance. Whatever it was these people were laughing at, she knew would be instantly overshadowed if she could just talk to them about something intellectual. She could lead a discussion on a great writer, a great composer— anything to win their acceptance.

Lillian noticed an empty seat at a table of about seven people. She walked to the table and addressed those seated.

"Good evening, everybody. I hope you won't mind if I join you."

All at the table looked at Lillian with blank faces but said nothing.

Lillian continued. "My what a lovely party. Words cannot express how excited I am to be here amongst all of you talented intellectuals. My husband told me all about you. He calls you the greatest intellectuals of the day. Just what do you do anyway?"

"We're writers," someone said.

"Writers! How wonderful," exclaimed Lillian. "As a matter of fact only four months ago I received a bachelors degree in English literature. I've longed so to discuss the great masters of literature with literary experts like you. Let's take Lord Byron for starters. Oh what a great zest for life he must have had, but paradoxically it was his colorful humanity that made him superhuman. The idea of the Byronic hero stems so clearly from his writings; it is of course the notion of physical beauty, strong emotion, and simple vitality in man. And then there's John Keats. 'I have loved the principle of beauty in all things,' he wrote. Like Byron, Keats had such a talent for descriptive verse. But his didn't arise from exuberance for life, I must add. It came from a state of mind that Keats dubbed 'negative capability,' or the quality of 'being in uncertainties, mysteries, doubts, without any irritable reaching after fact and reason.'"

Lillian paused for a moment to allow others to join in the discussion. But from their reactions, everyone seemed entirely bored with what Lillian was saying. No one responded as she would have expected.

Lillian continued with even greater enthusiasm. "Shelley of course differs from other romantics only in that he saw physical beauty as a clue to the true beauty, that of the soul. Oh but how can I even begin to talk about writers without mentioning Wordsworth, the early champion of romantic literature. Wordsworth, as I'm sure you all know, was from the beautiful Lake District of England. Although I've never been to Wordsworth's Lake District in body, I feel I've been there in mind just by reading his beautiful poetry."

Lillian smiled as though just reciting a Wordsworth poem had brought her much joy. She looked about at the others, hoping the poem had brought them equal joy. She saw instead sickened dismal expressions.

"I think Wordsworth stinks," said one man.

Lillian was a little perturbed at this response but made an attempt to rationalize.

"Oh but how rude of me. You're all Americans, and I've done nothing but talk about English writers. America can certainly hold its own when it comes to literature. There's Emerson, Hawthorne, Thoreau and all the other transcendentalists who believed there is truth in a spiritual level of existence that is beyond the mere physical word. There's Longfellow. There's Whitman who, seeing everything as part of a functioning cosmic system, revered nature as mother and brother to men. And of course my own personal favorite, Emily Dickinson. Although she spent most of her life a heartbroken recluse, the strong emotion, vivid imagery, and vibrant color depicted in her poetry reflect a spirit more alive and exuberant than I dare say most people can hope to experience during their life."

There was a moment of silence and then a man from across the table spoke frankly. "Lady, is there a switch on you so that one of us can turn you off?"

Lillian was stunned at this crass retort. At West Baden Springs she had long been accustomed to fascinating people by leading discussion on such matter as literature, art, and music. Not only were these people completely uninterested in her every word, but now someone was actually telling her to shut up! Lillian could not move or speak.

The group ignored Lillian and went on to discuss things totally alien to her, most of all current plays. Their language was strong and blatantly frank. Not once did Lillian hear anything vaguely resembling the gracious, refined manner of speech that she had been accustomed to at West Baden Springs. Their antithesis for *grand* and *lovely* was *lousy* and *stinking*. An occasional *hell* and *damn* were all too common. It seemed to Lillian at times the discussion was nothing more than a competition for bold and brazen talk. Around the table they would go, trying to outdo all others, trying to be modern, sophisticated, smart, to smash all conventions and to be devastatingly frank. And with a cocktail glass in one's hand it was easy at least to be frank.

One woman said, "A conversation in polite circles is like a room decorated entirely in scarlet—the result being overemphasis, stridency, and eventual boredom."

Lillian thought she had known everything about drama. But indeed the plays in discussion were as alien to Lillian as the erratic jazz band and the people's blatant mannerisms. They talked about a scene in a play called *The Road to Rome*, where it was the desire of a Roman matron to be despoiled by the Carthaginians. They talked in length about another play called *Strange Interlude* in which a wife who found there was insanity in her husband's family but wanted to give him a child and decided to have the child by an attractive young doctor instead of by her husband and forthwith fell in love with the doctor. *Strictly Dishonorable* apparently was the story of a charming young girl who walked blithely and open-eyed into an affair of a night with an opera singer. A play they discussed called The *Captive* revealed to Lillian the fact that the world contained such a phenomenon as homosexuality.

After exhausting the topic of current plays, the group then went on a rampage of "debunking." Lillian noticed with what great pleasure they defiled the names of great statesmen, military figures, kings, queens, writers, artists, scientists, musicians, and explorers from every period of civilization. One man pointed out that Washington had been a great card player, a distiller of whisky, a champion curser, and he danced for three hours without stopping with the wife of his principal general. In almost the same breath, he declared Lincoln nothing more than a stupid hillbilly. Other worthies were portrayed in all their erring humanity, but ironically the notorious rascals of history were rediscovered as picturesque and glamorous fellows. One man added that no intelligent person believes in God anymore. Another stated that under its ridiculous Puritan ethics America was an altogether impossible place for a civilized person to live.

Lillian left the table abruptly. She wanted to leave the place entirely but knew she must wait for Braxton. She waited at the bar, frequently peering out in search of her husband, trying to avoid the derisive stares.

Lillian noticed that next to her was standing the piano player of the jazz band. Apparently the band was taking a break.

"Excuse me," she said. "If I'm not mistaken, you're the pianist of the band."

"Yes, that's right."

"Do you know very much about music?" asked Lillian.

"Of course, didn't you hear me playing?"

"Yes, I heard you. But what I mean is, do you study the great masters of music like Beethoven, Bach, and Mozart?"

"Nah, I don't get into that stuff. I'm strictly jazz. To me jazz is all there is to music. All that classical stuff puts me to sleep."

"Let me introduce you to a one-time Parisian who hopefully won't put you to sleep."

Lillian walked across the room to the piano, seated herself at the bench, and with an air of confidence peered out at the crowd. At the first notes of Chopin's grand and noble polonaise in A flat, opus 53, the entire room fell to a hush. Everyone stared at Lillian as if mesmerized, as if experiencing something grand and wonderful they had never known before. Echoes of melodic beauty resounded and instantly captured a room that had been hitherto stagnating with vapid chatter and erratic jazz. Not one took their eyes or ears off Lillian as they looked and listened in fascination.

But halfway through the piece, just when spirits were swelling, Braxton appeared at the piano and hastily pulled Lillian away off the piano bench, forsaking the piece's magnificent ending.

"What the hell do you think you're doing," he yelled so that most everyone in the room could hear. "Can't I go away for just a few minutes with you making a spectacle of yourself! You have no business playing this piano. No one wants to hear you anyway."

Lillian spent the remainder of the night subdued in a remote corner. Braxton's action had so humiliated her that there was nothing she could say to anyone. She wanted to just fade into the darkness but knew it would be impossible in her white dress. The more she listened to Braxton's expatriate friends, the more she realized how stupid she had been for thinking she could win them over. It had been futile from the beginning because she tried to win them over with the very elements they opposed, and they had rejected her not likely out of sheer repulsion, however, but for fear they just might respect what they loved to disdain.

Lillian now saw the purpose for the smoke and darkness: to obscure the languishing faces of those who were forever doing battle with the world instead of playing a part in it. These expatriates talked forever about their struggle for freedom—freedom from the standards they hated, freedom for old fashioned manner and morals, freedom to do as they pleased and to be left alone with their iconoclastic views. Lillian suspected, however, that the freedom these people desired was freedom from responsibility. Even though Katia was dead, Lillian would always feel a responsibility to carry on her mother's tradition. Lillian would never want enough freedom to break her from this one ideal she loved and respected. She had built her life on it and it was her bulwark against the world.

The next night Lillian spoke with Braxton in the hotel room.

"Braxton, darling, I really don't think things went very well last night."

"How could you tell? You just sat there for most of the night and said nothing."

"That's because, ah, you see, Braxton, I really don't care for those people at all."

"Don't worry. I'm sure they don't like you either. Maybe it was all for the best that you did say nothing. Tonight you should probably do the same."

Lillian was horrified at the thought of having to go back there again.

"But, but, Braxton, I really don't wish to see those people again. Can't we do something tonight by ourselves—just the two of us?"

"That's impossible. I already told everyone I'd be back again tonight. But how inconsiderate of me! I should have seen the obvious disharmony between you and my friends. It was wrong of me to take you there in the first place. You shall never have to go back there again." Lillian was relieved to hear this, and she smiled. "Tonight I shall go alone. If you want something to do while I'm gone, I'm sure Hans is available. Goodbye for now. Don't wait up for me." Braxton left before Lillian could say a word.

There, alone in the hotel room, Lillian could think of nothing but how terribly frustrating it was to control Braxton. He always did just exactly as he pleased and never once considered her. With his glib way of talking and his sweeping charisma, he could manipulate people like puppets, but there was no controlling him. Lillian thought she had never seen anyone so self-centered. Since the wedding she had rationalized Braxton's behavior, but now she could plainly see that for some reason Braxton was avoiding her. But why? Could it be that he had lost respect for her somehow?

Just then Lillian had a frightening thought. If she did not appear at the party with Braxton, she would be admitting defeat to Braxton and to the group, and Braxton would respect her even less. She had to go to the party to show Braxton and the group that she was not afraid. The previous night the crass people had done their best to make Lillian feel unwelcome. If she did not come to the party, it would be victory for them. Lillian thought for a moment about West Baden Springs. It would not be long until she would be back again with those who loved and accepted her. Just thinking about

West Baden gave her strength and courage to stand up to the unruly crowd. It was they who were weak and not Lillian. She would show them this. She put on the same white silk evening gown of her mother's that they had so heartlessly derided the previous night. Lillian would show them that they had not won in injuring her with their crass behavior. She would show them that they had lost.

Lillian stood at the door to the dark, smoky room where she had stood with Braxton the night before. On the way over, she had purchased a single red rose from a flower stand. She fidgeted with the rose nervously as she stood there trying to conceal her fear. At the sight of her, the entire room immediately went quiet. The jazz band stopped playing. Everyone looked at Lillian with blank faces.

"Hello, everybody," said Lillian. "Sorry I'm late. I told Mr. Kingsley to go along without me and that I'd join him here later."

The room was without a sound.

"You'll find your husband through that door," someone said with a furtive grin, pointing toward an almost indistinguishable black door.

Lillian noticed that the others grinned as well in this same sort of sadistic way. There was a cold, wicked, and heartless manner about this grin, as if they wanted to hurt her in some way. Their sadistic grins told Lillian that they were waiting eagerly to be entertained by seeing Lillian hurt. She had to go beyond the door or else they would deem her a coward. She had to show them her strength. Her only defense against them was that she must not think about whatever lay beyond the door. She would think of it later, when she was out from under their animosity.

After meandering her way through the congested tables of people, Lillian arrived at the black door. With one hand placed on the door knob and the other tightly clutching onto her beautiful red rose, she hesitated for a moment, turning around to see again the sadistic grins and derisive stares. Slowly she went through the door and closed it behind her without a sound. She entered a small foyer, which allowed her to see nothing just then. But as she moved out of the foyer and into a room, she could see Braxton on a sofa, enjoying the pleasures of another woman. Lillian was paralyzed and did not know what to do. But suddenly a strange, supernatural force came to her rescue by pushing her back into the small foyer so that Braxton could not see her.

Lillian's only thought just then was to be gone from that place in the small foyer. She did not want to move but knew she must before Braxton discovered her there. The walk from that spot through the spiteful crowd and out of the building would be the hardest walk in her life. She dreaded it more than anything she had ever known. As she found herself trapped at a hopelessly difficult position, there was no easy way out. She certainly could not go the other way into the room. She wanted to despair. She knew, however, that the people on the other side of the door wanted just that. They were waiting for their victorious moment of seeing Lillian break down in tears when she passed through the door. The only thing Lillian could do to keep from breaking down was to think of West Baden Springs, to think of the friends and guests back home who loved and adored her. Only this could keep her from breaking down.

"Please, God," she whispered softly to herself. "Let this be alone in my thoughts."

Her heart rate racing, Lillian opened the door gently and appeared on the other side perfectly composed. She walked briskly through the jeering people but soon noticed that their faces had lost all expression as they saw her bravely make this walk of triumphant ignominy. It was not what they had expected to see, and they seemed confused.

When Lillian reached the street, she was disoriented. Could this really be happening to her? She was Lillian Everett of West Baden Springs, whom everyone adored like no other. Why should Braxton want to do such a thing? Why should his friends hold her in such antipathy?

As she walked along the avenue with tears blurring the bright signs and bustling traffic, Lillian was suddenly taken with a sense of alienation. Suddenly she missed West Baden Springs desperately and knew it was only there where she could cope with what she had just seen. She had to be on her own battleground to fight this thing. At West Baden she had friends and loving people to stand by her and make her strong. She must hold on somehow until she was home. She could not play the part of the injured lamb there in Paris, where she would find no sympathy.

Lillian walked down the avenue without the slightest idea of where she was going. Her only thought was to go as far away as possible from that horrible dark, smoky room. People crowed the avenue, but Lillian was lonely just the same. Just then Lillian heard a voice call out her name.

"Miss Lillian! Miss Lillian!"

It was Hans. Lillian was so glad to see anyone familiar that she quickly composed herself.

"Miss Lillian," Hans repeated. "Is something wrong?"

"Of course not," replied Lillian. "What could possibly be wrong? I just saw a sad drama at the theater, that's all. Sad dramas always make me cry. Hans, would you do me a favor and walk me back to the hotel?"

"Yes, of course. It would be my pleasure. But where is your husband?"

Lillian lied. "He had some business matters to attend to. I went to the theater by myself."

Lillian took Hans's arm and the two started walking.

"So tell me, Hans, have you been enjoying Paris?"

"To tell you the truth, Miss Lillian, I really haven't seen too much of Paris yet."

"We'll just have to do something about that. Tomorrow Mr. Kingsley has more business to attend to, and I had my heart set on seeing the Louvre. There's no point in my going alone, so why don't you join me?"

Lillian saw Hans's blue eyes twinkle at the prospect of accompanying her to the Louvre.

"I would be delighted, Miss Lillian."

As Hans escorted Lillian along the avenue, flashes of what she had seen in that small, dark room frequently appeared in her mind no matter how hard she tried to avoid thinking about it. Although this was the very young man whom she had tried so desperately to avoid throughout the trip, she now enjoyed his company immensely. His boyish giggles and grins and his simple way of talking were the perfect tonic to temporarily relieve the pain of that most lurid night. Hans was in fact her only link with home. She had no choice but to accept his friendship and hope that this chipper young lad could help her survive these next two weeks in Paris.

⊰ Chapter Nine ⊱

As THE TRAIN pulled into the valley, Lillian peered out the window in an effort to catch first glimpse of the Byzantine towers of West Baden Springs. A bright September day welcomed Lillian home as she squinted at the rapidly moving treetops. This was the moment she had longed for, ever since that degrading night in Paris—to see West Baden again in all its splendor. Never had she been so homesick; never did she want to leave her wonderful home again.

Had Braxton not consented to leave Paris one week early, Lillian could not have stood for much longer the way he would stay out all night and return to the hotel the next morning with the strong scent of liquor on his breath. On these occasions she had learned to awake early and leave the hotel before she could intercept her husband.

The sites of Paris would have seemed magnificent to Lillian at any other time: the awesome Place de la Concorde, the smart shops along the Champs-Elysees, colorful Montmartre, the treasures of the Louvre. But when she had stood atop the Eiffel Tower or had walked along the Rue Royale looking onto the imposing Madeleine, or along the quays of the Seine or the Grand Boulevards and the Sentier Quarter, something pained at her heart that would not allow her to enjoy the grandeur of these sites. Nothing in Paris seemed beautiful to her, not even the perfectly groomed flower beds of the Jardin des Tuileries.

But perhaps Hans mitigated some of the heartache. When he would appear at Lillian's door, ostensibly in search of his employer, Lillian would make up things to explain her husband's whereabouts: he had business matters, he was visiting some old friends, he had taken ill. And then the two would be off to a museum, an opera, a ballet, or a nightclub. Although when at the museums, Lillian had lectured Hans didactically about art and history, he always appeared interested. When at the opera or symphony, Lillian would talk to Hans about music. But the one thing Lillian would never discuss with Hans was Braxton. Hans had been her tool for pushing Braxton and that horrible night to the back of her mind, and thank goodness Hans had showed no inclination to ever bring up this most lurid matter.

Lillian thought it ironic that, having come to Paris with the intention of mixing with sophisticated, urbane people, she should have preferred the company of this simply country boy. She though it ironic again that, having been in a city unparalleled in style, refinement, and art treasures, she should have valued this humble young man's kindness above all else—above the chic, fashionable styles, the imposing landmarks, even about the art treasures of the Louvre. Hans was always cheerful, always considerate, treating Lillian as though she was a queen. Though Hans had made plenty a faux pas in Paris, especially when dining, his sweet, unpretentious ways always had a way of making the Frenchman's fastidiousness appear wasted.

Suddenly, at one blissful moment, the eight Byzantine towers appeared, and soon thereafter the train began to slow down. Lillian was so excited that she instantly stood up and walked toward the exit of the train. She had every intention of being the very first person off the train. As the wooden railway depot came into view, so also did the letters spelling out "West Baden Springs."

The train stopped and Lillian disembarked. Although she did not know exactly what she had expected to feel just then, as she stepped onto the platform, at the very least she hoped to have recognized a few faces. But as she looked about among the unusually large number of people standing at the depot and disembarking, nobody looked familiar. Everyone seemed as foreign to her as those she had seen when leaving Paris's Gare St. Lazare. These people she saw at the depot were not the usual West Baden clientele. The entire group was younger, more boisterous, and wore much more modern clothing. Lillian hated to think it, but some actually reminded her of Braxton's friends back in Paris.

Only days before, Lillian had sent a telegram to Rimsky informing him of their early return and on which train they would be arriving. As a decorous gesture, Rimsky always made it a point to welcome her home when she arrived at the depot, but apparently not this time. And what of Zelda? In the back of her mind, Lillian had been prepared for one of Zelda's dramatic scenes, where she would throw her arms around her "darling Lillian" at first sight. But Zelda was not there, nor were any of Lillian's friends, only these strange new people who stared at her as though she was an outcast. Lillian was mystified at the whole scenario.

Braxton then appeared before her. The two said nothing but gave each other cold glances and proceeded toward the hotel. As the two walked together in silence up the grand boulevard leading to the hotel, Lillian was suddenly taken with awe at the sight of the great domed structure with its Byzantine towers. Although she had recognized no one at the depot, this was one sight that was definitely familiar to her, and it made her heart sing with happiness. For several weeks she had fought a desperate case of homesickness to see this site. This was her fortress against the world, her royal castle where she was queen and her subjects bowed down to her. She gazed nostalgically at her hotel surrounded by the majestic gardens and forest. She could not look enough. Never had she been so glad to be somewhere in her life. After weeks that seemed like centuries, she had finally been delivered home, but with much heartache along the way.

Although she appeared composed as she walked besides Braxton, her insides were swelling with emotion at the thought of finally being free from a degrading episode in Paris. She wondered then how she had ever stood the ordeal. She swore thenceforth she would never take the things she loved for granted.

Lillian finally saw a familiar face. She saw Minnie standing on the veranda. The excitement was so great that Lillian immediately broke from Braxton and ran the rest of the way up the boulevard, passing many people along the way.

"Minnie! Minnie, my dear," Lillian ran calling. "I'm home."

When Lillian finally reached Minnie on the veranda, Minnie spoke with astonishment.

"Lillian! What are you doing here? I thought you weren't supposed to be back for another week!"

"I know. But I just got so homesick for West Baden and my darling friends like you. I could never leave again on a big long trip like that. Well, what's wrong? Aren't you glad to see me? I have so much to tell you and everyone about Paris. We saw every museum, every cathedral, and every opera imaginable. I don't think there's anything Hans and I did not see."

"Hans and you?" asked Minnie.

Lillian paused a moment at realizing her faux pas.

"I mean Braxton and me, of course. What was I thinking?"

When Lillian stepped into the lobby with Minnie, she expected all to throng to her in a fervent homecoming display. But of the great number of people in the lobby, she recognized nobody, and obviously nobody recognized her, for they completely ignored her. They were the same type of people as she had seen at the depot and in Paris. What an awful thought to think they had followed her home. Lillian noticed that the lobby was a great deal messier than usual. She could not believe Rimsky would let this happen. There had to be an explanation.

Zelda's uniquely boisterous laughter led Lillian to the atrium. There she beheld yet another perplexing site. Zelda, Violet, Pearl, Roy, Chuck, and Harold, along with several other strangers, were having a bash of a time, it would seem, decorating the atrium. For some strange reason they were jazzing up the place with glittering garlands and silver streamers. Lillian thought these cheap decorations distracted from the grandeur of the great domed room. A victrola sent the lively tune of a Charleston echoing around. A few people danced to this music. Lillian entered slowly and looked about in amazement. Person by person, her presence came to be known. She saw people scurry about and whisper things like "Oh my God, that Everett dame is back" and "What the hell is she doing here?" Someone turned off the victrola. Eventually the tremendous shouting and laughing died down to nothing. Everyone stared at Lillian in horror.

Zelda timidly spoke up in a quivering voice.

"Lillian, what are you doing here? You aren't supposed to be back for another week."

"We decided to return a week early," answered Lillian. "Well, why are you all staring at me like this? You looked surprised to see me. You must have known we were returning today. Didn't you get my telegram?"

"What telegram?" asked Pearl.

"The one I sent Rimsky."

All looked at each other in confusion and the Zelda spoke first.

"Well, you see, my dear, Mr. Rimsky has not been here in a while. He had a slight accident. He fell down some steps and is now recovering at Methodist Hospital in Indianapolis."

"I hope he's all right," said Lillian.

"Yes, I am sure he's just fine, but you know, Lillian, those old geezers that you're mother called friends could not put up with an instant of inconvenience.

Off they went in hordes! They didn't give a damn about you or West Baden Springs. Some friends! They left, but I stayed on to help West Baden in her hour of need, when Rimsky was not available to manage the place. There are plenty of people here now, and they'll be even more tonight. I say let them go. The place was never any fun with them anyway. Tonight we're going to have the biggest and best party this place has ever known, and I say it should all be in the honor of Mr. and Mrs. Braxton Kingsley."

Lillian took Zelda aside so that nobody else could hear.

"Zelda, I am flattered that you all these people would want to put on a party in our honor, but the truth is that I really regret having had such an ostentatious wedding, and I really don't want any more grand, elaborate events for Braxton and myself. You see, things aren't going as I though they would between Braxton and me. I think a big party in our honor would only aggravate the situation."

"Lillian, my darling, I simply will not believe there is anything wrong between you and Braxton. He simply adores you. He's a slave to you."

"I must tell you about something that happened in Paris, but now is not the right time. But I'll tell you soon. Then you'll understand why I don't want any more large, elaborate festivities for Braxton and myself."

"Lillian, don't be silly. I just wanted a tiny little gathering to show our affection for the Kingsleys. There'll only be a few people."

That night Lillian stood at the entrance to the atrium, making a pretense of receiving guests alongside Braxton and Zelda. The number of people entering the great room seemed endless. Already there were probably twice as many people there that night as at Lillian's wedding, and still the people kept entering. Braxton and Zelda failed to introduce Lillian to anyone, most likely because they themselves knew few of the people. And what atypical people they were for West Baden—so boisterous and effervescent, so loquacious and energetic. The women, dressed in glittering, avant-garde fashions, would enter vociferously chattering, never ceasing for a second, alongside stylishly dressed men who would frequently blurt out tactless comments like "Wow, what a classy joint!" and "Whoever owns this place must be rolling in dough."

In a flaming red dress, low-cut at the bust and very lascivious looking, Zelda at once established herself as the grand Madame in charge. Her dress, however, was probably no more salacious than those of the other women, all except for Lillian's. Her matronly frock must have appeared comical to the rest. Lillian tried to assert herself in a charming, demure fashion, but Zelda would always step forth in an obnoxious outburst to smother anything Lillian might wish to say. Even if Lillian was to shout, she could never hope to overpower Zelda's loud, brazen voice. True, throughout the summer Lillian had viewed Zelda as a novel spice of amusement at West Baden, but the entire atrium full of her kind was just too much.

In time, the vast mosaic floor was covered with wildly dancing people. Blaring jazz noise resounded amid a tumultuous clamor of voices. Lillian could not imagine what had become of the regular orchestra. Their sweet violins were now replaced with the harsh, blasting saxophone.

Gradually bottle upon bottle appeared in the hands of those gathered around the circumference of the atrium, and by the sluggish, staggered way these people were acting, Lillian knew what the contents of the bottles must be. West Baden Springs had not seen the stuff in some nine years, but now the drink had turned Lillian's hotel into the world's largest speakeasy.

Lillian could hardly comprehend what was happening. The events in Paris and the voyage home had completely enervated her. Perhaps this was all for the best. Her fatigue was in effect a shot of anesthetic that deadened the shock she otherwise would have felt concerning this wanton invasion of West Baden Springs. The unrestrained mob, guzzling gallons of spirits, grew drunker by the minute. But as drunk as they became, they would never match Lillian's feeling of drunken weariness. As she squeezed her way through the unruly crowd, she thought that at any time the pressure against their vibrating bodies would from all sides crush her to death. Even the frequent thunder of breaking glass could not revive her, nor their loud, clamoring voices. For a while their insane laughter rang and rang in her mind like screeching madness, but then all sounds gradually began to sound slurred together into one intense *bong*.

As they guzzled liquor down like thirsty cattle, their actions became more and more outrageous. One group had taken the trampoline from the gymnasium and was jumping onto it from the second- and third-story balconies. Others were sliding down the banister of the grand staircase. Still others were swinging from chandeliers in the lobby. Lillian viewed it all as a sick, nauseous nightmare. She wanted to leave and fall asleep in her own bed, but she knew the nightmare of what she saw then while fighting her way through the uncontrolled mob would be twice as bad in her sleep. She wanted to just faint or fall asleep in the middle of the noise and confusion but knew that their wildly dancing feet would trample her to death.

Lillian saw Hans across the atrium with Minnie, Violet, and Pearl. If only he knew how much Lillian wanted him next to her so she would not appear like a wallflower. But the three vivacious females completely dominated him with gesticulating chatter, laughter, and flamboyance. Eventually the three girls tugged Hans out to the dance floor and introduced him to the Charleston. Hans learned the dance very quickly, just as he had learned the waltz alongside Lillian in Paris. He smiled, laughed, and gave every indication that he was fully enjoying himself. Lillian was annoyed that Hans should appear to find pleasure in what she so disdained. She did not share the others' happy exuberance. Just as she had on that lurid night in Paris, she felt lost and alienated. Her wonderful home had become another place, a strange, erratic place over which she had no control.

The dance number ended with a loud squealing sound. Everyone stopped dancing while the band prepared for the next number. Apparently Hans must have caught sight of Lillian's forsaken expression because just then he did a most audacious thing. He left his three dance partners and boldly proceeded toward the band. Hans said something to the bandleader and then passed a handful of coins.

"Ladies and gentlemen," said the bandleader to everyone. "I have a request for a waltz."

The crowd moaned in disapproval, quickly withdrew from the center of the atrium, and began to accumulate around it perimeter. Hans walked straight across the newly hollowed center to where Lillian was standing. Just as he reached Lillian, the band began to play a number that was sluggish and unrefined, yet nevertheless a waltz.

"May I have this dance?" said Hans to Lillian with a boyish grin on his face.

Lillian found herself compelled into Hans's arms. Refusing Hans had never occurred to her, not after spending the evening as a wallflower. But out there in front of everyone, turning and swaying to the rhythm of the waltz, Lillian came to feel their sharp eyes staring at her in derision. She could hear snickers and laughter. She and Hans must have looked ridiculous to them all. If some others would take to the floor, maybe this would divert her terribly conspicuous position. But well into the number, it was still only Lillian and Hans who circled around the vast area under the dome. Lillian knew that Hans had only wished to be considerate by requesting this dance, but the time was not right. Lillian wished so much the waltz would end, but she could not stop dancing. This would draw even more attention. All she could do was continue dancing with Hans and hope that the dance number would soon end. Just when Lillian thought she could no longer stand the seething embarrassment, the waltz ended as inauspiciously as it had begun.

There was a lull of silence and then the band blasted into the next jazzy tune. The mob stampeded to the center again and, in retaliation for their lapse in excitement, became even more unrestrained.

Lillian took Hans's arm and hastily coaxed him away from the center.

"I'm amazed at how wonderfully you've learned to waltz, Hans," said Lillian, as if trying to create small talk.

"That's because I had a first-rate instructor in Paris to teach me," replied Hans.

"That's sweet of you to say. Hans, it's so noisy and congested in here. Let's go take a walk on the veranda."

Hans blushed. "I would be most honored, Miss Lillian."

As the two began to leave the room, Minnie, Violet, and Pearl popped up behind them.

"Here you are, you naughty boy," said Pearl.

"What's the big idea of dancing with Lillian?" cried Violet. "We thought you were all ours for the night."

"And besides," said Minnie. "Lillian is an old married woman now."

Lillian gave them all a cool look and then spoke. "Why should that make any difference, girls," she said in an unfriendly tone. "At this wild party of Zelda's, it would appear that anything goes."

"Why, Lillian Kingsley!" retorted Pearl. "Do I detect a note of disapproval in your voice. Why, this is the best party this place has ever seen!"

"Braxton told us that West Baden Springs will be like this from now on," said Violet. "Won't that be wonderful?"

Something occurring in the very center of the atrium suddenly caught everyone's attention. As a gap cleared, Lillian could see Braxton dancing wildly with a young girl in the center of gawking spectators. Lillian thought he looked like a fool as he thrashed his arms and hopped around like an idiot. About every minute, he would reach into the spectators for a different dance partner.

"Just look at Braxton!" said Pearl. "He's the life of the party!"

"He's so handsome and dreamy," said Violet in a high, breathy voice.

"Lillian you have to be the luckiest woman on earth," said Minnie.

Lillian agreed with none of them. She thought Braxton was behaving like a perfect fool, especially when he started dancing with Zelda. The two swung around together and created some new ridiculous dance steps that others immediately tried to imitate.

"Oh come on, everybody. Let's join in," cried Pearl enthusiastically.

"Yes, let's do," added Minnie. "Come on, Hans." She took Hans's hand and tugged him a bit. "Let's do Braxton and Zelda's new dance step."

Lillian intervened. "I'm sorry, girls, but Hans had already agreed to escort me outside for a night stroll on the veranda."

"Don't be silly, Lillian! Hans doesn't want to do that!" scolded Minnie. "Go take a walk by yourself. Come on, Hans." She tugged him again.

Reluctantly Hans left for the dance floor with the three flirtatious females, leaving Lillian standing alone at the edge of the atrium. Lillian was furious with Hans for leaving her. Could he not see that this had been a test of loyalty?

But the principal person toward whom Lillian's anger raged was Zelda. Zelda had probably been planning this party for weeks.

Thinking back, Lillian could recall so many indications that Zelda had been taking advantage of her, but Lillian always refused to see the truth about Zelda. Katia had never been friends with Zelda. Zelda had probably told Lillian nothing but lies all along. A strange, eccentric woman named Zelda Fairfax suddenly appeared at West Baden only mouths ago claiming to be Katia's dearest and closest friend. It all seemed so preposterous. Why did Lillian ever fall for Zelda and her lies?

Lillian painfully realized the answer to this question. She thought that all of Zelda's actions were out of adoration for her, just like everyone else who came to West Baden Springs. It was inconceivable to Lillian that people would do otherwise. Lillian avoided seeing the truth about Zelda in order to protect the Lillian who had long sheltered herself at this place of beauty and refinement where she could believe that anyone entering its gates could not help but love and adore her.

As Lillian looked about at the mess her beautiful Pompeian court had become, she became angry. The sight was repulsive to her. These people were not guests but invaders. They were invading the decent life that West Baden Springs stood for and the life that Lillian knew she would always want to preserve. Zelda and these others had poisoned West Baden with their vulgarity. This was Lillian's home, her sanctuary for all things noble and dignified. How dare they violate the sanctity of this place with their base ways. Lillian's parents had built West Baden for only decent, respectable people. This new crass crowd had no business there. The more she observed, the angrier she became. She kindled a fire of contempt for them that burned within her. Why should she stand for this? Was she not the owner of West Baden Springs? She wanted all of these people gone. She did not care by what means; she just wanted them gone.

She could call the sheriff. They were not acting like responsible citizens, so why treat them as such? Do responsible citizens jump from balconies, smash bottles and glasses onto the floor, and swing from chandeliers? They were no longer several individuals but instead one giant mob. And when each of them lost their individuality, they also lost responsibility for their own actions. There was no limit to what this uncontrolled mob could do. Lillian was the only person there who could impose a limit, and the only limit she could impose at the moment was to call the sheriff.

Lillian went into her office and picked up the telephone receiver. Although she was not certain whether she was making the right decision by calling the sheriff, she did know it would be the most efficient way to be rid of this new vulgar crowd that she hated so. After calling the sheriff, Lillian walked calmly back to her room with full confidence that the next morning she would wake up to her old, familiar West Baden Springs.

The shrill of the telephone woke Lillian the next morning. It was the sheriff rendering horrible details of the previous night's events and requesting information for his report. After hanging up the receiver, Lillian stared at the clock on her nightstand and was astonished at just how late she had slept. Never could she remember sleeping so late in the morning. By seven she was normally up and preparing for the day's activities. Never, as well, could she remember West Baden to be so quiet this late in the morning. By late morning the atrium's echoing traffic could be heard in her apartment through the French doors facing the great room. Lillian could remember falling asleep last night with irritating jazz noise and tumultuous clamor pounding at her brain. But now there was not a sound to be hear, only the gentle hum of the electric clock on her nightstand.

Lillian arose from her bed and opened the French doors to look out at the atrium. The sight was fantastic! It looked as though barbarians and vandals had plundered and sacked her great Pompeian court just as they had plundered and sacked Rome at the fall of the empire. Bottles and glasses had been smashed across the mosaic floor. Piles of empty bottles lay in great heaps. Band instruments were scattered in a sea of garbage and debris. Food was smeared all over the floor.

After she had dressed for the day, Lillian discovered that a desolate, somber mood crept with her when she stepped into the hall. The look of decay and ruin was not limited to the atrium but was ubiquitous throughout every place she walked. The entire hotel was still and empty like an effete civilization. No sign of life prevailed.

Several doors were open. Lillian went into one of the open rooms and turned on a light. To her great surprise, the room was covered with sleeping bodies in the very clothes they had worn the previous night. Many had fallen asleep with a bottle of liquor in their hands.

"Hey! What's the big idea!" someone shouted out. "Turn off that light. Can't you see we're sleeping?"

Lillian turned off the light quickly and left the room. No longer did a somber desolation follow her, but she almost wished it did rather than think the terrible thought that more rooms at West Baden looked like what she had just seen. How foolish of her for thinking the sheriff would just whisk them away and everything would be fine. The small force could probably do nothing more than control the crowd; they could not get rid of them. Lillian was still stuck with this irritating mob. Only now they were like a time bomb. Perhaps in another hour they would all awake and explode again, perhaps even above and beyond their usual intensity. Lillian did not want to set off the time bomb prematurely. Therefore, she took off her shoes and tiptoed down the hall as quietly as possible.

As she came close to another opened door, Lillian heard Zelda's unique laughter and the voices of those she recognized to be Minnie, Violet, Pearl, Roy, Chuck, and Harold.

"Everything was fine until Lillian, Miss Goody herself, had to ruin it all by calling the sheriff," said Chuck.

"What a bore she is!" said Pearl. "She makes me sick."

"I've never seen anyone so dull in all my life," said Violet.

"Why did she have to come back anyway?" added Harold.

"Just listen to this, everyone," commanded Zelda. "Nearly the moment our little Miss Lillian returned from Paris she whined to me, saying, 'Things aren't working out between me and Braxton, boo who! Something happened in Paris that I must tell you about, Zelda.' I can just imagine what she's going to say when she lets out this tear-jerking confession: 'All those mean, awful people in Paris didn't kiss my ass like they do at West Baden Springs and Braxton didn't do anything about it! Isn't that just awful! Boo who!'" Everyone laughed.

Minnie then added to the conversation. "You know what Braxton told me they called her in Paris? Lilly White!" Everyone laughed again. "That's because she wore that old white dress of her mother's. Can you imagine!

And in front of Braxton's friends. Braxton must have been embarrassed to death!"

"Let's face it, everyone," said Roy. "We're never going to have any fun at this place with Lillian around."

"Don't worry, my angels," said Zelda in a reassuring way. "Braxton is going to find a way to get rid of dear little Lillian forever. Just wait. In a few more weeks that bitch will be history around here, and after that we'll all have fun, fun, fun until we can't stand it anymore!"

Lillian tiptoed away in the opposite direction, her heart pounding, her body shaking. When she was a safe distance away from the door from where she had heard this unbelievable conversation, Lillian ran at full speed to her office.

In her office Lillian sat at her desk fidgeting and gritting her teeth. Never could she remember having been so nervous. What on earth was going on? What were they all planning out there? Over and over the conversation rang in her mind. She just could not go out and face them today or ever, not when they were saying such nasty things about her. Why should everyone suddenly turn against her? Why must she feel so threatened in her own home?

She understood very little. She was not brought up needing to understand things. The only thing she had always understood was that she was the star attraction of everyone with whom she made contact and everyone accepted her as thus. Without this acceptance she was lost and disoriented, just as she was at that moment.

About an hour after entering the office, Lillian could hear the rumbling of everyone arising for the day just as she had predicted. And gradually the rumbling increased until all at once, like thunder, Braxton stormed into the office and slammed the door behind him. Lillian had not seen him since last night. Very likely he had fallen asleep on a floor like the others. His angry look at that moment caused Lillian to stare at him like a scared cat.

"What the hell was the big idea of calling the sheriff last night?" scolded Braxton.

Lillian could hardly speak. She played dumb.

"The sheriff?" she said feebly. "Oh, did the sheriff show up last night? I wouldn't know. I went to bed long before everyone else."

"Come off it. You know you called the sheriff. Who else would have? If you do it again you'll be sorry. I'm leaving. I won't be back until tomorrow."

Braxton left the room abruptly, slamming the door behind him.

At first Lillian was so frightened she could not move from her chair. Finally she staggered to the door and locked it hastily. She wanted to lock out the world and stay in this small sanctuary of hers forever.

Suddenly she missed her mother desperately. She missed that beautiful, gracious, kind world of her mother's. In all the years that her mother had been dead, Lillian never fully realized the loss until that moment. Lillian knew she would forever be locked in that gracious world of her mother's.

Throughout the summer Lillian had let her college friends and Zelda run about West Baden in all their careless exuberance, but Lillian thought them innocuous, as nothing more than a colorful spice of life. She had never joined in their Jazz Age but had merely observed them from the side, believing only what she wanted to believe about them until their numbers had swelled to uncontrollable proportions.

Even with the door locked, Lillian did not feel secure. The door could not lock out the thumping, yelling, and jazz noise resounding above and all around her. Lillian had remained in her little office the entire afternoon, all except for a time during late afternoon when she went through a back hall to scavenge some food from the kitchen. She frequently paced back and forth, trying her best not to look at the Randreninoff portraits in their tiny gold frames. Staring out at Lillian with their stern, proud, pompous expressions, the Randreninoffs pictured here would not know vulnerability until later.

It had become evening. Lillian looked out the window and saw the sun setting peacefully in the distance. Just beyond the window lay serenity. The dim glow of the setting sun caressed her face. She could not stop watching the clouds swirl through the sky in warm tones of red, orange, and yellow. Just below, a gently breeze rustled through the trees. Suddenly a calm, peaceful spirit possessed her. This acted to blot out the irritating noises around her that had so tormented her that afternoon. But then all sunlight gradually disappeared so that nothing remained but the faint outline of trees and the headlights to four automobiles passing through the main gate. The small fleet proceeded up the grand boulevard and stopped in front of the hotel. Ten somber-looking men in black suits disembarked from the automobiles, joined in a group, and then walked toward the main door while looking around as if inspecting.

This strange group of men frightened Lillian. Aforesaid, the little office had been situated so as to allow a view of incoming guests, which also meant that incoming guests were allowed a view into the little office. Their countenance had so entranced Lillian that she did not realize she was standing conspicuously at the window, making herself a visual target for the somber intruders. Lillian knew they had seen her. Just then she wanted to be anywhere but at this place where she knew they could find her. Lillian left the office immediately.

She felt compelled to walk through the forest. It was not unusual for Lillian to take lengthy walks through the surrounding woodlands. Especially at evening, the forest offered her peace and tranquility. Lillian started off on a trail lit by lamps. At this time of the evening, the wooded trails were usually scattered with guests who had been drinking the spring waters. Apparently, however, the new guests at West Baden cared more for another drink to be found inside the hotel. Lillian walked along in much the same state of mind in which she had spent the afternoon. No matter how far she walked away from the hotel, she could still hear noise, even if nothing more than a faint squeal.

Having hastily left the hotel without a cloak or shawl, she then felt how chilly the night could be by mid-September. Nevertheless, she walked on.

Suddenly she heard footsteps behind her. Lillian turned around to see that it was Hans walking behind her at a fast pace, it would seem, in an effort to catch up with her. She did not want to speak with him, as she did not want to speak with anyone. But there was no way of avoiding him. All she wanted was to be left alone. Besides, she was still angry with Hans for forsaking her test of loyalty the night before.

"Miss Lillian!" cried Hans.

Lillian stopped and allowed Hans to approach her. Within speaking distance she addressed him coolly.

"Kind of you to finally remember our night stroll, Hans."

"Miss Lillian, I'm sorry about that but I must talk to you about something much more important."

"Thank you very much, but I don't feel like talking to anyone just now."

"Miss Lillian, don't you think I can tell that something is wrong?"

Lillian paused for a moment and looked over at the hotel.

"I suppose it would he hard to notice that something is wrong at West Baden," she said while pointing through the trees at the lights and noise coming from the hotel.

"Do you remember the last time we were alone together in the forest like this?"

Lillian knew what Hans was referring to, but she cared not to think about it.

"No, I remember nothing of the kind."

"It was early morning before your wedding. Do you remember what I said then?"

Lillian knew Hans was probing her on the very matter she had hoped to avoid all during their time together in Paris. Zelda's wild takeover of

West Baden had practically made Lillian forget all about Braxton and his misconduct in Paris. But she did not want to remember, nor did she want to remember that morning before the wedding when she had acted so conceited in front of Hans. She had been so dreamy, flowery, and self-confident on that morning, quite the antithesis of her present state. She wished Hans would not make her talk about it.

"No, I don't remember anything," she said, turning her face away."

"Miss Lillian, it must be impossible for you to imagine that any man could not fall in love with you. But that's exactly what I must ask you to do. You must acknowledge the fact that Mr. Kingsley does not love you, that he deceived you and married you in order to take control of West Baden Springs, otherwise ..." Hans paused for a moment. "Otherwise he will keep hurting you like he did in Paris. I knew something was wrong then, and I know something is wrong now."

Lillian said nothing for a while but instead paced back and forth in front of Hans in a nervous way that would indicate her intense frustration, frustration that could not stay bottled up inside her.

"All right, all right! I will tell you what you want to hear!" she said in a loud, irate voice. "Yes! Yes! It has come to my attention that my husband, Mr. Braxton Kingsley, has failed to demonstrate the conduct generally attributed to that of an affectionate husband." There was another lull of silence. "Well, just what did you expect me to do upon rendering to you this bold confession? Break down in a tirade of emotion? Whimper on your shoulder like a dying swan?" Lillian paced in front of Hans in jerky movements.

"The one thing you cannot do, Miss Lillian, is hide in your office like you did this afternoon. You cannot just stand by and let him get the better of you. Can't you see that what's come over West Baden is all Braxton Kingsley's doing?"

Lillian looked surprised.

"How do you know this for sure?"

"I don't know it for sure. That's why we must investigate."

"But how can we do that?"

"You must win Braxton's trust."

"Win Braxton's trust? Why, ever since Paris, Braxton and I have been playing nothing but cat-and-mouse."

"Then change. Go along with everything. Join their ranks. Learn how to dress like them, dance like them, walk and talk like them. Give Braxton the impression you approve of this new wild bunch at West Baden. Then he will have no reason for opposing you, and all along we will be investigating and plotting against him."

"I wouldn't know how to begin."

"All you have to do is imitate dear Zelda."

Lillian thought for a while, and then a slight glow of hope appeared on her face for the first time.

"I guess that wouldn't be so terribly difficult," she said calmly. Lillian thought some more. "Hans, come to my apartment tomorrow morning at seven. I need you to help me lift an old sewing machine out of the closet. Tonight go about the crowd and try to scavenge a bottle of liquor and some cigarettes. Also, see if you can find one of those cigarette holders like Zelda uses."

Lillian looked at Hans with a trusting face. She needed to trust someone just then.

⊰ Chapter Ten ⊱

THE GENTLE CLICKING sound of a sewing machine resounded about Lillian's apartment the next morning. Hans stood by as Lillian tediously blended fragments together into a single dress. Having stood at the apartment window the night before, peering out at the dancing crowd with a pencil and sketching pad, Lillian had copied their most avant-garde fashions onto paper and was now sacrificing three pink dresses in an effort to clothe the "new" Lillian. Lillian's regular tailor there in the valley would know nothing of the current style. Therefore, tomorrow Hans would have to go to Indianapolis with her measurements, an extensive list, and distinct orders that he ask for nothing but the latest fashion in all garments that he might purchase for her. Until he returned a day later, Lillian would have to make due with this hastily made improvisation. At any other time, Lillian would have agonized at the thought of ruining three of her finest dresses. But at that dire moment she thought of only one thing: outsmarting Braxton, Zelda, and their wild bunch.

At the final stitch, Lillian took her newly made dress into the next room and appeared several minutes later at the door.

"How do I look?" she asked Hans.

Hans observed Lillian with wide-open eyes. Never did he expect to see Lillian so scantily clothed. Now he was not surprised that so much of the three sacrificial dresses had been left over. The dress length, just above the knee, was scandalously short. There was nothing but two tiny straps over Lillian's bare shoulders. At no place did the tubular-shaped garment cling to her. A large sash covered the hip-level waistline. Fuzzy, frilly things adorned the dress.

"Well, I must say," said Hans in labored speech. "It certainly looks like something Zelda would wear."

"Oh dear, what am I going to do about jewelry?" asked Lillian rhetorically. "They always have on so much jewelry."

Lillian went to the jewelry box on her vanity and covered her fingers with every ring she could find. She then put about five bracelets on each wrist.

"All of my necklaces are much too short. I'll never be able to get away with these."

To solve this problem, Lillian cut several short necklaces and tied their ends together into one long one.

"There, this solves that problem!" she cried enthusiastically. Now it's time to do something with my hair and face."

Lillian went to her bedroom, returned with a handful of hairpins and cosmetics, and proceeded toward a large full-length mirror. She tried several experiments with her hair, but it always seemed her hair was too long to be in style. Finally she rolled her hair up into a bun at one side of her head and placed a glittering pink strap around her head. She then went to the closet, plucked out several large, red feathers from some old hats, and placed them inside the headband. She then carefully painted her face with flashy cosmetics.

"Now all I need is the cigarette holder. Here it is." She reached for the cigarette holder. "Light me up, Hans."

The two experienced great difficulty even in lighting up the cigarette. Only after the third try did the cigarette stay lit, and thereafter Lillian coughed and choked unrelentingly.

"What kind of image will I portray to them choking on a cigarette like this?"

"Try not to inhale it so much," advised Hans. "Take little, short puffs instead."

Lillian did as Hans suggested.

"Oh, yes. That's much better."

Although Lillian still looked awkward as she puckered her lips and grimaced after each puff, she nevertheless proceeded to the mirror in an attempt to imitate Zelda's flamboyant style.

"My dear Zelda," Lillian said in a low, dramatic voice. "You're simply my dearest and closest friend. I just don't know what I would do without you. If you hadn't have come along and put some zest into this dull place, I simply would have died of boredom. I can remember how dead it was around here before you came along. I don't know how anyone could have stood the place! I don't care if I never see any of those old people again. They would just sit there on the veranda morning, noon, and night, twiddle their thumbs, and watch the grass grow!" Lillian imitated Zelda's laughter.

Lillian then reached for the bottle of gin that Hans had scavenged. Tilting her head back, she took a giant gulp. Almost immediately Lillian began coughing and coking. It had obviously been her first taste of gin.

"It looks so much like water," Lillian replied in a hoarse voice.

"I know how we can solve that problem," said Hans.

He took the bottle of gin from Lillian, walked to the lavatory, and poured the contents of the bottle down the sink. He then replaced the gin with water and returned the bottle back to Lillian.

"Here, this should do the trick."

"Thank you." Lillian went on with her mimicking. "Oh, Zelda darling, and dearest Minnie, Violet, and Pearl, what on earth are we doing here standing around and chattering like fools? We should be drinking, dancing, and having fun." Lillian took a slug from the bottle and started dancing the Charleston with Hans. She then addressed Hans, pretending he was Chuck. "Oh, Chuck, you gorgeous thing, you." She squeezed both of Hans's cheeks with her hands. "You really have the most beautiful blue eyes." She then put her arms on his shoulders. "That fool Minnie doesn't know what she has in you. Oh if you were mine I don't think I would ever stop kissing you!"

Lillian kissed Hans passionately, but the two soon broke apart with red faces of embarrassment. Lillian resumed herself.

"Well, am I convincing enough?"

"Yes, very convincing."

"I just hope I can convince them as well," said Lillian in a serious tone.

Glancing at the clock, Lillian could see that it was a great deal later in the morning than she had thought.

"I suppose now is as good a time as any to introduce the new Lillian."

"May I escort you downstairs?" asked Hans. "No, I don't think it's such a good idea for us to be seen together, the way we're plotting against them and all. I know. I will come down about five minutes later and stand off at a distance from wherever you might be."

"Yes that would be fine, Hans. In fact it would be reassuring knowing that you're close at hand."

Lillian left the apartment. She passed several people while walking down the hall toward the staircase. Nobody gave her the slightest indication that they thought her appearance unusual. She then passed by a mirror. She did not recognize the person staring back at her. Why had Lillian dressed this way? Was not forsaking herself and yielding to others whom she despised as much as hiding in her office as she had done yesterday? No, the person inside the mirror was not Lillian, but the person outside the mirror would always be Lillian, and that was all that mattered to her just then.

As Lillian walked about the hotel, she noticed that the place was in nowhere near the forlorn condition as the previous morning. Perhaps Zelda's cleaning staff had at last responded. Or perhaps the cleaning staff secretly feared the thought of Rimsky's return.

Lillian walked through the entrance to the lobby but suddenly stepped back behind the wall adjacent to the entrance. From the brief exposure to the lobby, Lillian had seen Zelda surrounded by a great number of people among, some of whom were college peers. Most of the people, however, did not look familiar. Lillian could see that the lobby would serve as her stage. She could not have been more nervous. She had performed both on the piano and in dramas before much larger audiences. Only now she possessed only a tenth of her usual confidence. What if she could not gain their attention? What if they should all walk away as soon as she started to talk? What if they should all burst in to a clamor of chatter and not allow her to speak? Suddenly Lillian made herself think of nothing but the mission that she must accomplish. She closed her eyes for a moment and then walked briskly toward the cluster of people in the lobby.

"Hello, hello, hello, everybody," she said vivaciously. "How are each and every one of you beautiful people this fine day!" She walked about the people, flamboyantly waving her arms in an animated fashion. "Don't tell me. You've been waiting here all morning for me to make my grand entrance for the day. Well, here I am, full of pep and vigor, ready to conquer the world."

Everyone stared at Lillian in astonishment.

"Lillian!" cried Minnie. "You look different!"

"Of course I look different! I'm a whole new person inside and out. I've completely changed overnight! No more of that boring little mouse who used to sit in her stuffy little office and watch the world go by. I've fully awakened to the magical fascination of the Jazz Age. From now on I am completely reckless."

Lillian purposely walked right by Zelda, took a big puff from the cigarette Hans had lit, and blew smoke right into Zelda's face. Zelda coughed a bit. Lillian continued to circulate through the people.

Lillian continued. "And with the new Lillian comes also the new West Baden Springs, a West Baden of excitement, jazz, glitter, recklessness, and spirits." All were speechless as they witnessed Lillian guzzle from the bogus bottle of gin. "Let those spoilsports at French Lick say what they want. You know they actually had the nerve to call the sheriff on us the other night! I've never heard of anything so rude. Those people are nothing but bores. No more priggish Rimsky as manager. If Zelda had not taken over while I was absent, I never would have learned just how much was lacking at West Baden. I owe her a debt of gratitude for bringing life and vigor to West Baden. I will accept no one else but Zelda Fairfax as manager of West Baden Springs." Everyone in the room turned to Zelda and rendered unto her a tumult of applause.

Though surrounded by jubilant expressions, Zelda herself was left bewildered at the whole scenario.

"What's wrong, Zelda?" questioned Pearl. "Go ahead and accept Lillian's offer. It's what you've wanted all along, isn't it?"

Zelda still looked uneasy. "It's just such a surprise, that's all," she said awkwardly.

"Just look at the splendid job you've done so far," said Lillian. "We'd have to be fools not to keep you on. All of us have the same goals in mind for West Baden, don't we? Reckless fun, endless merriment, and sensational spirits?"

Lillian took another long swig from the bogus gin bottle but during the indulgence heard a great many footsteps behind her. When she turned around, Lillian was stunned at seeing Braxton coming toward her with the ten somber-looking men in dark suits that she had seen enter West Baden Springs the night before. Good heavens! This was much more than she had bargained for! She had only planned on confronting Zelda and her lively crew for now. Her first instinct was to retreat. Her office was very close by. She wanted to run into it and hide just like before. But this would ruin everything. Any hope of selling the new Lillian would depend on a strong offensive at this critical moment before all of them. No, she would have to find the strength somehow to confront Braxton and these truculent men as well.

"What it this?" Braxton questioned with a smirk. "Some sort of joke? Why are you dressed like that, Lillian?"

"Say hello to the new Lillian, Mr. Kingsley," exclaimed Pearl.

"And to the new West Baden Springs," added Violet.

Thank goodness the others were supporting Lillian. Lillian spoke up with confidence.

"Oh, Braxton, we must have fools here at West Baden for adhering to the dull, boring ways of the past, letting a whole Jazz Age of endless frivolity pass us by. We must change with the times or next thing you know West Baden will be a museum instead of a hotel. We need more parties, a younger, more dynamic clientele, and ..." For an instant, the cold, truculent expressions before her caused Lillian's mind to go blank. "And of course spirits as well."

For a third time Lillian guzzled from the bogus bottle of gin. There was a lapse of silence. All in the lobby, including Braxton and his ten mysterious men, Zelda and her children of the Jazz Age, stood by with faces of stone, giving Lillian their complete attention. This was exactly what Lillian had wanted. But now she feared she was running out of things to say. She must continue for just a few more minutes.

"Braxton, how mean of you to keep these terribly handsome business associates of your away from West Baden. Please, gentlemen, you must always feel at home at West Baden. It's the perfect place for you to conduct your business. Speaking of business, Braxton, I've come up with the most splendid idea. Since Zelda has been doing such a stupendous job as manager, why not keep her on? Rimsky's old and should retire, and I can't think of anyone more qualified to lead West Baden into the glittering Jazz Age than dear Zelda. It means so much to me to have my dear, loyal, devoted, adoring Zelda close at hand."

Braxton was hit with the same bewildered expression as Zelda had showed only minutes earlier.

"I suppose that would be all right," he said maladroitly.

"Oh, Braxton!" Lillian screamed in joy. "You're so good to me. You give me everything. I have to be the happiest woman on earth to have a husband like you. Now what are we all doing here chattering like fools. We have a new West Baden Springs to create. Run along, gentlemen, we must not just stand around wasting time when there's planning to be done!"

Braxton and the men said nothing as they stared at Lillian in a perplexed sort of way. All then turned away and walked sluggishly toward the North Conference Room.

Just then an idea flashed through Lillian's head. If she could just get them to assemble in the South Conference Room, she could listen in to everything through the dumbwaiter that went between this room and Rimsky's office. Lillian quickly raced before the men and blocked their entrance to the North Conference Room.

"You're not going in there are you?"

"What's wrong with that?" asked Braxton.

Lillian thought up a lie quickly. "The damper to the hot air vent is stuck open so that everyone on the entire second floor can hear everything said in that room. You certainly would not want that, would you?"

The men looked horrified at the prospect. Without saying a word, they proceeded to the South Conference Room.

This was Lillian's golden opportunity to investigate Braxton. But first she needed an excuse for Zelda and the rest.

"Now if all of you will excuse me, I must prepare Rimsky's office for our new manager."

Lillian charged into Rimsky's office before Zelda or the others could say anything. Hans was already there in the office waiting.

"Now is our chance!" exclaimed Lillian. "Braxton is in the next room with all those creepy men. We can listen to what they're saying through the dumbwaiter."

"What are we waiting for?" cried Hans.

The two scurried to the dumbwaiter and listened attentively.

One of the men was talking. "She doesn't seem anything like the girl you described to us. She's more like that Fairfax dame. I don't like things told the way they ain't."

"I can't explain it!" said Braxton. "She must have changed overnight. She used to be so proper and ladylike. I thought for sure we'd have to get rid of her. But now I don't know. Perhaps she might actually work to our advantage."

"Speaking of advantages," another man said, "so far I'm beginning to see less and less advantage in this West Baden place. Why, this place doesn't even have a gambling casino."

"I'll put one in immediately," said Braxton

"What if your adoring wife does not approve?"

"She's the least of our problems. I'll mention it to her tonight. If she doesn't like it, tough. There's too much money to be made in this place to let her stand in the way. This place is proving to be a gold mine. And this is only the beginning. We'll grow richer and stronger to take over more places in Chicago. Out here in the country we won't have to worry about the law as much either. These country bumpkins can be paid off, just wait. I propose that we make West Baden Springs our headquarters. Just imagine it—a profitable castle far off away from proper law enforcement with plenty of customers and no competition!"

"By the way," said one man. "Where do you keep all the stuff?"

"Come with me, gentlemen," said Braxton. "And you shall see my cleverly devised storeroom."

Lillian and Hans could hear the men shuffle out the conference room.

"Aren't we going to follow them to this storeroom that Braxton talked about?" asked Hans.

"How can we do that without being discovered?" replied Lillian. "No, not now, Hans. But we've got to find this storeroom one way or another. It could very likely hold the key to our investigation."

The two thought for a while.

"I've got it," said Lillian. "Wherever this room is at West Baden, it must have a key, and the key is most likely on Braxton's key chain. Tonight when Braxton is sleeping, I'll get his key chain and bring it down to your room. Together we can look for this mysterious room of Braxton's."

"That will be like looking for a needle in a hay stack."

"Hans, I've lived at West Baden all my life. I'm sure I would be able to recognize a West Baden key. They all have a distinctively rounded head and delicately detailed engraving. And the best thing is that all West Baden keys have the room number engraved on them. Unless Braxton has changed the lock to the door, I'm sure we would be able to find the room."

"But …" Hans looked embarrassed to speak. "Are you so sure that Braxton will be sleeping with you tonight?"

"I have all afternoon and this evening to make sure that he does," said Lillian with confidence.

Lillian spent the first part of the afternoon introducing herself to individual groups. All throughout the hotel Lillian would go—from lunch in the dining room to tea on the veranda, the lobby, the gardens, the horse stables, the bathhouses. She would force herself on as many people as she could find. She would flirt with the men, create scandalous gossip for the women, and regale all of them with fantastic stories of her exciting, reckless lifestyle. Of course the stories were purely fantasy, but to Lillian's amazement, all would listen seemingly without a twinge of skepticism. Lillian told of the time she had zoomed through the canals of Venice in a speedboat, the time she had performed in an airplane stunt show over Paris and had nearly crashed into the Eiffel Tower, the time she had been part of a safari in Africa and had been chased by a heard of elephants, the time she had been involved in a gangster shootout in Chicago, and of course, the time a circus had performed in the Atrium of West Baden and she was part of the high-wire act. Everyone was fascinated with Lillian's stories.

Lillian then went on to regale them with stories of her many love affairs all over the world: barons, princes, sheiks, cowboys and Indians, even the emperor of China and the Mikado of Japan! They believed everything and eventually became captivated with Lillian. Surprisingly enough, however, their biggest fascination came when Lillian told them she was the owner of West Baden Springs. Certainly in their eyes, anyone who could own such a wild and exciting place like West Baden, must be endlessly exciting herself. Most insisted that she spend more time with them and tell more stories. Many requested that she have dinner with them and join them for the big party that night.

All of them talked endlessly about these big nightly parties. Lillian knew an appearance at the party that night would be crucial. She would have to look dazzling and shine before all of them like a jewel. But what would she wear? She needed a flashy evening gown for the party—something that was the epitome of fashion, something that would glitter and attract attention. But turning to her wardrobe, she could see there was nothing that would serve as suitable material as before. But Lillian got an idea. What about the opera house? There were racks and racks of costumes backstage. Maybe she could find something there. When Lillian arrived backstage at the opera house, she wasted no time in sorting through the costumes. Luckily the women's costumes were hung separately from their male counterparts. She sorted through the costumes in haste, always with the thought of glamour and glitter in mind. But nothing seemed appropriate. Neither Susanna, a maid in *The Marriage of Figaro*, nor Dorabella and Fiordiligi, peasants in

Cosi Fan Tutte, would not do. Elsa's dress from *Lohengrin* was so horribly plain. Violetta's dress from *La Traviata* was very old fashioned. The oriental costumes from *Madame Butterfly* and *The Mikado* were much too exotic, as was Aida's Egyptian garment. Carmen's dress looked like a rag.

But in the dim light, Lillian noticed a twinkling coming from the male costumes. It was only a stupid black monster costume from that flop of an opera put on last spring. Although abhorred by the monster's head, Lillian could see that the rest of the monster costume was nothing more than a great mass of unshaped material. She walked over to the costume and observed the fabric. Tiny black glass beads, sequins, and palettes had been sewn onto a light gauzy fabric, covering the entire surface in a myriad of pattern and luster. Lillian draped the costume around her. It was perfect! She would not even need half of the material to make a dress.

That evening Lillian passed through the entrance to the dining room in a sparkling black *tube* dress. Although the fashionable dress had taken little effort to make, the results were astounding. Lillian knew this by the way people would stare at her with glowing eyes when she walked passed. "What a stunning creature!" people would say. To accompany the dress were long white silk gloves, high-heeled shoes, a long sparkling necklace, a bracelet and other shimmering jewels, flashy cosmetics, and a headband made of the same material as the dress. A long, flamboyant white feather protruded from the headband. Light reflecting off the dress scattered a bright array of tiny light beams throughout the room.

No one was more awestruck by Lillian than Braxton. He immediately broke conversation with those around him, stood up, and walked through the crowded room to intercept his wife. When reaching Lillian, Braxton did nothing for several seconds but look her over from head to toe, as if seeing her for the first time.

"You look beautiful," he said.

"Why, Mr. Kingsley," replied Lillian vivaciously. "How kind of you to escort me to our table." Lillian took Braxton's arm. He led her to a table for two that was in the opposite direction from where he had just come.

All throughout dinner Braxton did not take his eyes off Lillian, and he did not leave her side once. But strangely enough, the two could hardly say two words to each other all throughout dinner. This was because the people whom Lillian had met that afternoon continually came to the table. "Why, Mrs. Kingsley!" they would say. "What a great pleasure it is to see you again. We enjoyed so talking to you this afternoon. You look so glamorous, just like somebody in a fashion magazine. I can't remember when I've seen a more attractive woman. You must come and see us the next time you're in Chicago."

Lillian's efforts that afternoon had clearly paid off. People could not have said better things in front of Braxton even if Lillian had told them what to say. She played up to all of them just as she had done that afternoon, and never once did she cease to delight them with her new flamboyant style.

Braxton stood by and monitored. The only time anyone would talk to him was in reference to Lillian. "You must be the luckiest man on earth to have such a radiant wife," they would tell him. "She glitters and shines just like stars in the sky."

Lillian was no less popular at the party that evening. Although the tumultuous nature of the parties in the atrium had changed little over the past three nights, that evening Lillian made for a stunning addition to the jazz, glitter, and excitement. Her greatest apprehension at first had been dancing. But Lillian discovered that shaking around on the dance floor like an idiot was really very easy and that with each outlandish motion she would receive more and more attention. More than once Lillian recalled seeing great numbers of people surrounding her as she danced, and to her surprise, other dancers around her would even copy her stupidly improvised dance steps. As for Braxton, he continually lost her to scores of men who had insisted on dancing with the party's most sought-after woman. Face after face after face, Lillian's dance partners would change. In fact, sometimes she even danced with two or three men at a time.

It was not until very late at night that Braxton had managed to be alone with Lillian. He put his arms around her and kissed her gently.

"I didn't know you could dance like that," he said. "I was quite amazed."

"There are quite a few things you don't know about me, Mr. Kingsley, quite a few flagrant, wild, scandalous, and salacious things you don't know about me. You must have suspected before now. Surely, I did not fool you with that proper and prim imitation?"

"I'm afraid you did fool me, Lillian. May I ask why?"

"I had to maintain that dreary, dull image for all my mother's old friends and all the old guests of West Baden—you know, for business—for those sentimental old fools who never wanted West Baden Springs to change. But now they're all gone, and I no longer have a need to maintain that stupid image. You can't tell me, Braxton, that you prefer the old West Baden. Since things have changed around here, I've seen how you've been enjoying it all. And you seem to enjoy the new Lillian as well."

"Indeed I do," replied Braxton. "I was looking for you later this afternoon. I could not find you anywhere. What were you doing?"

Lillian had been making her dress during the late afternoon—making it in the alterations room backstage of the opera house so no one would find her. She had to think up a lie quickly.

"What else would I be doing, Braxton, but thinking up things for the new West Baden Springs?"

"Just what have you come up with, my dear?"

Lillian had not the slightest idea for the new West Baden. How could she? The changes that had already been implemented had distressed her enough! But then she thought back to what she had overheard through the dumbwaiter that morning. Braxton had told his business associates that he would put in a gambling casino.

"Here is my first idea, Braxton. The one thing West Baden needs more than anything in the world is a gambling casino."

Braxton eyes lit up. "That does not sound like such a bad idea at all. Maybe I could help. In fact, I know I could help. In fact, I could handle everything."

"Oh, Braxton, you're so good to me. You give me everything I want. It's getting late, Braxton. I believe I'm ready for bed."

"You don't look tired, Lillian."

"Did I say anything about being tired, Braxton?"

The two walked arm in arm to their apartment. This was exactly what Lillian had wanted. And to entice Braxton all the more, Lillian had the perfect thing to wear: a salacious-looking red silk undergarment with back lace stockings, quite like something a prostitute would wear. Some classmates had given the garment to Lillian at her graduation party as a practical joke. She could never have imagined then that someday she would find a use for the scanty piece.

Lillian could not say how long she had slept before she woke up in the middle of the night. For sure Braxton was sound asleep. Although it was near complete darkness, Lillian had not forgotten the table where Braxton had placed his key chain before turning off the light. She surreptitiously crept out of bed and extended her arms in search of this table. When finally reaching it, she swept her hand across the wooden surface until the feel of sharp metal reached her fingers. Lillian grasped the key chain tightly in her fist and then searched about for her robe.

After walking quickly and nervously, Lillian arrived at Hans's room. She did not bother to knock but went straight through the door into darkness, felt for the light switch, and turned it on.

"Wake up, Hans!" said Lillian while shaking Hans. "I have Braxton's key chain!"

Hans woke up. Lillian unfastened the key chain, allowing all the keys to fall freely onto the bed. The West Baden keys were not difficult to distinguish from the rest. Scrutinizing the keys carefully for the distinctively rounded heads with delicately detailed engravings, Lillian separated three West Baden keys from the remaining fifteen. She then observed the room numbers engraved on the keys.

"We can automatically omit this one," said Lillian. "Number 317 is the key to our apartment. And this one, 220, I'm pretty sure it's the key to Braxton's study. Lillian then observed the last of the three keys. It was key number 174. This must be the key we're looking for, Hans. Its the only one I cannot account for."

Lillian and Hans immediately rushed to the first floor. Lillian was almost certain room 174 was somewhere along an obscure circular hallway in back of some shops that faced the atrium. The smart, attractive shops around the atrium's circumference were leased out to individual proprietors. Since generally only shopkeepers used this hallway, it was not used very much; hence it was not decorated as ostentatiously as the rest of the hotel. The hallway was paneled in simple squares of wood with curved molding inside each square. The entire paneling was covered with white paint.

"The room has got to be down this hallway somewhere," said Lillian. They continued to follow the numbers on the right hand side: 168, 170, 172 … and then the numbers stopped! They looked on the other side of the hall at room 173 but could find 174 nowhere. The hall just suddenly ended with a wall where the door for room 174 should have been.

"Apparently there is no room 174," said Hans. "Check the key again. Are you sure it isn't 147 instead?"

Lillian looked at the key again. "The key reads 174, Hans. But where is the door for the key?"

The two stood bewildered, trying to solve the enigma.

"Maybe the numbers continue on the other side of that wall at the end of the hall," Hans suggested.

"That's impossible. The lobby is on the other side of that wall and a flower shop is on the other side of the wall to our right. The lobby is collectively room 100 and the numbers increase as one circles the building. The only place this room 174 could be according to the numbering system is right here—the last door on the right!"

"But where is the door?" asked Hans. "It would appear that we are looking for a room that does not exist." Hans thought for a moment. "Didn't the flower shop to our right used to be something else not too long ago Lillian?"

"Yes, it used to be a men's store. It was converted about three months ago."

"Around the same time you met Braxton perchance?"

"Yes, I would say around that time. What are you getting at, Hans?"

"Lillian, just consider the reduced volume of merchandise involved in running a flower shop as compared to a mean's store. What would a flower shop do with all this extra space? Lillian, I'm almost certain the room we are looking for lies beyond this wall somehow."

"But, Hans, there is really not much we can do without a door. We can't just knock down the wall in the middle of the night! Why don't we observe the flower shop from the atrium entrance?"

"That sounds like a good idea."

Lillian and Hans started back up the circular hallway, but then Hans suddenly stopped and turned around.

"Lillian, look at this hallway for a moment. Don't you notice a definite symmetry with the placement of the doors?"

Lillian looked down the hall.

"Yes, I see what you mean. All the doors are opposite to each other, except for the last door on the left. It does not have a door across from it. That disrupts the entire symmetry of the hall."

"Lillian, I know this sounds crazy, but I think there used to be a door there at one time. Let's see if we can find any clues." The two returned to the end of the hall and observed the wall just opposite room 173. It seemed futile, but they pounded and felt out every inch. Then suddenly a block of wood paneling gave way.

"Look Lillian," said Hans. "It's a keyhole. Give me the key and let's see if it fits!" With the turn of the key, the paneling opened like a door, giving way to darkness.

"Oh that sneaky Braxton!" cried Lillian. "He covered up the door with paneling and molding to make it look like the rest of the wall."

At the click of the light switch, the room became illuminated, revealing stacks and stacks of crates, stacked almost to the ceiling. The lid to one of the crates was opened. Hans reached through a thick layer of straw and pulled out a glass bottle.

"Does this look familiar?" he asked.

"Why it's a bottle of liquor just like the kind I've seen in the hands of all these people at West Baden. Braxton must be a bootlegger!"

After hesitating for several minutes, Hans spoke calmly. "As much as I hate to tell you, Lillian, this could explain why Braxton married you—to obtain West Baden Springs as a marketplace for bootleg liquor."

"If both of us were not so naïve about things dishonest, we would have figured this out a long time ago. It all makes sense now. Why could I not have seen it? Hans, what I am going to do? I don't want to live the rest of life in a giant speakeasy. There must be a way to outsmart Braxton."

"I know someone who can help."

"Who?"

"Rimsky."

"Rimsky!" cried Lillian. "That treacherous old man! How do we know he's not involved in all this?"

"Because I know Rimsky. He would never share power with Braxton or do anything unless he was completely in charge. That's why he's managed to keep bootlegging gangsters out of West Baden for all these years. Rimsky is due back in a few days. My suggestion is that the three of us assemble in his office the moment he returns and figure out a way to outwit Braxton."

Lillian thought for a moment.

"Yes, I suppose Rimsky might be able to do something. He's always had such staunch control over everything at West Baden. Yes, Hans, let's talk to Rimsky when he returns. But until then I'm afraid we have no choice but to capitulate to the new West Baden Springs."

⊰ Chapter Elevn ⊱

EVERYTHING ABOUT BRAXTON was clear to Lillian now. At last she had abandoned the foolish sentiments over him that she had clung to so tenaciously. By believing in Braxton's love, she had put herself at a great disadvantage. No matter how grim, it was better to face the truth about her husband than allow herself to be crippled by hopes and desires for him that could never be realized. Braxton was a bootlegger whose only reason for a marrying Lillian was to obtain West Baden Springs as a marketplace for his liquor. Only two weeks ago, there would have been nothing in the world that could have forced Lillian to believe this. But now events continuously flashed through her mind that reconfirmed Braxton's guilt to her all the more.

Of course the obvious blow to Lillian had been Braxton's infidelity in Paris. But even before this lurid event, there had been so many indications that Braxton's love was imitation and that he was nothing more than a con artist. All summer long Braxton had avoided the old guard because he knew the prominent businessmen among them could discredit him. That is why he had acted so nervous at Lillian's dinner party one week before the wedding. He had squirmed each time someone asked him to talk about himself and had changed the subject whenever possible. He had changed seating arrangements in the dining room so that he could be off by himself, away from questions. He had stumbled and stalled when these people asked him to stand up and talk about himself in front of them all. He had been absent during the week before the wedding so as to avoid contact with them. Lillian remembered how completely Braxton had ignored her after the wedding. The enormous number of liquor bottles should have triggered Lillian's curiosity. All of these things Lillian had casually ignored at the time, but now she could think of nothing else.

What a fool she had been for falling for Braxton. All summer long he had wooed her with a ridiculous fake charm that any rational person would have instantly dismissed, but that instead had put Lillian under a lovesick spell. Braxton must have thought her the biggest sucker on earth. Never did she show the slightest suspicion of how Braxton made his money. Back then she had lived in a careless world of sunshine and roses, believing only what wanted to believe about Braxton and trusting him fully. Along with many other documents, she had signed a prenuptial agreement granting him joint ownership of West Baden Springs. It seemed like such a perfect thing to do at the time, for in her mind she had thought it predestined that she and Braxton would live at West Baden in everlasting love and harmony, as if it had been planned in the stars. But now she could see that signing over West Baden to Braxton was the most foolish thing she had ever done, outside of marrying Braxton in the first place.

Why did Lillian ever fall for Braxton? She thought back on last spring during the months just before she had met Braxton. Her father had been all the world to her then, and his death had affected her deeply. She would have reached out for anything that would have relieved the pain of his loss. And then came Braxton—a dashing, debonair man with every trick needed to revive her spirits. How could she have known then the precarious position he was to place her in? Why, there was no telling what treacherous plans Braxton had in mind for West Baden Springs, and Lillian had made it all possible for him! To what extent would Braxton go to secure West Baden for his unscrupulous enterprise? Did he plan on going so far as murder?

Lillian could not afford to find out; in no way could she provoke Braxton, for even the slightest stand against him might result in a catastrophe. She had heard all about the extreme violence brought on by those battling for control of the liquor trade. Widespread lawlessness, murder, beatings, bombings, and bloodshed were common throughout many parts of Chicago because of power-hungry mobsters who would let nothing stand in their way. Their wealth and power enabled them to avoid arrest and to avoid conviction if arrested. They simply bribed or threatened government officials and sometimes even gained control of government positions themselves! How could Lillian oppose such power? Her only hope was Rimsky, just as Hans had suggested. Rimsky had long ruled West Baden with an iron hand. The thought that he would relinquish power in any way was inconceivable. Lillian knew Rimsky would find a crafty, sly way to thwart Braxton. After all, the stern old man had done nothing but thwart her own efforts at West Baden ever since she inherited the place.

But until Rimsky's return, Lillian had no choice but to play along with Braxton and his control over West Baden Springs. Why should Braxton not like the act Lillian was putting on? She was giving him everything he wanted at West Baden: loud, reckless parties; new amusements like the proposed gambling casino; hordes of people misbehaving, indulging themselves, and apparently buying Braxton's liquor in tremendous quantities. To escalate liquor sales even more, thus keeping Braxton very happy, Lillian could purchase sizable quantities herself and destroy the bottles whenever and wherever possible. Her game was to keep Braxton pleased with his West Baden enterprise and then, with Rimsky's help, pull the rug out from under Braxton just as he had done to her.

During the following days, not only had Lillian's popularity been steadily increasing, but at times she wondered whether she had not regained her one-time position as star attraction at West Baden Springs. The boxes of new clothes Hans had brought from Indianapolis had made a big difference. Although the capital of Indiana offered far less of the current fashions than, say, Chicago or New York, Lillian employed a few minor alterations to compensate for this, and the results were remarkable. Ladies would throng to her by day, and men would flock to her by night. All wanted a moment with the stunning Mrs. Kingsley.

All the while Braxton watched on in amazement as he saw his wife dazzle the very crowds who bought his liquor. He now showed a new interest in Lillian and competed with the rest for her attention. But more importantly, he was impressed with the new control Lillian seemed to have over the crowds—a control that just happened to support his own interests. Therefore, Lillian's efforts to please Braxton seemed to be succeeding. It might be that he had even fallen in love with her, or rather it might be that he had fallen in love with the way she was pleasing him.

Since her striking metamorphosis, everyone was now very pleased with Lillian—everyone except for Zelda that is. A younger, more beautiful, more glamorous prototype of herself was capturing the very crowds that Zelda had once ruled. For a while a fierce battle for popularity raged between Lillian and Zelda. But through it all, Lillian knew the ingredients for supremacy: imitate Zelda, but always do her one better.

At first Lillian had thought Zelda's loud, commanding voice was insurmountable whenever Zelda would lead people about the hotel from one amusement to the next. But Lillian did Zelda one better by using the megaphone Rimsky would use with the staff when setting up tables in the atrium or on the front lawn. Lillian always kept the megaphone well hidden from Zelda and pulled it out whenever it was necessary to gain command of the crowd. Such a time was when Lillian created new dance steps for everyone. In one turbulent scene in front of a great number of people, Zelda had tried to undermine Lillian's dances and employ her own.

"Oh, Zelda, we're sick of your dances," snapped Violet. "We've done them all summer long. We want to do Lillian's dances now."

Everyone else agreed as they rushed onto the dance floor, leaving Zelda standing alone, looking out at the others with sharp eyes of resentment and jealously.

Lillian's most original method of captivating the crowd was on the piano. The virtuoso on Chopin twisted her skill about to create, if not jazz, at least the illusion of jazz with rigorous rhythm and a barbaric sound. Whatever it was, the crowd went crazy over it and even danced to it.

"Come with us, Zelda, and listen to Lillian play the piano," Pearl had once said.

"You little idiot!" retorted Zelda. "I don't have time for such nonsense. Can't you see I have a hotel to manage?"

Indeed this was how Zelda lost the most ground in the battle over popularity: by demonstrating before everyone her complete incompetence as manager of West Baden Springs. It was not difficult for anyone to see that Zelda knew nothing about running a hotel. They would frequently find her hopping about to the tune of seething administrative pressures, all of which Zelda could not begin to handle. For the most part, Zelda was too busy struggling for popularity to notice that the hotel staff generally disregarded most of her harebrained instructions.

Lillian even began to play dirty. At the horse stables, she saw to it that Zelda was given a spirited horse. So while Lillian demonstrated to all her keen riding abilities, Zelda went charging off into the wilderness on a runaway horse. At the evening parties in the atrium, Zelda would often try to gain everyone's attention. But at each attempt, the jazz band would blast her away the moment she started to utter. Lillian had cleverly paid the band to do this!

Lillian was clearly winning the battle over popularity at West Baden, and no one could see this better than Braxton. On the day that Rimsky was to return home from Indianapolis, Braxton pulled up to the depot in his sports car in search of his wife. Lillian was there at the depot waiting for Rimsky, but she could not tell Braxton this. In no way could she cause Braxton to suspect a potential collaboration between herself and Rimsky. When addressing Braxton, Lillian denied that she was waiting for anyone in particular and used the excuse that she only wished to greet newly arriving guests. Braxton then insisted that she go with him for a ride in his sports car. After giving Braxton several excuses not to go, Lillian could see that her husband was not prepared to take no for an answer. Reluctantly she climbed into the sports car for a ride through the surrounding countryside.

"This little ride has lasted much longer than I thought it would, Braxton," said Lillian after about an hour in the automobile.

"Yes, I planned it that way," replied Braxton with a grin on this face. "I thought this would be the only way to have you to myself for a while. Your popularity at West Baden Springs amazes me. I've noticed the way all the guests admire you. In fact, you seem to have them all under a spell, a spell that allows you much control over them. Such control over people can be very helpful to me."

"How is that, Braxton?"

Braxton went on to explain. "Most people are like sheep. They aimlessly drift along in a heard, doing just exactly what everyone else does, never thinking about where they stand in this world in relationship to everything else. But there are a chosen few who are resourceful enough to see this mindless quality in people and have the good sense to make people work to their advantage."

"What does all this about sheep have to do with me?" asked Lillian.

"Lillian, my dear, I want us to work together like a team. As you said yourself, we have the same goals in mind for West Baden. Why shouldn't we be as happy as your parents were here? Only we'll try to make up for their big mistake."

"Mistake? How did my parents make a mistake?"

"By not realizing the money-making potential of their hotel. Why, they didn't even have a gambling casino at West Baden."

Lillian was annoyed at Braxton for implying that her parents should have forsaken honor and ethics for money. But she could not provoke an argument.

"West Baden guests did not involve themselves in such activities back then, Braxton."

"They do now, and we must make the most of it. You probably don't even realize the enormous benefit you have been doing West Baden these past few days. In fact, you, Lillian, are serving the function I thought Zelda would have served for me."

"Braxton, you mustn't flatter me by comparing me to Zelda." Lillian was being facetious.

"I do nothing of the kind. The more I get to know dear Zelda, the more I see her as neurotic and deranged. Her performance as manager has been a joke, although it was most admirable of you, Lillian, to give her a try. No, I'm afraid our dear Zelda will not do. You and I, Lillian, will have to take over management of the hotel until I can get someone new from Chicago. If you think you've seen changes at West Baden so far, just wait. There are many more changes yet to come, and after that, West Baden Springs will be known all over the country, maybe all over the world."

"Braxton, just what are some more of these changes?"

Braxton paused for a moment as if to avoid the question.

"My dear," he continued. "I want you to arrange a dinner for about twenty people. Three days should be enough time for adequate preparation. At this dinner all of my hopes, ambitions, and desires for West Baden Springs will unfold before your eyes."

"Just who will be at this dinner, Braxton?"

"Money, power, influence."

Although Braxton's answer was vague, the implication frightened Lillian.

"I suppose I can consult your business assistant for further details."

"What business assistant?"

Lillian was surprised that Braxton did not even remember Hans.

"He went to Paris with us. I believe his name is Hans."

"Oh him, He's just someone I hired as a cover. He won't do you any good. He's just a stupid little boy."

"He seems perfectly capable to me," replied Lillian.

"Oh, I'm sure the little guy tries his best. But let's face it. He just does not have what it takes. He strikes me as one of those idealistic fools who thinks you can just smile at the world and the world will smile back." Braxton then assumed a very serious tone of voice. "He'll find out soon enough that the world is an endless rat hole and that people are unfeeling, insensitive worms piled on top of each other in a murky sea of ruthless competition."

Lillian had never heard Braxton talk this way before. There was acrimony in the way he had spoken. This was not the man she had fallen in love with. Perhaps that man never even existed. Braxton's expression was now tense and very serious, not at all the jaunty, light-hearted face that had wooed her before. He stared straight ahead at the road as if lost in deep thought. The mood was so somber that Lillian could no longer resume the blithe spirit that had so captivated Braxton. The two said nothing for the remainder of the ride.

Lillian peered off to the side. It was a beautiful bright day in late September. As the open-topped automobile soared along the rolling countryside, only a slight chill could be felt, and only traces of autumn foliage could be seen among the miles of green trees. She was glad Braxton was now not inclined to speak, for Lillian was becoming lost in meditation. The soft wind and the sunlight against her face felt soothing. As she surveyed the acres of endless countryside, Lillian, all at once, remembered what a kind and beautiful friend nature could be. Lately she had become a distant stranger to life's milder elements and bedfellow to heartache and extreme tension. But now for nearly the first time since the wedding, Lillian felt almost relaxed as she leaned back and rested her head against the leather seat cushion. She wished the ride would never end. She wished she could sail and soar along the beautiful countryside like this forever and never have to return to her problems at West Baden Springs.

When Lillian saw the eight Byzantine towers in the distance, her heart sank just a bit, and how surprising that was, for only days ago she had longed for this sight more than anything in the world. But it was not West Baden she wished to avoid. It was the people now residing there whom Lillian did not wish to see. The struggle for popularity over the past few days caused her to grow tired of the very superficial people. She cared little for them. They were like children at play as they proceeded from one amusement to another, talking of nothing but money, the stock market, automobiles, and ways to have fun. Lillian's little act before them was actually very exhausting. She was tired of exerting effort; she wanted only to rest. What she would not have given just to be alone in her office for a few hours. But no one left her alone for a minute. Everyone wanted to be in the company of the glamorous Mrs. Kingsley.

When the automobile passed through the front gate, Lillian took hold of some binoculars in an effort to view the faces of those whom she would soon be confronting on the veranda. Among a number of people, Zelda's face flashed through the lenses only for a split second. Lillian followed Zelda with the binoculars to see that her expression was angry and frustrated-looking. Zelda paced about impatiently on the veranda floor, but when she caught sight of Braxton's sports car, she ran at full speed toward the front steps. Obviously, Zelda had been on the veranda awaiting their return.

"Lillian, my darling!" cried Zelda as Lillian stepped out of the sports car. Zelda embraced Lillian in a great display of emotion. Obviously Zelda was resorting to her old act of devotion.

Lillian played along with the act.

"Why, Zelda, what a rare pleasure!" she said with great zest.

The two walked up the front steps, arm in arm, in an animated way, both with broad, painted-on smiles.

"Yes, Miss Fairfax, what a rare pleasure," said Braxton facetiously, as if mocking the pretentious way Zelda and Lillian were behaving. "It's simply been ages. I would say a whole two hours."

"Every time we see Zelda is a rare pleasure, Braxton," added Lillian.

"Yes," continued Braxton. "A pleasure that we hope in the future to become even more rare."

"Ha, ha," laughed Zelda. "Oh, Lillian, your husband has such a sense of humor. Why your marriage must be one endless joke."

Lillian sensed jealousy and hostility leaking through Zelda's act, but Lillian chose to ignore this.

"Zelda, how pretty you look. What a lovely dress. I just can't take my eyes off it!"

"'Tis but a rag compared to all the latest fashions you've been wearing these past few days," said Zelda. "The only thing left for you to be in full style is to cut your hair into a bob. You'll have to let me do it for you."

"Oh, Zelda, I really could not impose upon you."

"It would be no problem at all, my dear. I'll do it tonight."

Braxton interposed. "My wife and I already have plans for tonight, Miss Fairfax."

"Oh nuts!" exclaimed Zelda. "You two are always together and you're always trying to sneak away from me. I've been nearly going mad looking for you two this afternoon. Sometimes I wonder whether you're not trying to avoid me."

"We *are* trying to avoid you, Miss Fairfax," said Braxton.

Zelda paused for a moment, as if absorbing Braxton's brash retort.

"No one could ever accuse you of not being frank, Mr. Kingsley," she said coolly. "The fact is, I have an obligation to Lillian's mother to make sure that her daughter behaves in a proper, ladylike fashion. From what I've seen of Lillian these past few days, I can hardly say that I've been living up to my obligation. I need to stay near Lillian to keep her from doing foolish things."

Braxton replied mockingly, "Maybe what you need, Miss Fairfax, is for us to leave you alone to all your ladylike ways. We would not want to be a bad influence on you."

"Don't be silly," said Zelda. "I've planned afternoon tea on the veranda just for the three of us."

"My wife and I are not interested."

Lillian could not help but notice the acrimonious climate between Braxton and Zelda. This had been the first time Lillian had seen Braxton and Zelda together since arriving home from Paris, and the combination of the two interested her. Hans had said something before the wedding about a conversation he had overheard between Braxton and Zelda that implied a possible collaboration between the two. Lillian wanted to keep them together longer.

"Oh, Braxton, Zelda went to all the trouble to arrange tea for us. The least we can do is accept."

The three sat down in a polite trio of tension. Zelda and Lillian smiled and laughed intermittently. Braxton looked totally bored, but the three said nothing for several minutes. Lillian wanted to say something just to get a conversation started.

"Zelda, what a beautiful ring you have on!"

"Why, thank you, Lillian. A very dear friend gave this ring to me. I can remember her at twenty-two in all her youthful beauty. At that young age she married a middle-aged man, oh I would say about Mr. Kingsley's age. Whenever they were together strangers used to mistakenly address them as father and daughter. Needless to say, the marriage was a complete disaster. It seemed like no time after they were married, the old man grew desperately ill, and of course, even to this day she plays nurse to an ailing invalid. Oh! I did not mean to imply anything by sharing with you this tear-jerking story. Your marriage might work out. People have bet on greater odds. Why, for centuries people believed in alchemy. Even though you two have hardly anything in common, you do have a lot of money. Well, as I said, you do have a lot of money. Just look at me here trying to pass judgments when actually I know so little about Mr. Kingsley's background. But for that matter, who *does* know very much about Mr. Kingsley's background? How unfortunate that your parents were not alive to investigate Mr. Kingsley for you, Lillian. Who knows? They might have found out many things about Mr. Braxton Kingsley that they would not have liked, would not have liked at all!"

Lillian sensed jealousy and intense resentment. Zelda's coy innuendoes caused Lillian to wonder whether Braxton and Zelda had known each other all along. It was perhaps no mere coincidence that Zelda just happened to present herself at West Baden at nearly the same time Lillian had met Braxton. By declaring herself as Katia's dearest and closest friend, Zelda hoped to win Lillian's trust and thus secure a stronghold for Braxton in his plan to take over West Baden Springs. Lillian wanted to hear more, but the three lapsed into another spell of silence. Lillian hoped to break the silence once again.

"Zelda, what a lovely necklace you have on."

"Why thank you, Lillian. A gentleman admirer gave this necklace to me not too long ago. He is a bootlegging gangster from Chicago who went into an old woman's house once with a machine-gun, shot plenty of bullets into the old woman, and tore this lovely necklace off her bleeding body. See, it even has her name engraved on it: Louisa Mae Crumpet."

Lillian gave an expression of half smile and half grimace and then replied, "What a pretty name."

Zelda continued. "I don't think there are any people on earth more treacherous than those battling for control of the liquor trade. Why the once pleasant streets of Chicago are nothing more than giant shooting galleries now all because of these hideous thugs." Zelda sat up in her chair as if preparing to tell a story. "One of the standard methods of disposing of a rival is to pursue the rival's car with a stolen automobile full of men armed with sawed-off machine-guns, to draw up beside it, forcing the car to the curb, open fire upon it, and then disappear into the traffic, later abandoning the stolen car at a safe distance. Another favorite method is to take the victim "for a ride." In other words, to lure him into a supposedly friendly car, shoot him at leisure, drive to some distant and deserted part of the city, and quietly throw this body overboard. Still another is to lease an apartment or a room overlooking his front door, station a couple of hired assassins at the window, and as the victim emerges from the house some sunny afternoon, spray the victim with a few dozen machine-gun bullets from behind drawn curtains. These are some of the more polite methods of disposal. There are much more ingenious and refined methods of slaughter. And the miracle of it all is how these unscrupulous thugs hide themselves in society, posing as honest, hardworking, and responsible citizens. And you never quite know who is involved in the underworld—a trusting neighbor, a loyal friend, even a beloved relative, perhaps even your very own devoted husband. On thing is for sure. They are all low-down, cheating, double-crossing varmints, not to be trusted under any condition!"

Zelda's tone had become acrid, and Lillian felt all hostility was directed toward Braxton. If Lillian could only hear Braxton and Zelda talking alone, this would surely confirm Zelda's involvement. Lillian noticed that the three were seated on the inside edge of the veranda, right up against the wall to the hotel. There was a window just about where they were sitting. If Lillian could only make an excuse to leave the two, she could enter the lobby and listen to them through the window.

"Lillian," said Braxton. "Perhaps you should waste no time in getting our little dinner party under way."

Braxton had given Lillian an excuse to leave and she must seize the opportunity.

"Braxton, that's a wonderful idea!" said Lillian with enthusiasm. "There are so many things I need to do in preparation. If you two will excuse me."

"Dinner party?" questioned Zelda. "What dinner party?"

"My wife and I are planning a dinner party for about twenty people who will no doubt prove to be very helpful to us and our beloved West Baden Springs," said Braxton.

"If there is anything to be planned around here," said Zelda vehemently, "I will do the planning. I am the manager of West Baden, remember?"

"You *were* the manager of West Baden, Miss Fairfax," Braxton pointed out. "Effective immediately my wife and I are assuming full charge of the hotel administration."

Zelda could not contain her temper. "Why of all the low-down, double-crossing …"

"Go right ahead, Lillian," said Braxton. "Miss Fairfax and I could use a little time to get acquainted."

"Very well, Braxton," said Lillian as she stood up slowly, trying not to show her extreme readiness to hear Braxton and Zelda alone.

When Lillian was sure she was out of Braxton and Zelda's view, she scurried through the lobby door. The lobby was cluttered with people. Lillian ducked her head down and quickly proceeded toward the windows along the front wall of the lobby. Luckily her window of choice was partially covered by a lofty palm planter, making the perfect cover while she listened through the window. Lillian could hear Braxton and Zelda talking now just outside of the window.

"All right!" said Zelda angrily. "I want to know just what's going on here. You'd better not be getting any funny ideas."

"Whatever to you mean, dear Zelda?" replied Braxton.

"You know perfectly well what I mean. We're planning to bump off that bitch and have the place to ourselves."

"Why, Zelda!" said Braxton in a playful voice. "What a horribly shocking mind you have. Why, I would not dream of such a thing. Why would I possible want to do such a thing to my dear, beloved little wife."

"You know this was all your idea to begin with. You'd better not be planning on double-crossing me, Braxton Kingsley. This whole affair has been nothing but one nasty trick after another. Like when you two came back from Paris a week early. I was nearly stunned out of my mind when Lillian strolled into the atrium that day."

Braxton continued jauntily. "I just wanted to see how Lillian would react to your charming little party, that's all. I had absolutely no idea she would have adapted so well to the new clientele. The truth is, dear Zelda, that you have exhausted your usefulness to me. In just a few days you have completely lost your popularity to Lillian. What possible use could I have for you when there is Lillian around completely supporting my every endeavor? Zelda, I believe it is about time you left."

Zelda went into rage. "I'm not giving up without a fight. You'll pay for this, Braxton Kingsley, you low-down, double-crossing rat. No one ever gets the better of Zelda Fairfax. I'll get you for this, just wait."

"Not unless I get you first," said Braxton with confidence. "I'm very good at making accidents happen. You so vividly described some just moments ago. Stay here as long as you like, Zelda, but don't be surprised if you should run into one of my little accidents."

Lillian turned her head from the window for a moment and looked about the lobby circumspectly. To her great dismay, several perplexed expressions had caught sight of her behind the palm planter. It would only be a matter of seconds before someone would begin to approach her, seeking an explanation for her curious position. Lillian had no idea what she would say in such a case.

Before she could be approached, however, Lillian walked briskly across the lobby toward her office.

Although several pondering faces had followed Lillian across the lobby, she arrived at the door to her office. There were voices on the other side of the door. Who could be in Lillian's office? She turned the handle slowly and opened the door. At the first crack through the door, Lillian was relieved to see Rimsky sitting at her desk in his characteristically solemn manner. After Lillian stepped into the room, she could see that Hans was the other voice she had heard. He was seated opposite to Rimsky and the desk.

"Rimsky! I'm so glad to see you!" said Lillian with vigor. "You can't imagine what has been going on around here." Rimsky gave Lillian a cold glance but said nothing as he continued to brood over the desk.

"I've already told Mr. Rimsky as much as I could, Lillian," said Hans.

Rimsky raised his eyebrows for an instant, as if surprised by Hans's familiar tone toward Lillian.

Lillian took a seat next to Hans.

"You told Rimsky all about how Braxton wants to take over West Baden and use it as a giant marketplace for his bootleg liquor?"

"Yes," replied Hans. "I even showed him the mysterious room 174."

"But however did you get in?" asked Lillian. "Mr. Rimsky used his pass key."

"There is one more thing, Hans," said Lillian impatiently. "Remember before the wedding when you told me of a conversation you overheard between Braxton and Zelda? Only minutes ago I, myself, overheard another conversation between these two that disclosed beyond all doubt that Zelda has been involved along with Braxton's scheme to overtake West Baden. It all makes sense, doesn't it? While we were in Paris with Braxton, Zelda was left at West Baden to initiate Braxton's plans. She caused an accident for Rimsky and then rallied together a mob of speakeasy-goers to drive out the old familiar guests and establish a climate of chaos and confusion all aimed at liquor sales."

"I just knew dear Zelda was involved in all this somehow!" said Hans. "Braxton needed Zelda to lure his Chicago customers on the train to her never-ending party at West Baden. Only one thing went sour for Zelda. She did not count on losing her widespread popularity to you, Lillian. Mr. Rimsky, you should see the way Lillian has captured this new clientele. They flock to her by day and by night. Why, no one hardly even remembers Zelda anymore, even though she is the manager."

Rimsky had been silent and subdued since Lillian's entry, but Hans's last words evoked a sudden surge of tension across his face.

"Zelda Fairfax is now the manager of West Baden Springs?" he whined loudly.

"Not any longer, Rimsky," said Lillian in a reassuring voice. "Braxton wants to bring in someone from Chicago to fill the job. Until then he wants me and himself to take charge."

"There you see, Mr. Rimsky," said Hans boldly, "even Braxton Kingsley has fallen for Lillian, and this time for real."

"Braxton would fall for anyone who would support his liquor trade," Lillian pointed out. "And that is exactly what I have been doing."

There was a spell of silence. Rimsky continued to brood over the desk in his usual somber way.

"So, Miss Lillian," he said. "It would appear that your husband and these new people here are quite pleased with you. Your dream marriage is perhaps working out after all."

"Rimsky, how can you say such a thing?" exclaimed Lillian. "How can you think for one minute that I am satisfied with the present condition of West Baden? I hate and despise Braxton and what he has done. I want him and his gangsters, Zelda, and that wild mob gone from West Baden forever. It's been nothing but one endless nightmare ever since I married Braxton.

The only reason I have been going along with him these past few days is to keep from being killed. Rimsky, surely you are aware of the ruthless ways bootlegging gangsters from Chicago dispose of those who stand in their way. In no way could I have opposed Braxton. My only choice was to play along and wait for you to arrive back."

"A very sensible thing to do," replied Rimsky. "But, I would have thought you would rather die than to abandon the mighty Randreninoff mystique so reminiscent of your mother. And just what did you think I could do to remedy the situation?"

Lillian was disappointed that Rimsky showed so little interest in helping her. But she knew that she must appeal to him somehow.

"Rimsky," she said with a touch of desperation in her voice. "You've kept gangsters out of West Baden for nearly a decade now. You've always had such staunch control over the place. Surely, there must be something you can do to ruin Braxton's treacherous scheme. There is not much time. Braxton wants me to plan a dinner party for twenty people. I am sure these are Braxton's fellow gangsters and business associates whose support Braxton hopes to gain. If we do not make a stand against Braxton and these people, they will become so powerful that heaven and earth won't stand a chance against them."

"How long until this dinner party?" asked Rimsky.

"Only three days!" answered Lillian.

Rimsky put his hand to his chin and thought for a good five minutes. Lillian and Hans looked on with tense expressions.

"There is only one force capable of destroying gangsters," Rimsky finally replied. "Not law enforcers, nor civic-minded do-gooders. No, the only thing powerful enough to destroy gangsters is other gangsters. I must leave at once for Chicago."

"But, Rimsky!" cried Lillian. "You cannot just leave us here alone with Braxton! You must stay and help us think of a way to defeat him."

"You shall be all right here at West Baden if you do exactly as I say." Rimsky's eyes were cold and serious. "I shall prearrange the dinner party before I depart and put my finest assistant in charge during my absence. You, Miss Lillian, however, shall tell your husband that you are solely responsible for the dinner and that you have had no contact with me whatsoever. I must depart before he even knows I have returned. The last thing you must do is determine the exact date and time of the event and send this information to me in Chicago via telegram. Mr. Kingsley is in for an evening he will never forget!"

⊰ Chapter Twevel ⊱

LILLIAN OPENED HER eyes to the stark whiteness of her bedroom ceiling. She could not decide which would be worse: to return to a very dismal nightmare in her sleep or to face the day that was before her. Only seconds after Lillian awoke did her heart start to tremble at the thought of what day it was. She could remember that when she had gone to sleep the night before she wished she would not wake up for this day. She wanted to sleep right through it and wake up later to find that all was well again. This was the day Braxton had set for his dinner party of gangsters.

The three days since her conference with Rimsky had whisked by quickly. What on earth was Rimsky up to in Chicago? Perhaps he did not realize the severity of her situation. Why would he just leave her at West Baden, dangling in apprehension? She cursed herself for not making the point stronger to him that if they did not take a stand against Braxton in due time, all of her efforts of appeasement would be in vain. Lillian would be handing West Baden Springs over to Braxton and his gangsters without the slightest resistance. If only Rimsky would do something to help!

Lillian had a sick feeling in her stomach that had been steadily increasing in strength the closer she had come to this dreaded day. Throughout the past three days, she was constantly reminded of Braxton's power over her. She envisioned the arrival of twenty, six-foot gangsters in dark suits slowly approaching her with machine-guns in hand. She would stand alone, quivering before them. But what would she say to them? How could she assume her careless imitation of Zelda when she knew all they wanted was to destroy her and her way of life at West Baden Springs?

Lillian looked over at Braxton while he was sleeping. He looked so harmless while sleeping. If only he could stay that way. Lillian had to admit that he was a handsome man with his dark features. How sad, she thought, that such a beautiful man could be so corrupted by the world.

Along with Braxton's new interest in Lillian had come also his new interest in sleeping with her. But Lillian no longer loved him, and if Braxton had any sensitivity at all, he would have seen this. Thank God he could not see it. Thank God he was insensitive; otherwise he surely would have noticed Lillian's obvious aversion to sleeping with him. It was more than an aversion. The thought of bearing any of Braxton's children distressed her terribly. This was but one of the many things, however, that distressed and frightened her during these tense days.

Lillian turned her attention back to the white ceiling above her. She was so terribly tired of everything: the play-acting, scheming, plotting, and fighting just to stay alive. Peace and contentment seemed so distant. For just now, all she wanted was to get through this day that was before her. She prayed that God would see her through it.

Braxton put his arm around Lillian. A chill went down her spine at his touch.

"What are you thinking?" he asked.

"Braxton, I did not know you were awake," said Lillian softy.

"You look worried about something. What is it?"

"Worried? What could I possibly be worried about? I was just thinking about … about how happy I am."

She said this even though nothing could have been further from the truth.

"Now don't lie to me. You're worried about something and I have a pretty good idea what it is. The dinner party tonight, right? Don't worry, my dear. Everything is under control."

"Yes, Braxton, everything has been under control these past few days, and the guests are so pleased with the changes that have already been made. Why, things just could not be better for West Baden," and then Lillian said emphatically, "just the way they are now. Don't you think so, Braxton?"

"You may think things are going well now, my pet. But just wait until after tonight. West Baden Springs will become a household word. It will become the most famous resort in the world!"

"Why after tonight?" asked Lillian. "Do you mean because of the dinner party? The whole purpose for this event remains a mystery to me. Can't you tell me more about it?"

"You shall see soon enough, my dear," said Braxton in a reassuring way. "Now don't worry about tonight. Just be yourself and they'll love you. You'll win them over just as you won over all my new guests from Chicago and just as you continue to win over me. It's funny. I did not think I would come to love you so much, my dear. You've brought much joy into my life."

Braxton's sentimental words were of little comfort to Lillian. Suddenly Lillian heard the main door to the apartment open in the next room.

"Hello! Hello! Where are you, my two angels?"

It was Zelda, and somehow Lillian was not surprised. Ever since their polite trio of tension three days ago on the veranda, Zelda had stopped at nothing to keep Braxton from being alone with Lillian. The reason was obvious. Zelda wanted to keep Braxton from falling in love with Lillian. By usurping Zelda's position as leader of the lively crowd, Lillian had put Zelda's part in the takeover of West Baden in jeopardy. Clearly Zelda was not prepared to have her plans altered, and Braxton's falling in love with Lillian had clearly not been in Zelda's plans.

So for three days Zelda had been hunting down Lillian and Braxton, forcing herself between them whenever possible. At dinner Braxton would always arrange a tiny table only large enough for just himself and his wife. But no sooner would Braxton and Lillian be seated than Zelda would appear before them with a table service in her hands, forcing all three around the tiny table. At the theater Zelda would always make it a point to sit right in between Lillian and Braxton. When Lillian and Braxton went out riding together, no matter how remote the trail, Zelda would always come galloping along to join them. And so it was no surprise to Lillian that Zelda had gone so far as to join them in their bedroom.

Without even knocking, Zelda whisked through he bedroom door.

"I hope I'm not interrupting anything," she said.

"Now whatever would make you think that, Miss Fairfax?" replied Braxton sarcastically as he covered his chest with the bedspread.

"It's no matter," said Zelda. "It's time for you two sleepy heads to get up anyway. Rise and shine! Rise and shine!" Zelda approached the bed and tugged on Braxton's arm. "Mr. Kingsley, you dress in the next room while Lillian and I have a few words of girl talk together. Now go along."

Braxton clumsily put the bedspread around him and stumbled into the next room.

Lillian was now left alone with Zelda. This was the first time the two had been alone together since the start of their popularity struggle. Zelda's expression was none too friendly as Lillian passed her on the way to the dressing partition. As Lillian started dressing behind the neck-high partition, she frequently glanced at Zelda and knew dear Zelda's insides were surely exploding with animosity. Lillian had put a snag in Zelda's plans to take over West Baden with Braxton, and now Lillian feared she would finally receive the wrath from Zelda that was long overdue. But Lillian would avoid this if possible. A confrontation with Zelda was not what Lillian needed just then. To relieve the cold, acrimonious mood, Lillian decided to introduce some small talk.

"So, Zelda," she said, making an attempt to be friendly, "just what sort of mischief have you been getting yourself into these days?"

"Apparently, my dear, not nearly as much as you!"

Lillian bushed. "Don't be silly, Zelda. It's not considered mischief if those doing it are married."

"Why, Lillian Everett Kingsley! I am appalled. How can you think that someone of my moral integrity would allude to such a thing! I am referring to your shocking behavior as of these past few days. I've anguished in silence long enough. I must speak out in disapproval of your actions! Where is the polite, demure princess I once knew who carried herself about the halls of West Baden Spring with grace and refinement? A strange, wicked spell has come over that docile one of mine, and I now see an erratic vision of ill manner on a dance floor, twisting and thrashing her body to abrasive sounds in a most unladylike manner. This is surely not my little Lillian, not this one who guzzles gin like water as she flagrantly breaks the prohibition law in front of crowds of dumbfounded spectators! What if the police should come to West Baden and find you guzzling the drink of sin? They would cart you off to jail, Lillian. I have a right mind to call them on you, to snitch on you, Lillian. But I will not because I know you have the good sense to reform yourself in due time. And as for the guests of West Baden, you think they admire you, don't you? You think they regard you as the epitome of style and fashion. But alas, Lillian, they jeer in fits of outrageous laughter at the thought of you in those ridiculous costumes, your face pointed so ostentatiously. Can you really blame them all for laughing at this new Lillian? She is a shocking creature. But I am only commenting on those actions of hers I can readily observe. I tremble to think of what she might be doing behind closed doors."

Lillian did not think she had ever heard anything so hypocritical. But sarcasm and fantastic verbal accounts were to be expected of Zelda. There was no point in arguing. Lillian could not afford a brawl with Zelda and had no use for one. She would dress quickly, pretend that she was hardly listening to Zelda, and then leave the room as soon as possible.

"And poor, dear Mr. Kingsley!" continued Zelda. "Lord only knows what he must be going through! How awful to think the person one marries is really someone else underneath."

"Yes, Zelda, how awful," muttered Lillian as if speaking from experience.

"Although quite naturally he would never admit this to you, my dear, your husband has come to me broken, in tears about your new shocking behavior. Yes, the poor dear! A stunning metamorphosis has come over the bright angel of goodness whom he thought he had married, whom he thought could deliver him from his salacious lifestyle of the past."

"Lillian," Braxton shouted from the next room. "I want you to see the new gambling casino. Remember, it was all your idea."

"Yes, Braxton," answered Lillian, shouting back. "I want to see it right away." This gave Lillian the perfect excuse to break away from her encounter with Zelda.

Lillian had thought little about the casino. But her nonchalance instantly changed to repulsion the moment she passed through its doors. No trace of the stately old billiard house remained. The handsome walnut paneling had been painted over in bright red with flashy gold trim. The large paintings had all been replaced with even larger mirrors. The delicately detailed plaster ceiling had been covered over with mirrors. The elegant brass chandeliers had been replaced with those of crystal that were much too large and elaborate to be in good taste. The oriental rugs and been removed and the beautiful marble floor had been completely cover over with thick red plush carpeting. All of the masculine eighteenth century English furnishings had been removed with, of course, the billiard tables. Lillian could not begin to know what all the gambling devices were but could see they were not the hastily made improvisations she had imagined.

What power and resources Braxton must command in order to make such a drastic change in only a few days! It seemed that in so much as a snap of his fingers Braxton had transformed Lillian's elegant billiard house into a cheap moneymaking outfit. From eighteenth-century Georgian to nineteenth-century western whorehouse décor, Braxton had carelessly butchered the place. Lillian shuddered to think what Braxton might do to the rest of the hotel.

Lillian moved about the many people, becoming more and more annoyed at their careless exuberance. Lillian wondered whether she had ever been so carefree as those she saw in the casino merrily moving from one game to another like children at a playground. She made no attempt to play up to them like before, for nothing could remove from her thought the dreaded hour that was quickly approaching. Moment by moment she could think of nothing but how much closer she was coming to Braxton's dinner party. She was sick with apprehension, and here were these fun-loving people before her, blithely tossing dice, playing cards, screaming, laughing, moving about as aimlessly as livestock, and greedily clutching onto gambling chips with tight fists.

Only days ago, when Lillian had struggled so to befriend the lively guests, she could not have imagined then the far greater struggle involved in merely tolerating them. All throughout the hotel that day, she encountered them with ever increasing aggravation. During a brief stint at the swimming pool, several spirited young men showed their admiration for Lillian by throwing her into the water while she was fully clothed.

Just as Lillian had walked passed Logan and Bryan Stock Exchange, a crowd of guests inundated her with jubilations of their newly acquired fortunes. "Look, Mrs. Kingsley!" said one woman in excitement while tugging onto Lillian's arm and showing her a piece of stock ticker tape. "American Can seventy-seven and one-quarter. I'm rich! I'm rich."

Another woman poked at Lillian from behind. "Mrs. Kingsley, Mrs. Kingsley! Look at what I have to show you!" When Lillian turned around, the woman opened her purse and pulled out a little glass bottle full of a dark substance. "It's oil from one of my oil wells in Texas." When Lillian finally settled down on the veranda with a large group, it dawned on her how completely uninterested she was in their every word. They spoke of nothing intellectual, nothing thought-provoking or stimulating, only insipid chatter about things such as money, automobiles, clothes, lifestyle, and ways of having a good time.

Lillian wanted to get away from people. But everywhere she went there were people—hundreds of people—with big smiles, laughing incessantly, playing like children. All throughout the hotel Lillian felt as though she was walking through a maze, and at each turn was a dead end full of people— clamoring, shouting, roaring, irritating, annoying people. Her office was no longer a suitable refuge, nor was her apartment, for both places had been discovered. Lillian would enjoy only a few minutes of solitude before someone would knock on the door or just barge in as Zelda had done that morning. More and more Lillian felt narrowed into a corner, until she arrived at the room of Hans.

"I don't really know what I'm doing here, Hans," she said. "I just needed somewhere to escape."

"Escape?" replied Hans. "Escape from what, Lillian?"

"What do you think, Hans? That horrible mob out there."

"These new guests are not so bad once you get to know them," said Hans flippantly.

"Hans, do you really believe that?"

"No, I just said it to calm you down some. You seem very nervous, Lillian."

"These people make me so nervous, Hans. They have infested West Baden with their vulgarity and have made everything so much worse. I do despise them. It is they who are the pawns in Braxton's treachery, they who reveal West Baden's openly visible wounds. It is they who kindle a fire of discontent in me that will burn until I have defeated every last vestige of their character."

Lillian moved about nervously, still pacing back and forth in a quick, short-tempered rhythm. She continued.

"True, West Baden Springs was designed for people to enjoy themselves, but did the party begin for this crowd upon arrival at West Baden, and will it end when they leave? Certainly not! West Baden is but a single link in their long geographical chain of frivolous amusements, and at every link, another inane episode, a continued inane existence. From Paris to Monte Carlo, Newport to Long Island, the party never ends as they globetrot from one party to another, always with a drink in one hand and a cigarette in the other, with nothing between themselves and the next person but smoke, darkness, vapid chatter, and blaring jazz. Before long they cease to be human beings with feelings and emotions but instead become self-centered, self-absorbed, party machines!"

"Lillian, you are being much too severe," said Hans. "You are taking these people much too seriously. Please, calm down and relax. Remember it is Braxton who is the enemy, not these guests. They are just innocent, harmless people caught up in Braxton's treachery just like us."

"These innocent, harmless people, as you call them, Hans, are the ones keeping Braxton in power by buying his liquor. They think it's cute and quite the fashion to break the law by buying bootleg liquor. Never has any one of them considered how many people Braxton and his gangsters have cheated, robbed, and killed to furnish them with their precious drink. Instead they choose to hide with impunity under a great pleasure dome with all their money and insensitivity and believe they are not their brothers' keepers."

Lillian paused for a while but continued walking nervously, now about the circumference of the room. She stopped, clutched some papers in her hand, and fanned her face with them. She took several long, deep breaths and then began to speak again.

"Rimsky assured me that he has everything under control, and you, Hans, tell me to relax. I will never relax until the lot of them are driven from my home. Twenty-two years at West Baden Springs have created someone who will not join in the whims of a fickle crowd who drift along in an endless quest for fun without regard to people they afflict along the way."

"Lillian," said Hans with great concern. "You must not talk this way. You must calm down. If your temper is shown at the dinner tonight, there is no telling what could happen. You simply must relax."

Lillian peered out the doorway of the private dinning room where Braxton's dubious dinner guests were to gather. She could hear a platoon of soft footsteps, soft muttering, and an occasional tingling of silverware and clanging of porcelain as the waiters scurried about with last-minute preparations. She fidgeted nervously while her mind tried to block out the agitating noises behind her. The sick, nauseous feeling at her stomach was at an all-time high, no thanks to the tasteless, lascivious-looking dress Braxton had selected for her to wear. She was frightened. More than anything, though, she felt so terribly all alone.

Just when Lillian's mind was sidetracked at thinking of how much she wished she was still with Hans in his room, her eyes caught the sight of some twenty men in black suits marching across the main dining room. She had not expected them so soon! Why, the waiters were not even finished setting the tables yet! Lillian braced herself as the mass of black came closer to where she was standing there at the entrance to the private dining room. Braxton was out in front leading the team. When the men finally reached her, Lillian made a feeble attempt to speak.

"How do you do, gentlemen? I am Mrs. Kingsley. I, I wish to cordially welcome you to West Baden Springs."

Lillian extended her hand to a tough, truculent-looking man who was out in front next to Braxton. To her dismay, the man did not accept Lillian's hand but instead stared at her with a blank expression.

Braxton interposed. "Lillian, this is only a bodyguard. So are all the rest of the men who are out in front."

Lillian turned red with embarrassment. "Oh, excuse me," she said.

The rest of the men looked at Lillian with the same blank expression and then the entire group walked right past her into the private dining room. Lillian was too embarrassed to speak. She wanted to walk off into the main dining room or lose herself among the workers in the kitchen. A chiming sound interrupted Lillian's thought as she trailed the men into the private dining room. Her ears followed the sound to a center table where Braxton stood with a spoon in hand, tapping it against a glass in an effort to gain his guests' attention.

"In Xanadu did Kublai Khan a stately pleasure dome decree," proclaimed Braxton. "Welcome, gentlemen, to the pleasure dome that is West Baden Springs. You know her from song and legend as a glittering lady, brightly adorned in Byzantine beauty, extending her arms out to Chicago's high society with all her appealing attributes. You envision West Baden Springs as an enchanted palace, crowned by the world's largest dome—a blot of civilization isolated in the Indiana wilderness, yet locked in a time zone far removed from the present and still under the spell of a storybook fantasy. But we, successful men of this day and age, cannot live in a storybook fantasy if we are to prosper. We must confront the real world at present, confront it and eke out every available opportunity and take every possible advantage in the greatest possible quantity. This we must do to achieve our goal of not only prospering, but to rule. I brought you gentlemen here this day to show you that West Baden Springs is no longer crippled under the curse of another age. An astonishing metamorphosis has ransomed this fair lady of a hotel from the clutches of a useless past and has revitalized her with a new style, a new look, new clientele, and everything needed to make her the perfect marketplace for our commodity."

While Braxton continued to talk, Lillian could not help but notice the alien environment of people. What was she doing here? But perhaps it was best that only strangers surrounded her. She did not want to have to explain her present misfortune to anyone she knew. She did not want the old familiar guests and friends of her parents returning to see her like this at West Baden. Surely they would notice the distressed look in her face. They thought that Lillian was guarded from the earth's more bitter elements and had every hope of her blossoming into a perfect rose. They did not know that weeds and thorns now proliferated around her and were competing for her plot of ground, blotting out life-supporting sun, seeking to destroy her in all her innocence. Much too vulnerable, she was easy prey to the likes of an unscrupulous opportunist like Braxton Kingsley.

Lillian turned to look out a large window at the vast forest that engulfed the hotel. It seemed a grand panorama of nature in perfect harmony, divine peace, and everlasting complacency. That is how it appeared from where she was standing there observing a gentle breeze rustling through the trees in graceful rhythm. But, looking deeper into the forest, she would find truth. She would find that nature is not so complacent, not so kind, and that every plant competes for a place in the sun, every animal struggles to eke out limited resources while being continually threatened by destruction. All creatures in the vast forest live a life of constant challenge and unrest.

Lillian thought about her life before marrying Braxton. Life had seemed carefree and effortless then. She used to spend days arranging concerts, dramas, and stupid amusements that were probably as much a waste of time as the activities of those she had encountered that afternoon. Everything she used to do back then seemed unimportant now: the hours of riding aimlessly through the woods on a horse as if there was nothing better to do, the hours of primping and preparing for grand social affairs where she would chatter insipidly with unconcerned people or dance all night without the slightest purpose. She remembered how she used to fuss so about particulars like table settings and flower arrangements and how she used to worry about perfecting her talents in art and music.

Now her life seemed a tense battle of wits, a battle for survival, a battle to fight for and preserve the life she had long known at West Baden Springs, the life that had become threatened at the sound of the tumultuous thunder that struck when Braxton had placed a wedding band on her finger. Lillian had since felt the reverberations of that moment. They never seemed to go away.

"So there you have it, gentlemen," Braxton said, still addressing the men but showing signs of finishing. "The perfect marketplace for our commodity—far removed from the flying bullets of our competitors in Chicago. A little money machine that produces big bucks in the middle of the Indiana wilderness."

"Although I have no doubt sold most of you on the idea of West Baden Springs, there is still one question in the back of your minds, isn't there? Just how, all of you ask, do I intend for us to get away with such flagrant schemes in this prohibition era? Or course the local authorities have been paid off substantially. But what about all those other people out there, the state and federal law enforcers and irritating civic-minded people. Don't you think they will try to ruin our lucrative enterprise? What protection do we have against them, gentlemen? I will tell you gentlemen what will be our protection: the memory of Katia Randreninoff Everett. People associated West Baden with her more than anything—that most pious of human beings. Do you think people would let the pristine memory of this saintly woman be besmirched? No, gentlemen, people will always remember the West Baden Springs of Katia. There is too much honor in the memory of her for people to ever conceive of dishonor in West Baden Springs, as if this place were forever blessed with eternal virtue. Don't you see, gentlemen? We can stuff our pockets at he expense of a dead woman. Sure we may get caught someday. But by that time we will have made so much money out of this place that we can afford to light a match to it and run back to Chicago. That woman insulted us with her superior virtue when alive, but she can prove to be a gold mine to us dead. We can do anything here at West Baden Springs with impunity, gentlemen, because we have the rump of the late, great Katia Randreninoff Everett to cover us."

The room exploded into laughter. Lillian looked around at the grotesque sight: a room full of fat-cheeked, double-chinned men chuckling, gurgling, squealing like pigs as they made fun of her late mother. Braxton had gone too far this time, and Lillian would not stand for it. A trembling anger the likes of which she had never known took control of her. Lillian did not care any longer. She would stand up against them even if it cost her life. Lillian rose from her chair abruptly. But just as she was on the brink of a defiant outburst, the kitchen door suddenly slammed. Lillian's eyes focused on Hans as he stood panting with a tense expression. When Hans caught view of Lillian, he ran to her at full speed, nervously tugged her by the arm, and coaxed her off in the direction from where he had come.

"Hans, what do you think you are doing?" cried Lillian in an irate whisper so that only Hans could hear.

"I don't have time to explain. Please, Lillian, come with me now!"

Grasping her tightly, Hans proceeded with Lillian across the private dining room. But when they reached the alcove of the recessed kitchen door, Lillian stopped.

"Hans, I demand to know the meaning of this!"

"A fleet of automobiles just arrived full of men dressed like waiters," replied Hans impatiently.

"What is so unusual about that? They are probably here to help with the dinner party."

"How many waiters do you know that carry machine-guns?"

Before Lillian could reply, about fifteen waiters marched through the main door and formed a line across the front wall. Several carried large silver trays covered by dome-shaped lids. Braxton's dinner companions took no heed to the waiters. But the dome-shaped lids were removed and, in an instant, machine-guns appeared in the hands of those lined across the front of the room. Without warning, the fifteen odd men dressed as waiters carelessly opened fire on the entire room, turning the once subdued dining area into a cataclysm of thundering gunfire. Luckily the alcove sheltered Lillian and Hans from the bullets, but from their protected position, both witnessed a bloody massacre more terrifying than anything they could imagine. One after another, men fell slaughtered on the tables in front of them, knocking the dishes and glassware to the floor in clamorous overtones.

Like Lillian and Hans, Braxton had stood separate from the tables of men. Braxton seized this advantage by diving out a nearby window, crashing through the glass in great haste.

After the first round of fire, the bodyguards attempted a slight counteroffensive but they were quickly overwhelmed. With all resistance smashed, the way was now clear for the invaders to search the room for those who may have survived the initial gunfire.

"We've go to get out of here!" cried Hans as he tugged Lillian and led her through the kitchen door. The kitchen staff had already evacuated. But much to Lillian and Han's disadvantage, the staff had had the good sense to lock the outside exit. "The only way out now is through the main dining room."

When Lillian and Hans passed into the main dining room, all was silent as the guests sat at their tables with fearful faces fixed on the door at a distance, where only moments earlier gunfire had resounded. The two quickly meandered their way through the tables of people when, all at once, the door to the private dining room flung open and the bogus waiters marched into the main dining room. At first sight of the machine-guns, the entire room panicked. The hundreds there in the main dining room stampeded toward the exit in a thunderous avalanche of bodies. Overturning tables along the way, crashing dishes, splattering food over the undulating floor, screaming with terror-stricken faces, the herd trampled right over those who had fallen during the hysteria. Had it not been for Hans's tenacious grip, Lillian might have fallen as well. The tight squeeze through the door was nearly unbearable. But when the hysterical crowd reached the atrium, they scattered like ants all over the enormous area.

Zelda stood in panic at the center of the atrium, screaming, "Braxton! Braxton! Where you are? What have they done to you?"

Lillian's immediate impulse was to seek refuge inside her office. She and Hans scurried through the nomadic confusion and then darted through the door to Lillian's office. Hans locked the door behind them.

"That was a close one," he said with a sigh of relief.

"Hans, they may be looking for me! After all, I am Braxton's wife. We've got to find a safer place to hide."

"Lillian, look!" Hans pointed out the window.

Hans and Lillian stood at the window and watched the men who had brought havoc to West Baden Springs. The somber intruders, still dressed as waiters, got into several back automobiles, and then the small fleet proceeded down the grand boulevard, through the arched gate, and then disappeared into the late September sunset.

⇥ Chapter Thirteen ⇤

THE WEST BADEN Springs Massacre, as it had come to be known, would prove to be a nightmare of adverse publicity. Papers and tabloids all over the country spared nothing in presenting to the public the sordid details of what many called the most brutal and savage gang violence yet to date. All twenty there in the private dining room had been killed, and more than fifty guests in the main dining room were injured during the mass hysteria. Such figures made the seven fatalities at last February's St. Valentine's Day Massacre in Chicago seem trifling. Lillian wondered whether the same mob had been involved in both killings; after all, the method of slaughter had been similar, only instead of the police uniforms in the Chicago massacre, the mobsters at West Baden had worn waiter's uniforms.

Once it was clear that Chicago gangsters had been involved, the Orange Country sheriff surrendered the investigation to authorities in that city. But the press would not surrender. For two straight weeks, reporters from all over the country inundated West Baden, collecting information mainly from those who had occupied the main dining room during the massacre. Again and again, Lillian denied interviews, saying that she knew nothing.

Only once did she appear before reporters. This was when a large, beautiful funeral wreath arrived at the front desk. Lillian's immediate impression was that some of her mother's old friends had read about the trouble at West Baden and had been gracious enough to render their sympathy in the form of this beautiful wreath. There was an envelope fixed to the wreath. Right in front of a crowd of reporters, Lillian opened the envelope, expecting the card inside to read something like "From all your devoted old friends during West Baden's time of dismay." But to Lillian's great terror, the card inside simply read, "From Al."

Lillian became flustered in front of the reporters. She crumpled the card tightly in her hand and then lied to the group, saying that the wreath was a gift from some friends. Obviously "Al" was unaware that Braxton had escaped the gunfire. Again, Lillian told the reporters she knew nothing about the incident and then quickly left the group in order to destroy the card that was crumpled in her hand.

Rimsky returned shortly thereafter and disclosed to Lillian that the massacre had been all of his doing. Having told Lillian before leaving for Chicago that the only way to destroy gangsters was with other gangsters, Rimsky had managed to pass to Braxton's opposition the information Lillian had sent via telegram, specifically the exact time and location of Braxton's dinner party. The rival in the Chicago liquor trade seized the opportunity to annihilate Braxton and his cohorts.

Lillian, of course, was horrified at Rimsky's method of operation. But what room had she to express consternation toward Rimsky? Did she not ask for Rimsky's help in fighting Braxton? Never had Lillian the slightest thought of how she could defeat Braxton and his seemingly intransigent rule over West Baden. She had relied solely on Rimsky, never questioning him once but trusting him fully and believing that he would find a way to thwart Braxton. What else would Rimsky have been doing in Chicago? Perhaps she had intentionally failed to figure out Rimsky's scheme. But now that Lillian had gotten just what she wanted, just what she had asked for, what right did she have to condemn Rimsky?

Braxton and his mob of gangsters were now gone. This was exactly what Lillian had wanted. No longer did she have to play Braxton's game or die. No longer was she a puppet on a string playing up to the children of the Jazz Age. Now she could tell them all to jump in a lake just as she had always wanted to say. She would be the old Lillian again and had every intention of restoring West Baden to the way it was before she married Braxton. Apparently Zelda had left with Braxton—a double blessing. Lillian never wanted to see either of these two characters again for as long as she lived. She did not care where they were or what they were doing as long as they never again returned to West Baden Springs.

But no sooner would Lillian drift on a cloud of reassurance than would an ugly thought spoil the euphoria. Lillian had told Braxton it was she and she alone who had planned the dinner party. For certain, no one else knew about the event, for Braxton had emphasized that the matter was strictly confidential. Therefore, Braxton had every cause to conclude that it was Lillian who had informed his opposition and had thus conspired against him. Braxton also had every cause to figure out that the *new* Lillian had been a fake all along. What would Lillian say to Braxton should he return? What if he should seek revenge? Lillian shuttered to think of what he might do. She wondered now whether it was *she* who needed a bodyguard.

At the county inquest in nearby Paoli, Lillian found herself in a tight corner. If she were to point the finger at Braxton, condemning him and his bootlegging before all the world, would she not be opening *herself* to scrutiny and investigation? After all, Braxton was her husband. She had done nothing but surrender to Braxton's Jazz Age frolics and had carelessly dropped sufficient evidence to link herself to Braxton's unscrupulous enterprise. She had sparkled as queen of the giant speakeasy. Hundreds had seen her guzzle from a gin bottle; but how could she prove that the clear liquid had been only water? The very capitulatory elements that had saved her from Braxton's destruction could now look like an involvement with him. Therefore, Lillian could not give up Braxton's cover. Besides, if she did, this would surely make Braxton seek revenge against her.

But Lillian's fears at the inquest had been in vain, for she was never called upon to speak. As chief administrator at West Baden Springs, Rimsky was the sole speaker on behalf of the hotel. Lillian was amazed at how Rimsky had mollified the county officials, saying that the hotel could hardly be responsible for a spontaneous outburst of gang violence. Rimsky pointed out that because gangsters battled for control of the liquor trade, the city of Chicago was afflicted with an epidemic of killings like no civilized modern city had ever before seen. Since much of the hotel's clientele comes from Chicago, he maintained that it was only a matter of time before West Baden would play host to such a shootout, despite his many efforts to prevent such an event. He likened West Baden's position to that of the Hawthorne Hotel in the Chicago suburb of Cicero. It had not been long ago that this famous old hotel had been sprayed up and down with machine-gun fire from eight touring cars passing by right in broad daylight. Gang violence had been the cause in that case as well.

The case incident report was completed. A copy was filed at the Orange County Courthouse in Paoli, and another copy was forwarded to officials in Chicago. As far as West Baden was concerned, the case was closed.

Lillian's next great effort was to return the hotel back to normal. Rimsky handled this well. Within a matter of days the main dining room was restored to even greater elegance. An orchestra replaced the dissonant jazz band. Every bottle of liquor was taken from the hotel and destroyed. The glittering streamers and other cheap decorations were removed. The wild, crazy parties were discontinued. The gambling casino was locked shut. An opera company arrived with a production of *La Bohème*. The entire hotel was cleaned from top to bottom. The grounds were groomed to near perfection. Every possible deficiency at West Baden was corrected.

Yet to Lillian's great amazement, the unruly crowd that had dominated West Baden since Lillian's return from Paris not only remained but continued to grow in number. Even every possible enticement was removed, these people still proliferated. Lillian was totally mystified until she discovered that it was the shot-up private dining room where most of them flocked. Apparently the macabre accounts of the West Baden Springs Massacre as portrayed by papers and tabloids had so fascinated people that hundreds found adventure and romance in the very thought of standing where brutal slaughter had not long ago taken place.

Rimsky's planning had done little to suppress this unexpected fascination. His plan had been to shut off the little-used private dining room to postpone the arduous task of cleaning and restoring it in order to concentrate full effort on correcting the rest of the hotel. But visitors cared little about the rest of the hotel. They cared only about this one room that still bore hundreds of bullet holes and had carpeting and tablecloths still stained with blood. Its floor was scattered with broken dishes and glassware and windows were shot out, letting in the chilly autumn air. There was virtually no way to keep people out of the room, because most would enter the infamous room via a shot-out window. Once inside, people would open the main door for others to enter. Even when clean-up and repair of the room had commenced, large crowds watched as the workmen replaced glass and covered the bullet holes with plaster.

Lillian was amazed and also disappointed that ever since her return from Paris she had heard nothing from the old familiar guests who had apparently left due to the new unruly crowd. While Rimsky had been busy restoring the hotel, Lillian had sent out hundreds of letters and advertisements in an effort to lure back these loyal patrons of the past. But three weeks after having done this, Lillian still received no responses. It was as though everything Lillian had sent out got lost in the mail. Each day she waited at the front desk for mail to arrive. But day after day, she heard nothing from the former clientele, many of whom had been good friends of her parents.

One afternoon Lillian was reviewing Rimsky's desk to see whether a letter or two may have somehow slipped passed her. During her search she inadvertently stumbled upon the hotel's master finance book. As Lillian casually glanced down the columns of figures, she was impressed that someone from the hotel staff had taken it upon themselves to mind the finance records even during Rimsky's absence and during Zelda's haphazard spell as manager. But then Lillian observed the figures in greater detail. Surely the bloated figures for September could not be correct. Why, they showed the hotel as making nearly twice the money as usual.

At first Lillian though a mistake had been made. But as she thought back, she suddenly recalled how readily Braxton's Jazz Age compatriots spent money. Right and left they practically threw money away, purchasing needless items along the atrium shops without even looking at the prices, handing out large bills as tips, paying top dollar for everything in their path. No wonder Braxton had wanted these people as clientele. They spent money like fools! Obviously they wanted to show their newly acquired wealth by spending big money. This was quite the antithesis of the conservation of the old guard, who were never the least embarrassed to show their thrifty habits. Perhaps the figures in the book were not so unbelievable after all.

A peculiar irony had arisen. Only weeks ago Lillian had cursed this annoying nouveau riche crowd without the slightest consideration that they were making her rich. As it turned out, she had actually benefited from Braxton's treachery! Why, the expenses for repairs of the private dining room would scarcely make a dent in the hotel's powerful income.

Well over three weeks had passed since Braxton's departure from West Baden. He was probably in Chicago, working out some clever way to end his marriage with Lillian and thus abort his West Baden enterprise. But Lillian tried not to think of Braxton. She only wanted things to return to normal.

She was short on patience and wanted quick results. Perhaps in another two months the fascination over the massacre would end. Until then she had no choice but to accept a slow transition and hope that the new season next spring would bring back some old clientele.

It was mid-October. After several days of wet, miserable weather, the sky finally cleared, the temperature warmed considerably, and a spectacular display of autumn foliage covered the countryside. Only the vibrant autumn color of New England could rival that of Southern Indiana. Lillian sat at the Oriental shrine on the bright Indian summer day. Practically all the guests were indoors watching the workmen remove the bloodstained carpeting. After weeks of endless stress, Lillian wanted only to sit at this beautiful spot and enjoy the peace and tranquility she had been without for so long. A warm, balmy breeze sent the smell of freshly fallen leaves through the air. The sky was blue and billowing with clouds.

Suddenly Lillian saw Hans walking across the lawn toward her. He was back again in his waiter uniform.

"Hello," said Hans in a cheerful voice as he approached Lillian.

"Hello," replied Lillian.

"I saw you out here by yourself and thought you might like some company."

"That was thoughtful of you, Hans."

"You're probably pretty exhausted after all you've been through lately."

"Yes, this seems like such a peaceful place to just sit and contemplate."

"Indeed it is. You're not likely to find many guests out here. They're all too busy observing the bullet holes. They're still so fascinated by the showdown. But what a showdown it was! I've never seen so many people die all at the same time! In fact, I do not recall ever seeing *anyone* die. Poof! All at once, dead people everywhere! And the blood … our white linen tablecloths will never be the same again. And to think the blood staining them was nearly ours!"

"You acted very heroically, Hans. You saved my life and I am very grateful."

"Don't mention it, Miss Lillian. When I heard a bullet whisk past my ear, I thought I'd better do something fast. Mr. Rimsky is a sly old codger, but he should have told you about his plan to eliminate Mr. Kingsley and all of those gangsters. Maybe then you would not have been such a nervous wreck those days before the shootout."

"I think I would have been nervous anyway. And please call me Lillian. There is no need to be formal."

"No, I guess there's not."

Lillian observed Hans. He was a good-looking young man. Lillian wondered why she had never noticed this before. Before, the very thought of being alone like this with a common waiter would have been inconceivable. But she had lost faith in much of what she had known before. It would have been easier for Lillian to believe the sky was falling than to believe that West Baden Springs would ever endure the disturbing hiatus it had known these past weeks. And the fabulously wealthy, dashing Braxton Kingsley: to call him a disappointment would be an understatement. Lillian had once thought her marriage to him had been planned in the stars, but now she knew it as the biggest disaster of her life. And Zelda's deep, motherly concern: what a joke that had been as well. At one time Lillian would have done anything for the acceptance of her six college friends, but now she never wanted to see them again. After such disillusionment, who was to tell Lillian she could not have affection for this caring young man who was so unlike the vogue, stylish people who had wronged her. While she stared into Hans's sincere blue eyes, the affection seemed more and more likely all the time.

Hans continued. "Well, it looks like Mr. Braxton Kingsley's bootlegging empire is gone forever. Hallelujah!"

"Yes, Hans, but Braxton still has plenty of money in stocks, bonds, and other things. He's still a very rich man, and he escaped the bullets. The others were not so lucky. Braxton brought them here to West Baden to get their money but got their blood instead, only he ran away like a rat so quickly that the strong stench of their blood never penetrated his nostrils."

"Braxton and Zelda are at this very moment probably involved in some new deceitful scheme to get easy money. Cheating, lying, and deceiving are their food for life."

"With absolutely no regard for the piles of injured people that it costs to obtain their easy money. I wonder what their new scheme will be now that they have left West Baden. I'm sure it is well under way."

"Maybe they're starting a charity for gangster victims, only they plan to pocket all donations," Hans suggested. "Braxton could dress up like a priest and Zelda like a nun."

"Zelda as a nun!" Lillian began to laugh. "Just imagine it!"

"She'd be the only nun with rouge, lipstick, and eye shadow."

"And perfume! Lillian added. "Oh that strong perfume she always wears would make her victims so delirious they would be more apt to part with their money."

"Think of the long-winded, tear-jerking speeches Zelda could give."

"Yes, poignant speeches that would melt people's hearts and their pocketbooks as well." Lillian imitated Zelda. "Ladies and gentlemen, have you no heart for the endless multitudes who lie vanquished due to the evils of gang violence?"

"They could get musical instruments just like the Salvation Army."

"Form a band and parade down the streets."

"Braxton could lead with a piccolo."

"And Zelda would follow with a base drum."

"And a kazoo in her mouth."

"But alas!" cried Lillian. "They would not have a free hand to hold the collection plate, the most important item of all. Let's see. Where could they place that?"

Hans bent over and whispered into Lillian's ear. "They could fasten it to Zelda's derriere!"

The two broke out in laughter.

"Oh, Hans, I haven't laughed in such a long time," confessed Lillian.

"There will be much more laughter for you from now on, Lillian, now that West Baden will return to normal."

"Yes, but how far removed I feel from it now—the West Baden Springs of my childhood. I grew up thinking nothing could ever change this magnificent place. Although I will make every effort to restore West Baden to the way it was before Braxton and Zelda, somehow I don't believe this magnificent place will ever be the same again, nor do I think I will be the same again either. How sheltered and naïve I was only a short time ago. I've learned much in a sort time about things I never wanted to know but was forced to learn. How foolish of me not foresee that it would enter West Baden someday."

"What would enter, Lillian?"

"The rest of the world, Hans. Yes, for so long only the people whom I thought acceptable entered West Baden Springs, only the lifestyle I thought proper prevailed, only the art and music I deemed superlative flourished. And I had wanted to keep it this way forever—yes, enclose only pleasing elements within this mighty fortress of mine and form a bulwark against the baser elements remaining outside. Only perhaps remaining outside was something quintessential but inextricably linked with the rest. My need for it made me victim to encroaching power."

"Power, Lillian?"

"Yes, Hans, Braxton's power over me. I was completely unprepared to deal with it. Braxton thoughtlessly and maliciously imposed his power on me, power that hovered over me like a black cloud and shook me in desperate measures to rescue myself from its encroachment. I had not the resources to oppose his power, only the wrath to disdain it and the fear to see how easily it could destroy me. I could do nothing but appease and trust that Rimsky would bring deliverance. I appeased by forsaking my own principles, ever enduring Braxton's heartless rampage over West Baden. But now Braxton has every reason to suspect that I was false all along and that I conspired against him. There is no telling what vengeance he might seek. Perhaps this moment of peace I share with you now, Hans, is but a calm lapse before a violet storm."

"Now that Braxton's aspirations for a liquor empire in Southern Indiana are destroyed, Lillian, he no longer needs you. He will slyly work out a divorce or annulment and then scurry back to Chicago to conduct some new method of corruption. After that you will probably never see him again. A man like Braxton Kinsley would never waste time over that which can no longer produce. Forget Braxton, Zelda, and all the madness that went on. Don't permit torments of the past to block the road to happiness in the future. There is much happiness to be enjoyed, Lillian, if only you will permit it to exist."

Lillian placed her hand close to Hans's, hoping he would be forward enough to take hold. After a long silence, Hans finally took her hand, and with his touch a tingle went through Lillian. His touch was soft and gentle, his face warm with sincerity as Lillian looked into his entrancing blue eyes. The two stood up and embraced. The warm Indian summer breeze gathered around them, as did the scent of newly fallen leaves. All was quiet and peaceful, the surrounding woodland bright with autumn color.

Lillian whispered into Hans's ear, "You would be very easy to love, Hans."

⊰ Chapter Fourteen ⊱

LILLIAN SAW HANS often. Just as he did in Paris, he had mitigated a great deal of heartache. Time with Hans was an escape from the torments and pressures Lillian had know since her marriage to Braxton. Gone was the sick feeling of insecurity that had haunted Lillian. Hans was always happy and totally unconcerned about problems. Perhaps he was irresponsible just as Rimsky had always said. But that was just what Lillian wanted: to be irresponsible. She was tired of burdens and the fight for survival that Braxton had forced upon her. Lillian wished only to live and be happy again, to enjoy the pleasures of old West Baden Springs again in all its peace, serenity, and carelessness.

Hans made this possible. He and Lillian were frequently seen together throughout West Baden. They would take long walks together about the grounds and then sit together on the veranda and chatter. Hans took time off from his duties as waiter to share a table with Lillian in the formal dining room, and during his hours on duty Lillian helped him with things such as setting tables and other kinds of work they could do together. When Hans returned to the kitchen, he would find Lillian waiting there, eager to help by either adding or removing dishes from his tray. Once Lillian had even been audacious enough to deliver dessert to one of Hans's tables. Outside of the waiter's job, Lillian was teaching Hans to ride and to play croquet. The two were practically the sole audience for the West Baden premiere of *La Bohème.*

Lillian sensed strong disapproval from the hotel staff. The other waiters ostracized Hans and treated him with jealousy and resentment. Certainly Hans's performance as a waiter was lacking. But who was to reprimand him with West Baden's owner always close at hand? The hotel guests, on the other hand, saw nothing unusually about a married woman of aristocracy befriending a common waiter. Nor were they shocked at always finding Hans in Lillian's apartment and seeing Hans enter the apartment at night and leave in the morning.

"One must be a little scandalous to be in style these days," most maintained.

Lillian was surprised Rimsky never voiced his disapproval or showed the slightest objection to Lillian's relationship with Hans. Nevertheless, Lillian felt Rimsky was conscious of everything. Perhaps his golden opportunity had at last come to see Lillian's saintly image besmirched. Perhaps he was patiently waiting, observing the two from afar, jotting down things to use against Lillian at a later time. But Lillian did not care. Hans made her forget all her worries, even her acrid relations with Rimsky, even the vengeance Braxton might be seeking against her. Sure she would have to confront a divorce sooner or later. But for now she wanted a break from all problems and cares.

Lillian could not be sure when her six college friends had left West Baden. They had just disappeared without saying goodbye. This was typical of them.

Even though the repairs were not yet completed to the infamous private dining room, crowds no longer flocked to this room. They now flocked to another instead: the Logan and Bryan Stock Exchange on the first floor just off the atrium. Although the broker's branch office had gained an enormous amount of business since the change in West Baden's clientele, people were now waiting in line to speak to the brokers while others clustered in large groups to watch the ticker tape. Lillian knew little about the stock market and could not imagine what was happening. All there in the exchange were solemn and serious, quite the antithesis of their usual blithe character. While walking back to her office, Lillian passed a broker she knew from the exchange.

"What seems to be the trouble at Logan and Bryan?" she asked the broker.

"A break in the stock market, Miss Lillian," the broker answered.

Lillian had no idea what the broker meant but listened on nevertheless.

"A bad break, to be sure," the broker continued. "But there have been other bad breaks lately, and the market always recovers. Besides, when there is a break it is a good time to buy. You can't go wrong with Anaconda at 109 and three-quarters or American Telephone at 281—mighty wise investment, first-class bargain levels at that."

"Just what caused this break?" asked Lillian.

"Oh the wiseacres of Wall Street have been looking about for causes. Some say the collapse of the Hatry financial group in England led to a lot of forced selling among foreign investors and speculators. The refusal of the Massachusetts Department of Public Utilities to allow the Edison Company of Boston to split up its stock also probably contributed to the break. The steel industry is undoubtedly slipping, and of course there is a mighty big accumulation of undigested securities. But no real alarm. The market is merely readjusting itself into a more secure technical position."

Lillian understood nothing of what the broker had said.

"If you want to know more, Miss Lillian," the broker continued. "I suggest that you take a look at some of the business journals in the exchange. They are on the bookshelf in the waiting area. Good day, Miss Lillian."

Lillian returned to the stock exchange around noon, not out of interest in the stock market but because she discovered the waiting room there provided the perfect place to meet Hans to go for lunch. She had grown to dislike waiting for Hans in the dining room and lobby. In the exchange she could at least preoccupy herself with some business journals.

All Lillian really knew about the stock market was that if one owns stock, it's good if the price goes up and bad if the price goes down. She saw from one of the business journals that during the first part of October stock prices had fallen a great deal since the year's highest levels on September 19. Steel, after having touched 261 ¾ in September, had dropped as low as 204; American Can was nearly 20 points below its high for the year; General Electric was more than 50 point below its high; Radio had gone down from 114 ¾ to 82 ½.

Day after day, Lillian returned to the exchange, hearing people around her talk of nothing but the "recovery" in stock prices—over and over again, the recovery, the recovery. Day after day, Lillian glanced through business journals there in the exchange that indicated a recovery was just around the corner and that prosperity was here to stay.

Tuesday, October 15, 1929, Colonel Leonard P. Ayres of the Cleveland Trust Company stated, "There does not seem to be as yet much real evidence that the decline in stock prices is likely to forecast a serious recession in general business. Despite the slowing down in iron and steel production, in automobile output, and in building, the conditions that result in serious business depressions are not present."

Wednesday, October 16 a *Broad Street Gossip* column stated, "Business is now too big and diversified, and the country too rich, to be influenced by stock market fluctuations."

Thursday, October 17 Professor Irving Fisher, a leading economist, was reported as telling the Purchasing Agents Association that stock prices have reached "What looks like a permanently high plateau." He expected to see the stock market, within a few months, "a good deal higher than it is today."

Friday, October 18 Charles D. Mitchell, chairman of the great National City Bank of New York, was positive that despite the stock market break: "The industrial situation of the United States is absolutely sound and our credit situation is in no way critical… The interest given by the public to broker's loans is always exaggerated," he added. "Altogether too much attention is paid to it."

Saturday, October 19 an editorial opinion of the *Boston News Bureau* stated that "whatever recessions [in business] are noted, are those of the runner catching his breath … The general condition is satisfactory and fundamentally sound."

Monday, October 21 Charles D. Mitchell spoke again to the press: "Although in some cases speculation has gone too far in the United States, the markets generally are now in a healthy condition. The last six weeks have done an immense amount of good by shaking down prices. I know of nothing fundamentally wrong with the stock market or with the underlying business and credit structure … The public is suffering from 'broker loanitis.'"

Tuesday, October 22: For a week Lillian had returned to Logan and Bryan each day between noon and 1:00 p.m. The business journals she had read predicted a recovery in stock prices, as did the brokers and clients in the exchange. And sure enough, on this day a recovery came. By the time Lillian left the exchange with Hans, prices had risen gradually since the previous day.

Wednesday, October 23: Lillian and Hans went on a picnic, thus missing the midday activities at the stock exchange. But when the two returned to West Baden in time for dinner, Lillian noticed something strange.

"Look, Hans," she said. "There are lights on at Logan and Bryan. Why, they should have closed hours ago. I'm going to see what the matter is."

"I will meet you in the dining room, Lillian," replied Hans.

When Lillian entered the brokerage, she saw every broker slumping in exhaustion over desks piled high with papers.

"Just what is going on here?" she asked one of the brokers.

"A perfect typhoon of liquidation today, Miss Lillian," the stockbroker answered in an exhausted voice. "The volume of trading was over six million shares, and the tape was almost two hours late when trading closed for the day."

"Does that mean stock prices have gone down?"

"I should say so, miss—18.24 points for the fifty leading railroad and industrial stocks. The worst break to day."

"But how could that be?" asked Lillian, perplexed. "Just yesterday prices were recovering."

"All the gains made yesterday were lost during the last hour of trading. And then this morning this happened!" The broker threw some papers up from his desk. "But don't worry. You know what they say. The time to buy is when things look blackest. Perhaps the turn will come tomorrow. After all, things couldn't get much worse."

Thursday, October 24: Lillian entered the Logan and Bryan Stock Exchange around noon, just as she had done for more than a week. Only things were dreadfully different on this Thursday the twenty-fourth. A climate of fright shook the brokers' branch office as never before. Large crowds of tape-watchers stared at the figures on the shining screen as if stunned. Others inundated the brokers at their desk, bombarding the beleaguered men in a roar of panic.

Lillian observed the large board, covering one wall of the room, on which the day's prices for the leading stocks were supposed to be recorded. For more than a week she had stared blankly at the board while waiting for Hans, and during this time, she could hardly remember the figures to have moved at all. But now the boys who slapped into place the cards that recorded the last prices shown on the ticker were scrambling about the board like chickens.

"There's no point in looking at that board, miss," a voice sounded behind Lillian. "They lost track of the figures hours ago."

Lillian then turned to the shining screen across which ran an uninterrupted procession of figures from the ticker. Even with what little she knew about the stock market, Lillian could see that the stock prices were going down with an altogether unprecedented and amazing violence. Once more, without use of the board, when viewing a run of symbols and figures, she could not be sure whether the price of "6" shown for Radio meant 66 or 56 or 46, whether Westinghouse was sliding from 189 to 187 or from 179 to 177.

Lillian addressed a man next to her who was mechanically tearing a piece of paper into tiny and still tinier fragments.

"What on earth could be making the stock prices fall so drastically?" she asked.

The man did not answer right away but stood motionless, as if looking defeat in the face, his eyes fixed blindly upon the moving figures on the screen. Then he uttered in a somber voice, "Forced selling."

"That's a fancy way for saying that the bottom is dropping out!" another man said hysterically and then continued in a frightened, bewildered way. "The price structure's crumbling to pieces! Why, the leading stocks are going down two, three, and even five points between sales. Look at those prices go down. Where are the bargain-hunters who always come to the rescue at times like this? Instead it's a made scramble to get out from under. Where are the investment trusts, which are supposed to provide a cushion for the market by making new purchases at low prices? Where are the big operators who always claim to be bullish? Where are the powerful bankers who are supposed to be able at any moment to support prices? Why, there's no support whatsoever. Down, down, down. The prices just keep going down! And right now the ticker is an hour and a half late! Why, all this before our eyes is ancient history!"

Lillian had never seen so many people tremble in fear. Only weeks ago they had behaved as though they hadn't a care in the world. But now rows of them stood stunned with strained faces fixed upon the moving figure on the screen, those innocent-looking figures that meant the smash-up of the hopes of years:

$$GL_{8.7.5.2.1.90.89.7.6}AWW_{3.21/2.2}JMP_{6.5.3.21/2}$$

Lillian did not feel comfortable around these people. With all thoughts lost in hysteria, there was no telling what some might do. When Hans finally arrived, Lillian was glad to leave with him. But eventually she found it made little difference, for a climate of fright had permeated throughout the entire hotel. Fantastic rumors spread wildly all afternoon—that fortunes of even the rich and powerful had been smashed to splinters, that the Chicago Stock Exchange had been closed, that troops were guarding the New York Stock Exchange against an angry mob, that an epidemic of suicides had swept the country one end to another. None of these rumors could be confirmed, because telephone and telegraph to every financial center in the country was still jammed with orders to sell. The discomforting stock ticker remained West Baden's only communication with outside world. Everything else remained a mystery. It is the unknown that causes real panic.

Only after the financial crisis had claimed its first victim upon West Baden Springs did Lillian begin to share the others' fear. A man had plunged to his death from a sixth-story atrium balcony, causing those below to cringe in horror. Shortly thereafter another jumped from an even higher place, a Byzantine tower facing the main entrance. Lillian went directly to Rimsky's office.

"Rimsky!" cried Lillian as she entered his office. "What the devil is going on? Two men just killed themselves!" Lillian was frantic, but Rimsky remained unperturbed as always.

"It would appear that we are experiencing a bit of a financial crisis," he said calmly. "More specifically, the gigantic edifice of stock market prices that we have seen during the past two years was in reality honeycombed with speculative credit and is now breaking under its own weight. But what would one expect when ignorant, ill-bred, common people have the audacity to buy into major corporations. They have no business doing such things, and they should be prevented from doing so. Vulgar people like those now at West Baden, all of them—the masses. How they do resemble a great herd of cattle, doing just exactly as the others do. At the slightest disturbance they all stampede in a great cataclysm of forced selling! Only a chosen few should be allowed to determine what is good for the masses. The thought of common people buying stock is ludicrous. But then again, they, themselves, never bought the stock at all. They borrowed money from bankers who are just as stupid, bankers who must now assume the responsibility of millions of dollars worth of loans secured by collateral which will soon be completely worthless!"

Friday, October 25: Stock prices miraculously held, thus ending the frightening descent of the day before. Lillian had learned that in the midst of the seething hysteria on the floor of the New York Stock Exchange, on that black Thursday the twenty-fourth, six major banks had formed a 240-million-dollar pool to make purchases in a desperate effort to steady prices and to regain a semblance of confidence. From point to point, representatives of the bankers' pool had scrambled about the floor of the exchange, bidding at each point the price of the last previous sale for thousands of shares. The desperate remedy had apparently worked well, at least for the time being.

Saturday, October 26: Newspapers carried a very pretty series of reassuring statements. Herbert Hoover himself, in a White House statement, pointed out that "the fundamental business of the country, that is, production and distribution of commodities, is on a sound and prosperous basis." The Harvard Economic Society delivered the cheerful judgment that "despite its severity, we believe that the slump in stock prices will prove an intermediate movement and not the precursor of a business depression such as would entail prolonged further liquidation."

Monday, October 28: The pundits of Harvard were to be proven ludicrously wrong. Another avalanche of forced selling plunged right through the prices that the bankers' pool had so desperately fought to steady. Even six great banks could hardly stem the flow of liquidation from the entire United States. Once more the ticker dropped ridiculously far behind. The losses registered at the end of the day were terrific: 17 ½ points for Steel, 47 ½ for General Electric, 36 for Allied Chemical, 34 ½ for Westinghouse, and so on down a long and dismal list. The lights at Logan and Bryan burned until dawn, as did those of every broker's office across the country. Telegraph companies distributed thousands of margin calls and requests for more collateral to back up loans at the banks. Bankers, brokers, clerks, messengers all over the country were almost at the end of their strength. For days and nights they had been driving themselves to keep pace with the most enormous volume of business they had ever encountered. Now that every effort to steady prices had failed, there was nothing to stop the tremendous juggernaut of liquidation. Certainly the worst was yet to come.

Tuesday, October 29: Reports from the New York Stock Exchange were horrifying. The big gong had hardly sounded before a storm on the floor broke out in full force. Huge blocks of stock were thrown upon the market for what they would bring. Five thousand shares, ten thousand shares appeared at a time on the laboring ticker at fearful recessions in price. Not only were innumerable small traders being sold out, but big ones, too, protagonists of the new economic era who only days ago had rejoiced in the golden future of American business. Specialists in any given stock were beleaguered by brokers fighting to sell—and nobody at all even thinking of buying. Orders to sell came in the New York exchange faster than human beings could possible handle them. Within half an hour of the exchange opening, the volume of trading had passed three million shares. By twelve o'clock it had passed eight million, by half past one it had passed twelve million, and when the closing gong brought the day's madness to an end, the gigantic record of 16,410030 shares had been set and the average prices of fifty leading stocks, as compiled by the New York Times, had fallen nearly forty points!

The big bull market was dead. Billions of dollars worth of profits—and paper profits—had vanished. As a result, a new round of terror struck West Baden. Suicides from falling became so commonplace that the top floors and the Byzantine towers had to be closed off. Where only weeks ago laughter had flooded every space of the hotel, now only sobs of grief prevailed. Crowds of people sat in the lobby with backs slouched over and heads bowed. Gradually a mood of despondency and deep depression replaced the hysteria, as poisons gradually seep through the human system after a vital organ has been struck. In a matter of days, those at West Baden had plunged from showy affluence into debt and even destitution. Houses, automobiles, radios, and other symbols of prosperity would have to be repossessed. Those who had dreamed of retiring to live on their fortunes now found themselves back once more at the very beginning of the long road to riches. Life on Easy Street had become normal. It would seem alien to live any other way than in the secure, comfortable world that had suddenly slipped out from under all of them during their stay at West Baden Springs.

As Lillian looked about the languishing faces throughout the hotel, she knew that the big bull market had been more than the climax of a business cycle. It had been the climax of a cycle in mass thinking and mass emotion. There was not one of them there at West Baden, nor hardly a man or woman in the entire country, whose attitude toward life had not been affected by the stock market in some degree and was not now affected by the sudden and brutal shattering of hope.

For four days people left West Baden in a solemn exodus. There were not nearly enough porters to go around, so clerks, cooks, waiters, janitors, and any other able-bodied young men were used to carry luggage. Contrary to Rimsky's advice, Lillian gladly let go any outstanding balances. She knew the guests were certainly in no position to be pressed for money. For those who had been wiped out and completely penniless, Lillian even furnished free meals and train tickets home.

Lillian thought little of these small acts of amnesty, seeing she really had no other choice. But the financially ruined responded with overwhelming gratitude, coming to her in tears and saying tings like, "Oh, Mrs. Kingsley, you're kinder than a saint." Suddenly Lillian was treated like an angel of mercy. As every train departed, she stood alone at the depot, bidding farewell to a train full of waving people who were sure to encounter more disappointments at their final destinations. After one such departure, Lillian returned to the lobby's front desk to discover that not a soul was registered at the hotel. Every single guest had left West Baden Springs.

Lillian had never known West Baden without people. It seemed a different place as such. From room to room, she would find the entire hotel still and stagnant, suddenly haunted by an insufferable silence. As she walked the large vacant rooms, Lillian was now conscious of sounds she had never thought anything about: the rustling of her clothes against her body, her very own breathing and heart beating, unexplained cracks and snaps coming from the walls, the popping and crackling of the fireplace. Her once delicate footsteps now seemed loud as elephant treads.

The hotel staff had initially seized the lapse in business as their golden opportunity to catch up on those jobs that normally get put aside: polishing door handles, reorganizing storage shelves, recovering furniture, doing inventory. But after two weeks, every piece of metal in the hotel had been polished time and again, even the pedals of every piano and the brass plates at the bottom of every door. Every item of every shelf had been removed and replaced in meticulous order, even if the order had been the same as before. Furniture had been refinished and recovered and had been disarranged then rearranged. Floors had been scrubbed down to the finish and had then been resealed and waxed again. The entire hotel was immaculate and glistened like never before. Every conceivable job had been completed. Suddenly there was nothing more that could be done. The staff gradually slowed down from their usual bustle, and as much as they tried not to show it, sighs of ennui became contagious.

Each time Lillian looked out a window, she saw that the dismal mid-November landscape matched the hotel's apathetic mood: gray skies, brown grass, dark trees whose bare braches rattled angrily to a cold, fierce wind.

Outdoor activities at West Baden were now rather limited because of the cold weather. Hardly anyone every left the main hotel building since the opera house had closed. Every day boredom and apathy increased. Lillian tried to stimulate things with a piano concert, but the hotel staff had been generally unenthused when Lillian played for them. She thought they would be more interested in a folksong sing-along, but their voices, sounding weak as newborn kittens, told Lillian that spirits had not risen greatly.

Lillian never realized just how uninteresting were the members of the hotel staff. She could get hardly any of them to say more than two words. They knew nothing of art, music, literature, or other things that interested her. With the way Rimsky worked them all like drones, it's no wonder they were so dull. Even after jobs had been completed three and four times, Rimsky would insist that the job be done again, just to get work out of his staff.

Now with the lapse in business at West Baden Springs, Lillian saw Hans more than ever. It was easy for the hotel staff to see the two had fallen in love but easier still for Lillian to perceive the staff's strong disapproval. No longer could the peccadilloes of a salacious crowd overshadow Lillian's relationship with Hans. She was now alone at West Baden with Hans and the sharp eyes and brooding scowls of an entire hotel staff. Ignominy was at its highest on mornings after Hans had spent a night in Lillian's apartment. Lillian knew her affair with Hans was the talk of the servants' quarters. After all, there really was not much else to keep the staff entertained.

Lillian sat with Hans at the piano in her apartment. She had just played for him a minuet.

"I wonder whether they're listening behind the door," replied Lillian.

"Whether who's listening?" asked Hans.

"You know perfectly well who I mean, Hans—the staff."

"Lillian, are you still worried about the hotel staff?"

"I can't help it, Hans. Every time I leave this apartment I feel like Hester Prynne on her way to the platform to be shamed before all of New England. I used to be such an example to the hotel staff. Now they treat me as though … as though I've let them down. I might as well save them the trouble and furnish my own scarlet A."

"But, Lillian, they don't know the story behind Braxton."

"There's nothing I can do about that. If only there were just a few guests here, just some people to keep them busy, maybe then they would not be so preoccupied with gossip. Where are all the guests anyway? The stock market crisis should not have taken everyone. What about all the old familiar patrons that I always call the old guard?"

"It is the end of the season you know, Lillian."

"Yes, but even in cold weather people are attracted to the thermal baths. There must be something we can do to get the old guard back at West Baden and keep the staff busy."

Lillian and Hans thought for several minutes.

"Hans, I've got it!" exclaimed Lillian. "I can contact my old drama professor from college, Professor Thornsbie, to revive something I did with him in college. Its was a sort of Shakespeare variety show comprised of a series of famous scenes from Shakespeare plays—you know, the balcony scene from *Romeo and Juliet*, the ghost scene from *Richard III*, the witches scene from *Macbeth*, Hamlet's soliloquies, the trial scene from *The Merchant of Venice*, the murder of Desdemona from *Othello*, you know."

Lillian sounded so excited that she did not give Hans a chance to reply as she continued with enthusiasm.

"Professor Thornsbie could come down to West Baden with some players and costumes. Oh, Hans, I'm sure the show would be a sensation. We could get the hotel staff involved in the production. That would give them something to do and would perhaps solve the problem of apathy at West Baden. The entire hotel would be working together on something and we could have so much fun. I remember the success the show had the first time when I played Desdemona in college. I am sure people will return to see it. Oh, Hans, I've got so much to do to get ready. I must wire Professor Thornsbie at once."

Lillian immediately stood up from the piano bench and, with great enthusiasm, whisked out the door of her apartment, leaving Hans at the piano, playing a steady round of chopsticks.

⊰ Chapter Fifteen ⊱

WITHIN DAYS AFTER Lillian's proposal, Professor Thornsbie arrived from Indiana University with his players. The players were greeted at West Baden Springs with jubilation, and all attention instantly turned to the opera-house-turned-theater. Two weeks of intense rehearsing were producing not only a fine show but also a great deal of laughs. The laughter was mainly due to the hotel staff's involvement in the production. The stage crew had left when *La Bohème* closed, thus leaving many members of the hotel staff to take command in a series of technical blunders. During rehearsals props fell; lights blazed around the stage, shining everywhere but on the players; costumes became mixed-up; but eventually the novice stage crew came about.

On the day of dress rehearsal, Lillian remained alone in the lobby while the others rehearsed in the opera house. Among other things, she was busy planning a reception for the Shakespeare show. Despite extensive advertising and promotion, no guests had yet registered at the hotel. Nevertheless, Lillian was determined to make the show a success, even if the audience included only staff members, even if the reception included only staff members and players. When Lillian would see all of West Baden laugh and smile over an innocuous mishap at rehearsal, she knew the show had already proved a success. Spirits had lifted dramatically since rehearsals began. Everyone at the hotel was busy with the show in some capacity. Just as Lillian was prancing about the lobby, thinking of nothing but the Shakespeare show, a loud voice sounded.

"Hello, Lillian. Remember us?" said Zelda.

Lillian turned around quickly, caught by surprise. "Braxton! Zelda!" she cried in quivering voice, her face stunned at the sight of these two dubious characters.

So much had made Lillian forget Braxton and Zelda: her affair with Hans, the stock market crash, the Shakespeare show. More than anything, though, the torments and pressures of her last tense days with Braxton and Zelda caused Lillian to hope she would never see these two again. Lord only knows why they had returned to West Baden Springs. Both looked haggard and untidy. Lillian was petrified and did not know what to say.

"What's wrong, Lillian?" asked Zelda in a harsh voice. "You look at us as though we've come back from the dead. Surely you must have thought we would return to West Baden Springs. After all, Braxton *is* your husband. Remember? This place is like a tomb. Where is everybody?"

"I … I think most of the guests were pretty hard hit from the stock market crash," answered Lillian timidly.

"Thus explaining their departure from this carefree pleasure dome," said Zelda. "But you, Lillian, escaped unscathed I'm sure."

"Well,, I … suppose so."

"You see, Braxton," continued Zelda. "I told you we'd come to the right place. Lillian, in the tradition of the great Randreninoffs, could never be without money. It's simply not written in the stars. And your prudent and loving father, Lillian, no doubt left you with vast properties and investments *outside* the stock market. Mr. Everett was a wise one, Braxton. You see, he did not put all of his eggs into one basket."

"I don't rightly know what you mean, Zelda," said Lillian.

Braxton suddenly assumed an animated style, walked briskly to Lillian, and took her hand.

"All Zelda is trying to say, Lillian, my darling, is how fortunate for you that I've returned just in time to save you and West Baden Springs from financial ruin. With my expertise in business and financial affairs, you are now safe from the encroaching financial despair that has stunned many tragic souls throughout the country. Woe to all those pitiful creatures who jumped to their deaths off Chicago's towering buildings. And to think you could have been among them, Lillian, had I not returned to take over your finances."

Braxton put his arm around Lillian. When he did this, Lillian noticed that under Braxton's jacket a revolver was strapped to his waist. Lillian became even more frightened, but Braxton continued.

"Though these past weeks I was bound to business matters in Chicago, I thought of nothing but you, Lillian, and how much I love you. I never called you, because I thought the sound of your sweet voice would cause an uncontrollable yearning for you. But I turned my back on Chicago business for you, Lillian. I shall never return to my vast enterprises in that city no matter how lucrative. You and West Baden Springs are more important."

Just as Braxton attempted to kiss Lillian, Zelda suddenly broke into laughter while lighting a cigarette.

"Oh that was good, Mr. Kingsley," she shouted so that her voice echoed throughout the large, empty room. "I was curious to see just how deviously you would circumvent the disparaging yet vital facts. Let's see if I can remember a few." With cigarette in hand, Zelda walked casually about the lobby, talking loudly in every direction but toward Braxton and Lillian. "Your lucrative bootlegging empire is destroyed forever. How disheartening! The big bull market completely devoured your vast wealth. How devastating! And now you, the great Braxton Kingsley, have no choice but to hope that your mousy little wife will support you. How humiliating!" Zelda started to laugh.

"Why don't you shut your stupid mouth," scolded Braxton as he approached Zelda.

"That is if she'll even take back, the broken dog that you are."

"I told you to shut your mouth!"

"You don't have the power anymore to tell anyone to do anything, Braxton. From the way it looks, your little wife does not seem even interested in your welfare. I'm sure deep down under her mask of virtue, dear Lillian, would like nothing more than to throw you out this very instant."

"Oh no, Zelda, you're very wrong," interrupted Lillian, as if decorum had called for it. Still in a daze, she let out a feeble lie. "I've been very worried about you and Braxton these past few weeks."

"Oh is that so, Lillian?" retorted Zelda in a mocking, sarcastic manner. "It grieves me to think just how sick with worry you must have been these past few weeks over Braxton and myself. You must have bit your fingernails every damn day, bit them so frantically and furiously that your fingers started to get numb with pain, perhaps with so much pain that you could not bear to pick up the receiver to this telephone." Zelda picked up the telephone behind the front desk. "And dial Braxton's office in Chicago to find out anything about us that you would wish to know. Yes, Lillian, I guess that shows just how worried you were about us."

"I meant to call, but … I've been so busy lately."

"Busy? In this morgue? Doing what, pray tell?"

"I've been putting together a sort of Shakespeare variety show made of famous scenes from Shakespeare plays. I thought it might attract some business."

"What I charming idea," said Zelda with sarcasm. "I am sure every person in the Midwest will want to come and see it. Just when is this charming little show of yours, Lillian?"

"Tomorrow night. Tonight is dress rehearsal."

"Then we've returned just in time, Braxton," continued Zelda, still in her sarcastic mode. "Let's start learning our lines and forget everything that has happened lately, just the thing Lillian Everett would do. Now come along, Braxton. We have no time to waste. We must give our parts the once over before dress rehearsal."

Zelda whisked behind the front desk, casually snatched a key for one of the rooms, threw it to Braxton, and then snatched a key for herself.

"We shall see you for dinner at six in the dining room, Lillian," said Zelda as she left the lobby.

In the enormous main dining room, Lillian, Braxton, and Zelda sat together surrounded by a vast sea of empty tables and chairs. The tense silence of the large room with its towering pillars and countless chandeliers served only to reinforce the cold, distant mood between the three.

Braxton was unshaven and wore a wrinkled suit. His tie was loose and crooked, his hair uncombed. As Braxton slouched over his plate and picked at his food, Lillian could see this was a completely different man than the one who had left only weeks ago. No longer did he speak in a glib, poetic voice and move like a panther. His voice was now soft and full of grunts, his movements sluggish and lethargic.

While Zelda rattled on with talk of social eminence, Lillian sat jittering like a suspect on trial. Although Lillian was convinced Braxton did not suspect the plotting she had done against him, this did little to suppress the extreme discontentment she felt just being in the company of these two. All the tension and torments of the past flashed through her mind as Zelda indefatigably talked and talked in her characteristically derisive, mocking, and sarcastic way, on and on with intense, maddening overtones.

"Lillian, if you don't mind my saying so, the food tonight is exceptionally wretched. Oh, I'm sure you did not plan on it being that way. But I can understand how in the raw wilderness of Southern Indiana one would have difficulty providing the finer things. I'll just have to take into consideration, my dear, that you do not frequent the great centers of refinement like I do—you know, London, Paris, Monte Carlo, Baden-Baden, the *real* Baden as far as I am concerned. What you need to do, Lillian, now that your West Baden Springs has fallen into this new abyss of decay, is to get around to some of these places. It would do you a world of good. A year would just barely be enough time. I could map out the whole tour for you, and Braxton and I could hold down things here at West Baden. Oh, I would not mind too much looking after the place for you, Lillian. It might be an interesting change to live the primitive lifestyle of Southern Indiana after having been emerged in refinement for all these years. In fact, they say Abe Lincoln spent his boyhood in a log cabin not too far from here."

Hans was the waiter for the meal. Having heard Zelda as far away as the kitchen, he passed Lillian a tired expression as Zelda continued to talk and talk and talk.

"That was the problem with your mother, I dare say. She never got away from West Baden to see real refinement, manner, style, and culture. Of course I would never begin to deny that in her day Katia Randreninoff Everett was all the rage. As far away as Chicago people did not think they would ever hear the end of the legendary Katia of West Baden Springs and the mysterious Randreninoff jewels. To these churlish locals, Katia must have seemed like a misplaced queen. Everyone bowed down to her as if she were royalty. But I knew better. I knew if Katia ever went out from her pleasant little realm of admirers into the aforementioned great centers of refinement, she would be a complete nobody. In fact, I'm sure she knew that as well. That's why she rarely left West Baden Springs. If ever she would have left this great heap of stone for, oh, let's say the French Riviera or Newport or Long Island, she would have seen instantly how vastly inferior West Baden Springs is compared to them. Just look around you, Lillian. Obviously others must have made the comparison, for you don't see anyone here, do you? They've all left West Baden Springs for better places."

"But the stock market—" Lillian started to say.

"Oh that's right! You're going to blame everything on the stock market. It's very healthy to rationalize, Lillian, because it helps one deal with desponding failure. Mr. Kingsley should know all about that. But, yes, I do agree the stock market fall was a devastating affair. You should have seen the Chicago Stock Exchange. The brokers there were raising such a huff! I do hope things weren't too unpleasant for you here at West Baden, my dear."

"Things were very heated here during that time, probably as bad as anywhere in the country," said Lillian timidly.

"How dreadful!" continued Zelda, "I did not think unpleasant things were supposed to happen at West Baden Springs. But then I'm being forgetful. We left you at West Baden in the midst of a very unpleasant incident. You must have had a pretty little mess to clean up, but I'm sure you and Rimsky managed. But if you don't mind my saying so, Lillian, the place still looks a little haggard. You can never really repair the damage that was done here, can you? And oh what the Chicago papers had to say about the great West Baden Springs Massacre. I didn't think I would ever hear the end of it. And to think this place hasn't made Chicago news since the death of your mother. One of the worst outbreaks of gang violence yet to date, that's what the Chicago Tribune said. Of course, the police blamed the whole atrocity on old Scarface Capone. Thank goodness for Braxton that neither you nor Rimsky released the other party involved. I am sure that Braxton is eternally grateful. Yes, Lillian, if you have not figured it out by now, your husband was a bootlegging gangster before his great demise."

Zelda had hit right on the matter that Lillian was hoping to avoid. Lillian's only thought was to blurt out anything that would change the subject.

"Oh, is that so?" Lillian said uncomfortably. "Well, I know very little about gangsters. So how was everything in Chicago? Chicago must be very windy this time of year. I suppose that's why they call it the Windy City."

Lillian giggled a bit.

Zelda mimicked Lillian's giggle. "How coy and cute you are Lillian—the sweet, innocent princess of West Baden Springs. Whatever happened to the *new* Lillian, the wild and reckless child of jazz and salaciousness?"

Lillian was caught in a trap. Her pulse rate increased rapidly and her body and expression became tense. She had forgotten all about the *new* Lillian.

Zelda continued. "Very peculiar how you managed to change your entire character practically overnight in order to, you might say, *adapt* to West Baden's new clientele. It was all a fake, wasn't it, Lillian? Now that I think of it, there are so many anomalies that have gone on unexplained. How did Braxton's competition from Chicago just happen to know the ideal time to strike West Baden with full force? Perhaps you're not as sweet and innocent as one would suspect, Lillian."

There was an unbearable silence. Lillian was nearly petrified at what Zelda had alluded to. From Braxton's now truculent expression, Lillian could tell that suspicions had entered his head. She braced herself for the worst. Luckily, Hans, having just refilled Braxton's glass, responded to Lillian's desperate predicament by purposely nudging Braxton so that his beverage spilled onto Zelda.

"You idiot! Look what you've done!" scolded Zelda to Braxton. "The only decent dress I had left in the world completely ruined!" Zelda stood up quickly and frantically attempted to blot off the stain with a napkin. "Really, Braxton, lately you've grown into such an imbecile. You do nothing but sit there like an oaf and spill things. Why, you haven't said a word all night. Honestly, Braxton, sometimes I think you're half deranged!"

"I'll say a few words right now, dearest Zelda." Braxton stood up and faced Zelda. "I am sick and tired of that jaw of yours reverberating at full speed and that tongue of yours waddling around in your mouth, saying things that could prove dangerous to your health. You have no room to insult me, Zelda. London, Paris, Rome, huh! Besides West Baden, you haven't been outside the south side of Chicago. And as for being a friend of the fabled Katia Randreninoff Everett—she loathed, detested, and despised you. You've never been anything but a phony all your life. And now you have the gall to insult *me*. Remember, dear Zelda, I was something at one time, and that's more than I can say for you!"

"Oh, you were something all right, Mr. Braxton Kingsley—public enemy number one! You couldn't make it the honest way, dear Braxton, because you don't have what it takes to be a success. So instead you had to cheat like a rat. You thought the whole world was your private little game and all the people in it your toys, puppets to manipulate and mutilate. And when the world put you in check several weeks ago, Braxton, remember how you cried on my shoulder—yes, cried like a big baby! For once the poor, spoiled little boy was not getting his own way. The world suddenly deprived you, Braxton, of what you see as your right to take all for yourself and leave others with nothing, your right to rule, your right to destroy. And what is destroying you now, Braxton? That you see the cold, ugly truth that you can no longer rule and destroy!"

"Shut your mouth," scolded Braxton.

Throughout Braxton and Zelda's bitter arguing, Lillian gradually developed a sickened expression.

"If … if you two will excuse me," Lillian said timidly. "I'd better be getting along. You see, I have to organize some things before dress rehearsal."

"What's wrong, Lillian?" shouted Zelda. "It's all a bit too much for you to stomach, ah? The big bad gangster from Chicago and his scarlet woman have returned to ruin your darling little fairyland called West Baden Springs. And oh the ghastly thought of being stuck with this loser of a husband for God knows how many years!"

"That's enough, you loud-mouthed wench!" shouted Braxton. "Shut that ugly mouth of yours before I smash one of these against your head!"

With great force Braxton violently smashed a plate on the floor.

Lillian jumped at the tumultuous sound of the shattering porcelain and began to tremble.

"Oh, now he's getting violent!" Zelda broke into sarcasm. "Oh my! I'm so scared! Let's hide under the table, Lillian, before he beats us!"

"I've had enough of this," yelled Braxton. He then turned abruptly to exit the room.

Zelda followed behind him.

"Sound the alarm," Zelda yelled. "Braxton Kingsley is on the loose! Everybody find a place to hide from his monstrous temperament! Lock your doors, everybody in the goddamned hotel!"

Zelda stopped, rested her head on a column, and then broke into tears.

Dress rehearsal had started, but Lillian's mind was in another place. All she could think about was her fear of Braxton as many things thronged into her head at once: the tempestuous quarrel during dinner, the revolver at Braxton's side, and above all, Braxton's expression when Zelda had all but accused Lillian of plotting against them. Lillian did not want to be alone but had no choice, for Hans was on the lighting crew and players were all busy with the show. Dressed as Othello, Braxton kept staring at Lillian in a mean, vengeful way, and as a result, she became flustered as Juliet and even forgot her lines. This of course sent Professor Thornsbie into a huff, but Lillian thought little of it, for something occurred to her that frightened her terribly: she would have to appear alone on stage with Braxton in Desdemona's death scene.

Just what sort of ruse were Braxton and Zelda formulating by getting involved with the show so late in the game? They could not possibly learn their lines so fast. They were up to something, all right, but it was impossible to predict what. Indeed that was the most aggravating thing about these two: their spontaneous and unpredictable nature.

Zelda again showed her spontaneity. After no more than a few unpolished lines as Lady Macbeth, she suddenly lapsed into dialogue of her own while all the players and crew listened in amazement.

"All within this fair kingdom of West Baden Springs, lend me your ears. I am someone who will never be forgotten at this mighty place, a character even the great bard himself could not have imagined, and my name is Katia Randreninoff Everett. There is no one of greater beauty, brains, and breeding than myself, no one of greater social eminence, and no one so greatly admired than myself. For all of you wealthy people of Chicago, I am your patron saint. I, and my West Baden Springs, are your refuge from the filth that your factories create for all humanity. Your smokestacks billow up black clouds to the sky, blotting out the life-giving sun to all those lesser sort of people. The sweatshops, the slaughterhouses, and the incessant mind-breaking clang of the shop machinery: this whole cesspool of toil can make for such an ugly picture. But it's no matter. Your pockets bulge with money at their expense. You should be glad. You should cheer. You should come to me at West Baden Springs. A simple train ride can deliver you from these ugly surroundings to a world where life is beautiful and pleasant all the time. I open my arms out to you in all my beauty and splendor, oh great wealth of Chicago. You have the money I like, and I have the tricks you need to desensitize you: the soothing hot mineral water, golf, tennis, magnificent banquets, grand balls where you can spin in delirium to the entrancing music and forget all about the ugly world you created in Chicago."

Lillian was sitting on the main floor when Zelda suddenly addressed her from the stage.

"So what do you think, Lillian? Is it a pretty good likeness? Although I'm sure you would never know. *I* would know how to do your mother, for I idealized her more than anyone back during the golden age of West Baden. What a royal queen she was, coming from the famous Randreninoff dynasty and all. Oh, and the life she must have led as a child at the magnificent estate—servants waiting on her hand and foot, beautiful clothes, beautifully decorated rooms to live in, and of course the famous family jewels. How completely different was my childhood from hers.

"Alas, the truth comes out! I was born the daughter of a foundry worker in the south side of Chicago. My parents were as happy as any young couple could be, until my mother felt the joyful innocence of youth waning, being displaced by the cold, harsh fact that she would never go anywhere being married to a foundry worker. And so when I was five my mother left my father and me. I never saw her again. She very likely wanted to go off and be a Katia Randreninoff somewhere out where the grass was greener. Thenceforth, night after night for a year, I would wake in darkness and hear my father crying alone—until one morning, I opened the bedroom door to see him hanging there dead by a pair of my mother's stockings.

"I was shifted around amongst the relatives for the remainder of my childhood, and then married an old goat with money. He left me plenty of the stuff after he died just four years later. I came to West Baden Springs in hopes of establishing myself among high society. All at this splendid place immediately rejected me, especially her highness Katia. Oh, I did manage to find acceptance within some vulgar new money in Chicago, but, however futile, I was always drawn back to West Baden because I was hopelessly fixed under Katia's spell, as was everyone back then."

Braxton approached Zelda on the stage.

"What do you want?" asked Zelda with a smirk.

The moment Braxton reached Zelda, he brutally slapped her, causing her to fall to the floor in tears. While crying profusely, Zelda lifted her head and looked at Lillian.

"Lillian," she said softly. "I'm so sorry for everything."

"I'll tell you what I want, dearest Zelda," said Braxton. "I want you to get the hell out of West Baden Springs and never come back. You've been nothing but trouble. You have until tomorrow evening."

"But, Braxton," said Zelda while rising up from off the floor. "I don't have anywhere else to go, and I don't have any money or any prospects. What would become of me?"

"You can lie in the gutters of Chicago for all I care, or sell apples on a street corner. I no longer have any use for you, Zelda. Any more you're nothing but a loud, irritating eyesore."

"Please don't say these things, Braxton. I'm sorry for the way I've been treating you lately. I don't know what's come over me. I don't really mean any of the things I say anymore. I love you, Braxton. I've always loved you and no one else. Let's leave this place together, Braxton. Surely in all the world there must be a place where we can find happiness. We were never meant for West Baden Springs. Happiness and peace await us beyond its borders. Please, Braxton, come away with me."

"Away with you, Zelda? You're a miserable wreck. Just look at you. Why would I possibly want to go away with you?"

"Because I can't live without you, Braxton. Only your love can ransom me from the woes the world has placed upon us. There is nothing else left for me, nothing else that matters.

"Oh, Braxton!" cried Zelda.

Zelda fell frontward onto Braxton and embraced him around his waist. She locked herself there, sobbing for a while, then quickly jerked away. To everyone's great surprise, she now held a revolver in her hand and was pointing the weapon to her head. Braxton must have carried the revolver even under his costume.

"I'll use it, Braxton, right now on this stage in front of everyone. I told you I had nothing else to live for. If I don't receive your love, Braxton, I'll kill myself with this gun, and everyone out there will know you will be responsible."

"Braxton, stop her!" cried Lillian in terror from the main floor.

"Don't worry," replied Braxton. "It's another one of her phony stunts. That's all Zelda is—one phony stunt after another."

"No, Braxton, I think she's serious! Please don't let her do it!"

"She's not going to do a damn thing, are you, Zelda?"

"Yes, I will, Braxton. I'm serious this time."

"Zelda, don't!" cried Lillian in desperation. "Let's talk things over, just the two of us."

"You stay out of this, Lillian," scolded Zelda. "This is between Braxton and me."

"Go ahead, Zelda. We're waiting," said Braxton with a grin. There was a tense moment of silence. "No, you won't do it, dearest Zelda, because you don't have the guts to do it. You've never had anything but a big mouth."

"Yes, I'm going to do it. You'll see. I'm going to shoot myself in the head right now."

"No, Zelda!" cried Lillian.

"Go ahead then, Zelda," continued Braxton. "For once, let's see a decent show on this stage. Go ahead, do it."

A thundering shot went off. The entire opera house went into a frenzy of screams.

"Wow, she really did it!" said Braxton as if stunned. "I don't believe it!"

"Rimsky," said Lillian with one hand on her forehead, as if on the verge of fainting. "Call the sheriff. If anyone needs me I'll be in my apartment."

⊰ Chapter Sixteen ⊱

LILLIAN SLEPT LITTLE during the night and remained in her apartment for the greater part of the morning. Over and over impressions of Zelda's strutting and fretting upon the stage flashed through Lillian's head: the boisterous way Zelda's voice resounded about the opera house; her neurotic, abrupt movements; the thrashing of her arms; her wild gesticulation; and most of all, her desperate pleading to Braxton during the final moments of her life. There was a knock on the door. Lillian answered it.

"Good morning, Rimsky."

"Good morning, Miss Lillian."

"I suppose you're here to tell me the details on, on ..."

"On Miss Fairfax's dramatic performance last night?"

"Yes, Rimsky. It was quite a traumatic experience for me. I still can't believe it happened."

"Please spare me your tear-jerking sorrow. She was a neurotic, unstable creature who possessed an indefatigable drive to spread her vulgarity through the world like poison. She was out to destroy your precious West Baden Springs from the beginning, and if you were not so hindered by foolish sentiments you would see the practicality in this convenient suicide. You would see that it was the only was to remove that deranged woman from this place. Otherwise she would have stayed around forever, like a curse over the place. You know you wanted her gone."

"Rimsky! How can you say such things! Have you no respect for the dead? I am appalled!"

"It's no matter. I did not come here to challenge your storybook values. As far as I am concerned, your dear Zelda is not even worth talking about. Instead I have something much more important to discuss."

"The funeral, no doubt."

"What funeral?"

"Zelda's funeral. Surely, we're going to have a funeral for her."

"I sent the body to Chicago on the morning train. Let her relatives there worry about the funeral. She's caused us enough trouble. Besides, we have a show to put on, remember?"

"Rimsky, how can you think I would give that stupid Shakespeare show the slightest consideration after what has happened?"

"Rubbish! The dress rehearsal has been rescheduled for this afternoon. The players will be ready by tonight as planned."

"But Zelda—"

"That wretched woman is gone forever, and you now have a much more serious problem to face."

"What are you talking about, Rimsky? How important can that silly show be?"

"I am not referring to that ridiculous thing. I am referring to Mr. Braxton Kingsley."

"Braxton? What about Braxton?"

"He wants to kill you."

These words from Rimsky should not have been a total surprise. Nevertheless, Lillian was stunned as she listened to Rimsky.

"He understands that he possessed great wealth and power only weeks ago, and that you, Miss Lillian, are responsible for taking it away from him. A seemingly innocent girl destroyed him and all his imagined strength, and now the neurotic disease of vengeance has struck your husband. I can tell. Like a rabid animal he sits and growls, his mind having gone wild in a frenzy of short-circuited pride. The growls are only a forewarning of the rampage in which he will destroy his victim at all costs. And you, my dear Miss Lillian, make such a perfect victim—always so completely unaware of evil lurking closely around you."

"Rimsky, what should I do?"

"My reason for not canceling the show was to keep plenty of people around to serve as a deterrent."

"That was good thinking, Rimsky. There is safety in numbers." Rimsky pulled out a revolver. "Rimsky, that's Braxton's revolver! However did you get it away from him?"

I told him the sheriff needed it for an investigation since the gun was Miss Fairfax's suicide weapon."

"How clever of you, Rimsky. At least that limits one method for Braxton to use."

"I want you to keep this weapon in the drawer of your nightstand in case he should try something during the night."

"Oh, Rimsky, I don't know. I've never handled a gun before."

"You will if your life depends on it. All you have to do is aim and pull the trigger." Rimsky placed the revolver in the drawer of the nightstand. "Keep it here at all times. For now, all you can do is prepare for tonight's show. I wanted to replace Mr. Kingsley as Othello, but he insists on doing the part. The last I saw of him he was memorizing his lines."

"I don't see how Braxton could harm me on stage in front of an entire audience, and I'll be with the players for most of the afternoon."

"That is exactly what you should do. Stay with the players. Try never to be alone with your husband for an instant."

Rimsky started toward the door.

"All right, goodbye, Rimsky, and thanks ever so much."

Again it was Braxton's unpredictable nature that disturbed Lillian. Just where was he at that moment? What was he doing? What was he thinking? And most importantly, what was he planning? Rimsky's admonishment was probably warranted. Yet, at the back of Lillian's mind, there were tenuous hopes that Braxton might reason with her. Lillian did not want to be alone with Braxton. In fact, she was afraid to leave the apartment for fear of engaging him at some point through the hotel. Early that morning Lillian had sent a note to Hans, instructing him not to come to her apartment, saying that she would see him later in the day. She could not risk Braxton discovering the extramarital relationship, for it was something he could use against her.

While walking down the grand promenade en route to dress rehearsal at the opera house, Lillian passed the billiard-hall-turned-gambling-casino. On the dark November day, it was easy for her to notice a light from within. The door was ajar, as though someone had recently entered. Lillian entered the building surreptitiously, noticing with a sudden jolt of fear that Braxton occupied the building by himself. But Lillian's fear gradually subsided when she noticed Braxton's plaintive demeanor. This was not the angry man she had feared but rather a man looking very depressed and sorrowful. He sat at a poker table, dolefully hunched over, apparently memorizing his lines for the show. He was still unshaven and wore the same wrinkled suit. Lillian approached Braxton cautiously.

"Braxton, are you all right?" she asked.

"Leave me alone." Braxton said in a gruff voice.

Braxton looked up from the script but did not face Lillian. As he leafed through the script, trying to find where had had left off. A photograph of Zelda fell out and landed on the floor in front of Lillian. Lillian picked up the photo and placed it on the table where Braxton was sitting.

"You really loved her, didn't you, Braxton?"

There was a moment of silence as Braxton's face drifted into a pensive expression.

"I suppose so," he answered. "Bad lots both of us—both born in dirt and raised in dirt. We'd never learned anything else. Even after we'd grasped hold of some money, we were still dirt. But neither of us would accept this fact, and that's why our love was doomed from the beginning. I was hopelessly obsessed with money and power. She was ever trying to establish social parity with the elite while dominated by the mystique of your mother. No one will ever know the strength it took for her to say her final words, when she at last defied Katia and confessed her love to me."

"Why, Braxton, why? Why close your eyes to love close by and reach out for something so far off at a distance that it hardly can be seen at all? You ought to have married Zelda and not me. You ought never to have come to West Baden Springs."

"Ah, what pathos, Lillian! Alas, the final judgment over that untidy group, that wretched lot you would politely refer to as the nouveau riche. You stand over me now, high and mighty, triumphant, representative of your noble, well-bred establishment. You look down and weep at the dismal tragedy. Children—unfit, unthinking—children having awkwardly dressed themselves in adult clothing, comically parading about, stumbling, tripping in the long trousers and skirts in front of crowds of jeering adults. Children now at last severely disciplined for their impudence, stripped of their borrowed clothing and returned to their lowly ascribed level. When will they ever learn? you ask. When will they learn to stay within the confines of their playpen off somewhere not visible to the honorable ruling class?"

Braxton paused for a while and then continued.

"But remember those words of yours, Lillian. Perhaps soon you too will be answering to them. Do you really think your precious old guard will accept you now? What sort of reputation do you think West Baden has got lately— first a giant speakeasy and then playhouse to the notorious West Baden Springs Massacre? How socially unacceptable! Those old goats probably avoid this place like a whorehouse, regardless of the famous Randreninoff mystique. Where have all these gracious friends of yours been anyway? Why, you have not seen any of them since the wedding, have you? I'll tell you where they've been—clustered at their clubs, cackling and sneering at West Baden Springs in all her ill-repute."

"Braxton, you know nothing of the special relationship between me and, and—"

"The old guard?"

"Yes. They would support me until the end. Once I get West Baden back on its feet, I'm sure I'll be seeing them again regularly."

"You really think so, ah?"

"Of course, Braxton."

"So confident you are. What fortitude! No, you're not the little mouse I thought you were."

"Braxton, why keep passing extraneous judgments? Why create such indifference when our lives may as yet be bridged somehow? Haven't we both been through enough these past months? Somehow there must be a way for us to find peace."

"Sure, you want peace now that you have the advantage of being in the ruling position. Now that I am stripped of money, power, and influence, you want me to make peace, to sit back and accept my new lowly lot. Only weeks ago, when I was running things around here, when this great hotel had fallen short of its civilized air, you did not want peace then. No, you fought instead.

Remember what you did to secure the removal of all the undesirables, Lillian? Remember what you did?"

Braxton became angry and spoke harshly. Lillian became nervous and flustered. Her heartbeat raced rapidly.

"Braxton, we must be off to dress rehearsal. Everyone is waiting."

"Remember what you did?" Braxton repeated.

Lillian said nothing but turned toward the door and began to walk rapidly.

"Remember what you did, dear, sweet, innocent Lillian?" shouted Braxton from across the room.

Once outside, Lillian ran to the opera house for fear that Braxton would catch up with her. When Lillian entered the opera house, Professor Thornsbie approached her at once.

"Miss Lillian, where on earth have you been? Everyone's been waiting for you. You are on now as Juliet. Oh dear, you still have to change into your costume."

"Professor Thornsbie," said Lillian, almost out of breath. "Have you seen Hans?"

"Hans? Hans who?"

"He's on the lighting crew. I must speak to him immediately. It's very important."

"Important!" exclaimed Professor Thornsbie. "You're too young and unthinking to know what's important. I have a show to put on. That's what's important." Professor Thornsbie took hold of Lillian and oriented her toward backstage. "Now quickly change into your costume. We have no time to waste."

When Lillian slipped into her costume as Juliet, she wished she could have slipped into the part permanently. She wanted to be anybody but Lillian Kingsley just then. Thankfully the backstage climate provided a buffer between herself and Braxton. Professor Thornsbie made a show in himself by shuffling around backstage, fussing about particulars, and behaving as though the group was to perform before the crown heads of Europe. Lillian spent most of her time between performances in the women's dressing room amid the commotion of females rapidly changing costumes, primping with makeup, and fixing their hair. She tried to talk to Hans backstage, but each time she left the women's dressing room, Braxton followed her around. And so Lillian always returned to the dressing room, where she knew Braxton was not allowed. Her dress rehearsal performance as Desdemona opposite Braxton's Othello was innocuous enough, if incredibly dull. Braxton talked his way through the lines like he was giving an ill-prepared speech.

Lillian would not always enjoy the benefits of playacting against her husband. After the show, words between the two would become real and tensions would almost certainly swell. Lillian hated to think of the show ever ending, of the time when the players would leave West Baden Springs, leaving her alone with Braxton and his monstrous temperament.

Time seemed to zip by in a maddening countdown. Dress rehearsal ended before Lillian knew it. Lillian had dinner alone in her office, claiming she still needed time to memorize her lines. But before she could even finish her meal, the time had come for her to report to the opera house for the evening performance. The audience was sparse and consisted mostly of hotel staff. One by one the scenes passed like lightning: the trial scene from *The Merchant of Venice*, Prospero's farewell from *The Tempest*, the balcony scene from *Romeo and Juliet*, the murder of Duncan from *Macbeth*, the ghost scene from *Richard III*—until there Lillian was in Desdemona's bed, soon to be smothered by her husband, Othello. Rimsky had just finished his part as Iago, and now Braxton took command of the stage.

"It is the cause, it is the cause, my soul," recited Braxton as Othello. "Let me not name it to you, you chaste stars! It is the cause. Yet I'll not shed her blood; nor scar that whiter skin of her than snow, and smooth as monumental alabaster. Yet she must die, else she'll betray more men. Put out the light, and then put out the light: If I quench thee, thou flaming minister, I can again they former light restore. Should I repent me: but once put out thy light, thou cunning'st pattern of excelling nature, I know not where is that Promethean heat that can thy light resume. When I have plucked they rose, I cannot give it vital growth again. It must needs wither: I'll smell it on the tree."

Braxton as Othello kissed Lillian as Desdemona.

"O balmy breath, that dost almost persuade justice to break her sword!—one more, one more. Be thus when thou art dead, and I will kill thee, and love thee after—one more, and this the last: So sweet was ne'er so fatal. I must weep. But they are cruel tears: this sorrows' heavenly; it strikes where it doth love. She awakens."

"Who's there?" said Lillian as Desdemona. "Othello?"

As Lillian exchanged lines with Braxton, she was amazed at how Braxton's acting had dramatically improved since dress rehearsal only hours ago. He spoke with such anger now, as though he was not play acting at all but really speaking every word for himself.

"Sweet soul, take heed," continued Braxton as Othello. "Take heed of perjury; thou'rt on thy death bed."

"Ay, but not yet to die," continued Lillian as Desdemona.

"Yes, presently. Therefore confess thee freely of they sin; for to deny each article with oath cannot remove nor choke the strong conception that I do groan withal. Thou art to die."

"Then, Lord have mercy on me!"

"I say, amen."

"And have you mercy too! I never did offend you in my life."

Braxton's realistic acting made Lillian suddenly realize with great horror that she might very well reenact this same scene for real in her own bed that night. Thank goodness Rimsky had placed a revolver in her nightstand.

"O, banish me, my lord," continued Lillian as Desdemona. "But kill me not!"

"Down strumpet!" continued Braxton as Othello.

"Kill me tomorrow; let me live tonight!"

"Nay if you strive…"

"But half an hour!"

"Being done, there is no pause."

"But while I say one prayer!"

"It is too late."

Braxton placed the pillow over Lillian's face just as before. But to Lillian's great surprise, he suddenly began to press down with all his titanic strength. Lillian began to panic. The applause of even a scant audience was loud enough to cover her faint, muted cries. She pictured the lights dimming, the curtain falling, and knew it would not be long until the next scene could move into place. Perhaps this was Braxton's forewarning to Lillian, for surely he must have known the period between scenes was not nearly a long enough time to smother her to death.

Lillian heard Professor Thornsbie approach.

"Come, come you two," he said. "We must be on with the next scene. Don't dawdle now."

When Braxton removed his hand from the pillow, Lillian stood up abruptly and panted uncontrollably. She gave her husband a contemptuous look and then walked off stage. All Lillian could think of was how she wanted to be locked up somewhere away from Braxton. Her office at the hotel could suffice. Only when she was sure to be out of Braxton's sight did Lillian retrieve her coat and depart the opera house. Walking quickly but surreptitiously down the grand promenade toward the hotel, Lillian tried her best to conceal the sharp crackle of fallen leaves. Her dark coat effectively concealed Desdemona's white nightgown so as to make her less visible on the somber November night.

It was when Lillian was almost at the hotel steps that she heard the faint sound of a door slamming far off in the direction of the opera house. *Good*

Lord! she thought. *What if that were Braxton!* It would hardly be wise to wait there and find out. Lillian entered the hotel lobby. Everyone was gone from the hotel and most certainly at the opera house for the show. She crossed the lobby quickly and arrived at her office door. She entered the office, locked the door behind her, but did not turn on the lights. If that noise she had heard outside was Braxton, her unlit office as viewed from outside might deter him from coming there to find her.

Lillian went to the window. Sure enough, there was Braxton, still dressed as Othello, walking down the grand promenade toward the hotel. As Braxton came closer, Lillian backed away from the window more and more. She thought she had left the opera house unnoticed, but Braxton probably found out she had gone from someone who had seen her leave. The show would end in less than an hour. If she could just hide there in her office until that time, she could join the others in the lobby just beyond the office door.

A tense half hour went by. Lillian imagined Braxton searching the hotel for her, hunting her down by whatever possible means—in their apartment, in the library, and perhaps soon there in her office. She dared not turn on the lights; light could be seen from under the door. Lillian peered out the window at the lighted opera house, hoping that people would soon exit and come to the hotel. She knew this would not happen though for at least another thirty minutes.

Suddenly Lillian heard footsteps. The doorknob rattled fiercely. Someone was trying to get in. Who else but Braxton? He knocked three times and then rattled the doorknob again. Lillian nearly collapsed in fright. She thought about hiding in the closet, but before she could move, Braxton broke down the door like thunder, instantly flashing light into the once dark room. Lillian stared at him as if petrified. The Othello costume made Braxton appear even more formidable.

"Well, well, what have we here?" said Braxton in a hostile voice. "Dear Lillian locked in her office with the lights out. One would think you were trying to hide from someone."

"Braxton, you tried to smother me."

"Why, Lillian, you're trembling. You act like someone who had double-crossed someone else and now fears retribution. You made sure to it that Al and his gang knew right where to find me and my cohorts, didn't you, dear, sweet Lillian? The wild new Lillian of jazz and reckless fun! What a sham that was. How much did he pay you for the whole job Lillian? It must have been quite a sum!"

"No, Braxton, you have it all wrong. It was Rimsky who arranged everything."

"But I'm sure it was you who put him up to it, dear Lillian."

"So what if I did. What was I supposed to do? Stand by and watch you and Zelda take over the place in a wild rampage? Why shouldn't I protect myself and my home against an unscrupulous opportunist like you?"

"It is the cause, it is the cause, my soul," said Braxton while approaching Lillian. "Let me not name it to you, you chaste stars! It is the cause. Yet she must die else she'll betray more men."

Lillian reached for the telephone on her desk.

"Braxton if you come one step closer I'll call Rimsky at the opera house, and he'll come right over with ... with a shotgun."

Braxton violently ripped the telephone cord out of the wall.

"Sweet soul, take heed. Take heed of perjury; thou'rt on they death bed."

Lillian backed up against the bookshelf.

"Braxton, I'm warning you. I wouldn't try anything."

"Down strumpet. Being done, there is no pause. It is too late."

Braxton grasped Lillian around her neck, choking her mercilessly. Backed against the bookshelf, Lillian moved her arms frantically up and down the shelves, searching for anything she could use to afflict Braxton. Her right hand came upon a porcelain object. She wasted no time in dashing the object against Braxton's head with all her strength. Braxton yelled, removed his grasp, and placed both hands on his head as if stunned by the blow.

Lillian tore out of the office with only one thought in mind: to get to the opera house where there were people. But no sooner did she cross the lobby than did Braxton start out after her.

Lillian ran out of the hotel. It would be a long run down the grand promenade to the opera house, but she had no other choice. With the wind swirling the leaves about, the cold night mist obscuring the brick walkway, Lillian ran though greatly hindered by Desdemona's long nightgown. The white fabric fluttered in all directions as Lillian ran down the grand promenade. The opera house was brightly lit in the distance. If only she could reach the great illuminated building! But Braxton was gaining on her terribly, even to the point that she could hear his heavy breathing. Lillian knew she could never outrun him to the opera house. It shimmered in the distance like an unreachable star. Her only alternative would be to run into one of the bathhouses alongside the promenade.

Lillian was out of breath when she arrived at the door to the nearest bathhouse. She entered and quickly locked the door behind her. Within seconds thereafter, Braxton began to pound and rattle the door. It would not be long until he broke the door down or broke through a window. Lillian needed a placed to hide. She did not turn on the lights, because Braxton could then see her through the windows. There was certainly no place to hide in the open bath area. Her only hope was down below in the basement, which housed the machinery and piping for the facility.

Lillian walked quickly down a spiral staircase all the way to the basement. While feeling her way around the confusing network of pipes and large metal objects, she suddenly heard footsteps from above. Apparently Braxton had found another entrance since there was no sound of a forced entry. With her nerves rattled, Lillian accidentally ran into some metal objects, sending them clanging and banging to the cement floor. Braxton was sure to have heard this. He would be on his way down any second. Lillian was paralyzed with fright. Perhaps he had her now. She grasped a large board she had found and braced herself for Braxton's descent.

But with great luck, Lillian stumbled upon a large metal mixing tank used to mix cold water to the scalding hot spring water for bathing purposes. She opened the hatch with care and climbed down a small metal ladder, taking the board with her. The tank was completely dry. Lillian could just barely stand in it. She waited there shaking with fright, trying still to suppress the heavy breathing brought on by the long run down the promenade. Braxton's footsteps pounded above for several minutes, then he found the spiral staircase, for Lillian could hear the vibrating metal answer to Braxton's heavy footsteps.

Braxton shuffled around for a while, but then his sounds became violent, no thanks to the frustration brought on due to his inability to find the light switch. In a thunder of sound, Braxton tossed and turned objects in a mad search for Lillian. The clanging, banging, and crashing went on for several minutes. And then the fury ended. There was a period of silence.

"Hello down there!"

Lillian cringed at the sound of Braxton's voice coming through the hatch of the mixing tank. She gripped the board in her hands tightly. Without even using the ladder, Braxton jumped right into the tank, causing the great metal structure to bong loudly. Hunched over, trying not to knock his head on the tank's ceiling, Braxton came toward Lillian with arms extended. Now Braxton's great height was to his disadvantage. Lillian smacked the side of his head with the board, lunged forward on to the ladder, and then tossed the board out of the hatch. While striving desperately to climb the ladder in Desdemona's long nightgown, Lillian deterred Braxton's grasp by kicking whenever possible. Lillian climbed out the tank and quickly slammed the hatch on Braxton's arms as he tried to climb out. She then tightened and locked the hatch. Braxton continually pounded.

Without a second thought, Lillian went to the control valves and turned only the valve for hot spring water. As the torrent of 150-degree water poured into the tank, Braxton screamed like a wild animal and continued to pound at the hatch.

"Lillian, you're a dead woman! I'm going to get out of this thing and kill you!" cried Braxton angrily.

The tank would fill up completely and then drain off through a pipe that led to the bath. Lillian made sure the valve that drains the tank was closed. Had Braxton known the mechanics of the bathhouse, Lillian may well have played victim to such a seething death. Braxton's screams continued but softened the closer he came to death. When the tank was nearly full, all Lillian could hear was a faint whine. When Lillian began to hear water rush through the discharge pipe, she knew the tank was full and that Braxton was drowned.

Lillian cautiously opened the hatch. While steam rushed out of the tank, Braxton's clamming, hot hand suddenly grasped Lillian's arm and held on to it like a vice. Lillian was stunned out of her mind as she saw the red, chapped skin on Braxton's hand and saw his scalded, twisted body floating around below the steam. In a short time, the hand loosened its grip and slowly sank back down into the scalding water.

Lillian kept assuring herself that this had been the only way. This aggressive man called Braxton Kingsley was out to destroy her long before they had even met. She thought of the hours he must have spent planning and dreaming up his own West Baden Springs—his own palace of liquor, jazz, and glittering excitement that was vastly different from Lillian's stately birthplace. He had viewed West Baden as *his* for the taking, plundered and pillaged the place, and then became wild with vengeance for what he saw as Lillian's taking away what he perceived to be his. Lillian thought there could never be anyone so maliciously selfish, anyone so completely absorbed in his own unscrupulous pursuits, anyone so spiteful and contemptuous. All Lillian ever wanted was peace. But Braxton never offered her peace, only confrontation. Had Braxton lived, there would have been no end to the suffering he would have caused Lillian.

"It would appear that you have just murdered your husband, Miss Lillian."

Lillian jumped at the sound of Rimsky's voice. She turned to see his old, wrinkled face emerge from the clouds of steam. In all the commotion, she had not heard Rimsky enter the building.

"Oh, Rimsky, thank goodness you're here. You were right. Braxton *was* trying to kill me," replied Lillian, nearly at the end of her strength.

"But *you* managed to kill him instead."

"Out of self-defense, of course."

"Oh really? I am not so sure of that. I followed you and Mr. Kingsley into this building. I have been keeping an eye on the two of you."

"Rimsky, what do you mean? What are you saying?"

Rimsky did not answer right away but instead paced the floor a few times as if preparing a long explanation.

"I knew your mother's family quite well in Russia before the revolution. They were the fabulously rich and famous Randreninoffs, one of the greatest names among the Russian aristocracy. The Randreninoffs were known for one thing more than anything else—their family jewels. Diamonds, rubies, sapphires, emeralds, the likes of which few have ever seen, made the Randreninoff jewels one of the world's greatest treasures. As all the world well knows, the jewels have been missing now for some sixteen years, ever since the revolution. There have been many theories as to their whereabouts, but one theory had always held firm to me more than any other. When you were a girl your mother took you on an extended journey to her native city of St. Petersburg."

"Yes, I remember. I must have been about seven at the time."

"I remember meeting you then for the first time, although I am sure you don't remember me. Nevertheless, you and your mother came to Russia during very precarious times. The Czar's government was in chaos. Revolutionaries thronged to the street in protest. And war had been declared only a month prior to your departure. With Russia in such an unstable state of affairs, the Randreninoffs needed a hiding placed for their precious jewels. How convenient for them that you and your mother were on your way back to America."

"Rimsky, you mean that—"

"Yes, the Randreninoff jewels are here at West Baden Springs."

"But, Rimsky, that's just a silly legend."

"The jewels are here, my dear."

"What makes you so sure, Rimsky?"

"Because I have seen them. After years of searching, I finally discovered them last spring, just after the death of your father."

Lillian looked amazed. Rimsky continued.

"When your mother arrived back after the arduous journey to her homeland, she at once commissioned more mosaic floors and walls to be built at West Baden. What better way to hide the jewels than in a mosaic? I knew all along the jewels were here at West Baden Springs. If in 1920 your mother would have told me where she had hidden them, I would not have had to spend nine years searching for them, and also, I would not have had to kill her."

Lillian was stunned. "You killed my mother?"

"Yes. She would not tell me where she had hidden the jewels, so I smothered her with a pillow there in her bedroom right where your father found her on the eve of a grand ball to celebrate the postwar reopening of the hotel. If only she would have told me where she had hidden the jewels, she might still be alive today."

Lillian was in a daze, trying to comprehend what was being told.

"Of course, even though I had discovered the jewels, there really was no clandestine way of just chiseling them out of the walls. I needed to gain ownership of the hotel. Then came the perfect opportunity—Mr. Braxton Kingsley. And of course I should not forget his illustrious compatriot, Miss Zelda Fairfax. I knew what those two were all about from the moment I laid eyes on them—a couple of ill-bred, money-grubbing Americans out for a cheap shot at anything they could get. I had the dashing Mr. Kingsley checked out, and I certainly did not have to dig very deep. I knew why he wanted West Baden—for his all important liquor trade. I knew he wanted to kill you in order to get West Baden. Those two would do my dirty work for me. Only I would make sure they would not get away with it. They would hang for your murder, Miss Lillian, and then West Baden would be open for me to purchase. I played along with their scheme. I willfully relinquished the hotel management to Miss Fairfax. I pretended that her stupid, little accident had disabled me for a proper duration in Indianapolis. When I returned to the hotel, I quite expected to find you dead, Miss Lillian. But you ruined everything for me. You managed to play-act your way around Kingsley's treachery in a way I could never have imagined. I needed an alternate plan. That of course was to invigorate Kingsley with vengeance for your having destroyed his bootlegging prospects as a result of the West Baden Springs Massacre. Only *he* was supposed to have killed *you* instead of the other way around. Finally, though, I believe I have the matter under control."

"Yes, and just what is your diabolical plan this time?" asked Lillian.

Rimsky pulled out some papers.

"Here are a few notes that you wrote to your sweet, little Hans while Kingsley and his gangsters controlled West Baden. 'Hans, I have an idea of how we can get rid of Braxton. Come to my apartment as soon as you can.' And another one. 'We must think of a way to get rid of Braxton. Perhaps Rimsky can help.' Among many others, all are written in your beautiful handwriting, signed, and even dated. And of course here too are also many sickeningly sweet love letters to your pretty boyfriend, as if your infidelity needed any more proof. You and that young man have been the scandal of the servant's quarters for weeks, and now you have just completed the murder of your husband to make the romance fulfilled."

"But those notes were written completely out of context," said Lillian. "Hans and I were trying to get rid of Braxton's gangsters before they got rid of me. Again, it was self-defense."

"You had every opportunity at the inquest to turn your husband in to the authorities, but you did not because you cowardly chose not to be found guilty by association."

"All right, Rimsky. I am tired of your games. Just what do you want?"

Rimsky pulled out another paper.

"Sign this transfer of title to the property of West Baden Springs, and I will gladly give you all of these silly notes and stupid love letters in exchange."

Lillian was amazed at Rimsky's flippancy. So casually did he speak of events that had brought Lillian great torment: the murder of her mother, Lillian's struggle with Braxton, the defaming of herself and West Baden Springs. And casually as well did Rimsky reveal his plan for Lillian's destruction, as if all along she had been nothing more than an insignificant cog in his perfectly mechanized plan, as though her only purpose for living was to be used as a device to fulfill his ambitions. Rimsky's tone was triumphant, arrogant, and spiteful, addressing Lillian as though she were a frail flower that had no choice but to get stepped on or blown down. But why should Rimsky think otherwise. For nearly ten years, he had observed Lillian at West Baden playing the role of a carefree princess, admired by all and lost in a world of her own fanciful endeavors. What pleasure he must have taken these past few months at seeing Lillian and West Baden defiled and defamed.

Lillian had been born and raised at West Baden Springs. She had long thought the place a part of her. Signing the property over to Rimsky and leaving the great place seemed inconceivable. But then Lillian thought more deeply. What was to keep her at West Baden? She had no family or friends, only a brooding hotel staff that would never accept Hans if Lillian married him, as she had intended on doing. The old West Baden Springs was dead and gone forever, but Lillian was alive. Yes, she was alive and breathing and she must make the most of it rather than bury herself in past sorrows at West Baden. Where was it written that she was destined to play princess to Chicago's high society and then forever anguish in infamy at having lost their favor? West Baden was nothing more than a great heap of stone, and she, Lillian Everett, was a human being with feelings and emotions and dreams that she could renew once again with the help of Hans. She would begin anew and Hans would lead her. Just then Lillian looked to Hans as one looks to the faint amber rays that streak eastern skies after a long, gloomy night.

"Do you have a pen?" asked Lillian. "Where do I sign?"

"You don't have to sign anything, Lillian," interjected Hans, calmly walking down the spiral staircase from above. Lillian was surprised. "Very entertaining speech, Mr. Rimsky. You see, sound resonates from this small basement room like a giant musical instrument. But I am sure that the all-knowing, all-powerful Mr. Rimsky has certainly studied enough physics to know that."

"What do you want, you foolish creature?" said Rimsky angrily. "So what if you heard me. What could anything possibly mean to you?"

"You still think you are a powerful land baron ruling over the miserable masses, ah, Mr. Rimsky?" continued Hans. "You are in a different country now, and if you are representative of the Russian aristocracy, it's a good thing those people overthrew you and your kind. You see, your treachery does not work here. There is such a thing called the law. I supposed it never occurred to you that for all of these years you have been the leading suspect in the murder of Lillian's mother. Your arrogance made you believe that you were above the law. But your nasty disposition, manner, and conduct certainly did not make you a favorite at the local sheriff's office. Now they have a confession, and when the jewels are found in the mosaic, they will have a perfect motive for the district attorney."

Suddenly two more men began to walk quietly down the spiral staircase.

"I am sure you remember Sheriff Arnold C. Palmer and his deputy, Peter Sinclair," said Hans.

"Igor Sergeavich Rimsky," said Sheriff Palmer. "You are under arrest for the murder of Katia Randreninoff Everett."

Sheriff Palmer and Deputy Sinclair approached Rimsky, handcuffed him, and then proceeded to escort him up the spiral staircase.

"This is preposterous," said Rimsky while being taken away. "Take your hands off me, you vulgar animals."

"Don't worry, Miss Lillian," said Sheriff Palmer. "This monster will not harm you any longer. We'll be back for Mr. Kingsley."

Deputy Sinclair looked down into the scalding tank at Braxton's drowned body and added, "It doesn't look like he can harm anyone either."

When Rimsky and the local authorities were a sure distance away, Hans gentlemanly escorted Lillian up the spiral staircase and out of the bathhouse. While the two walked arm in arm down the grand promenade, they could see that the Shakespeare show at the opera house had let out, and the small audience was gradually dispersing out onto the grounds of West Baden Springs.

"How did you know where to find me, Hans?" asked Lillian.

"We heard Mr. Kingsley screaming from the bathhouse."

"But what made you fetch the sheriff?"

"When I saw you and Mr. Kingsley on stage together, I knew he was smothering you for real. No one else could tell, but I could. I had gone to the sheriff the day Braxton and Zelda arrived back. I knew he would want to get even. Although Braxton had paid the sheriff off to keep quiet about the liquor at West Baden, murder is quite another matter. The sheriff told me to come back when I had something more solid. So I telephoned him when I saw Braxton smothering you on stage. After I made the telephone call, I looked all around, but I could not find you or Mr. Kingsley. I decided to wait down by the front gate for the sheriff. When the sheriff and his deputy arrived, as soon as we proceeded up the drive, the three of us immediately heard screaming from a bathhouse. We entered the bathhouse quietly in case Braxton had a gun. But then we started to overhear Rimsky's arrogant oration. And don't worry about those silly notes and love letters. The sheriff knows all about Braxton's bootlegging. After all, Braxton was paying him off to keep quiet about it. The sheriff told me that the FBI has been investigating Mr. Braxton Kingsley for years, long before Braxton ever met you, Lillian. They all knew you were in trouble here when Braxton controlled the place. But they could do nothing without more evidence. And everyone knows how good gangsters are at concealing evidence."

"I should have known, Hans, that you would come to my rescue somehow," said Lillian. "And now we must pack. We have no time to waste. Tomorrow we are leaving West Baden Springs for good and we are never coming back."

"Lillian, why should you want to leave West Baden Springs when you have fought so hard to save it?" Hans asked. "You fought against Braxton and his gangsters, Zelda, and all those wild people, Rimsky and everyone else. This should be your moment of victory. And what about the Randreninoff jewels?"

"I will see that they are returned to their proper place – a museum in Russian or some place like that. After all, the Randreninoff jewels are a great part of Russian history and culture. And as for West Baden Springs – there was once a time when I thought I could happily bury myself at this place, enjoy a carefree life of poetry, art and music, beautiful gardens … long lazy afternoons on the veranda among beautiful, fine people who would adore and admire me. But now I realize eventually something would have made me see those days at West Baden Springs could not have lasted. If it were not Braxton, the stock market crash, Rimsky, then something else would have made me see. But it does not matter now. All that matters now is that I know and I am thankful for knowing."

"Yes, Lillian," replied Hans. "I believe I understand now. The world begins just beyond West Baden's front gate."

It was a cold November night. The bare trees of the forest rattled angrily in the wind as Lillian and Hans encountered swirling leaves on their walk back to the great domed structure. A cold, wet mist gathered around them.

As Lillian looked at the Byzantine building for one of the last times, she felt none of the nostalgia one would have expected. These were the walls that had sheltered her and had kept her from seeing the world as it really is. Fate had since forced her to develop all her sympathies, to play a part and live among others in human joy and sorrow. For this then nothing had been in vain, and she would leave West Baden Springs and all that it stood for.

They reached the atrium under the dome.

"The atrium is so still and quiet now, Hans," said Lillian. "How different it used to be only a short while ago. So much merriment and laughter used to fill this great room. I remember how shocked I was when I returned home from Paris to find that a provocative, livelier crowd had replaced the conservative old guard that had long prevailed at West Baden. But now I see that they were all the same, as I believe people are all the same. I suppose everyone longs for a West Baden Springs of their own, a secure plot of ground where they hope to loll in ease, hide from the world's uncertainty, and pretend to be happy. But you know what I think true happiness is, Hans? True happiness is realizing there is never a world without problems, pain, or sacrifice, and to deal with things as best as humanly possible."

The years passed by. Like a green, creeping scourge, nature came into its own about the empty and abandoned grounds of West Baden Springs.

Seedlings grew into trees to eventually eliminate the road through the forest that had carried Lillian away from her home. Weeds grew to conceal the rusted rails that were forsaken for an alternate route. The beautiful acres of gardens quickly fell victim to nature's tougher strains. The rugged flora of the wild devastated the delicate flowers and other cultivated plants. Twisted, jagged thorn bushes, tenacious vines, prolific weeds, endless patches of tall grass now prevail. And in the middle of all this stands the great Byzantine structure with its eight towers and enormous dome. No matter how sickly and effete looking, the building nevertheless stands, and probably always will—a wonder of the world, sealed off and buried behind dense brush and forbidding woodland, forgotten and neglected, but never losing hope that someone might discover her once again.

IND
F
KIL

WEST BADEN SPRINGS
$ 15.00   1-22-09

Printed in the United States
132076LV00006B/225/P

9 781434 339546